An Interactive Fantasy Adventure

Enter the prolific worlds of...

SAVAGE REALMS GAMEBOOKS

Book 0 - Balance of Fate: The Legorian Kings Saga
Book 1 - What Dreams May Come
Book 2 - Malivor: Cataclysm's Edge
Book 3 - The Tavern on Gallows Hill

BALANCE OF FATE
The Legorian Kings Saga

Written by TroyAnthony Schermer

**Cover artwork by Vincenzo Pratticò
Interior artwork by Ilya Shkipin
Fillustrations by Pat O'Neill**

THE LEGAL STUFF

Story by Brian Henson and TroyAnthony Schermer
Cover artwork by Vincenzo Prattico̓
Interior artwork by Ilya Shkipin
Fillustrations by Pat O'Neill
Puzzle illustrations by NiKayla Schermer
Character Log Sheet by TroyAnthony Schermer
Game Mechanics by Michael Lee and Peter Agapov

Contact us at: savagerealmsgamebooks@gmail.com

Follow us on Twitter: @SGamebooks

Follow us on Instagram:
http://www.instagram.com/gamebook_adventures/

And be sure to join our Facebook group to stay up-to-speed on all things Savage Realms:
Savage Realms Gamebooks

For my baby brother, Colt...
There isn't a day that goes by that you don't
cross my mind. I miss you deeply. You will
always, always be my hero! Until we meet
again, lil bro...

This book is also dedicated to my wife, Shar...
Here's to many more great adventures
with you, my love!

And finally, a special thanks goes out to
Michael Lee and Peter Agapov for their
tremendous help in creating the game
mechanics for this book and the
ones to come!

"Fantasy is escapist, and that is its glory. If a soldier is imprisoned by the enemy, don't we consider it his duty to escape?... If we value the freedom of mind and soul, if we're partisans of liberty, then it's our plain duty to escape, and to take as many people with us as we can!"
— J.R.R. Tolkien

THE

SAVAGE REALMS

AWAIT....

SAVAGE REALMS

NAME:

LIFE FORCE (LF SCORE): **25**

CHARACTER CLASS:**FIGHTER ADEPT**

COMBAT SKILL SCORE (CSS):

SKILLS AND ATTRIBUTES

STEALTH:

INTELLECT:

LOCK PICKING:

STRENGTH:

PICKPOCKETING:

AGILITY:

CHARISMA:

RESISTANCE:

LUCK:

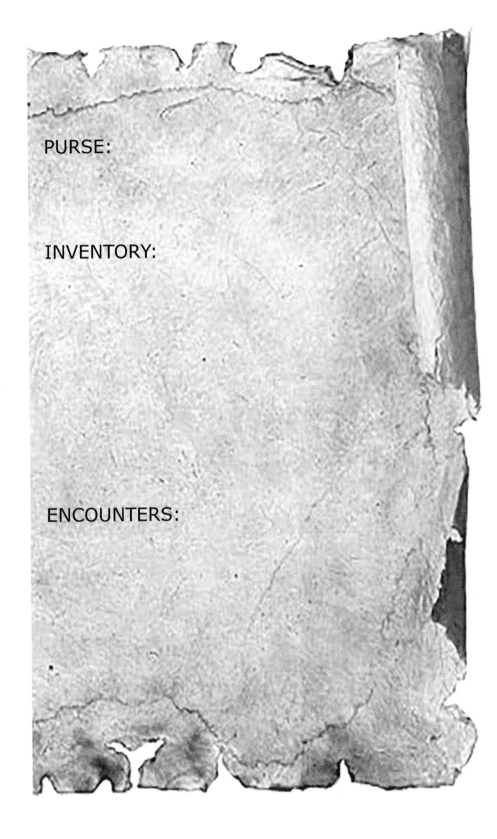

PURSE:

INVENTORY:

ENCOUNTERS:

RULES OF PLAY

The book you are holding in your hands is unique. Not extraordinary by any means, but unique in the fact that it is a role-playing game as well. It is also different in the sense that YOU choose your own destiny — that by your own choices YOU determine the direction and outcome of this story! In fact, sometimes your very fate might even depend on the roll of the dice themselves!

WHAT YOU WILL NEED
In addition to a copy of this gamebook and the CHARACTER LOG sheet contained within, you will also need a pencil with an eraser and two six-sided dice (one for yourself and one for your opponent(s). The only other thing you will need for gameplay is a blank sheet of paper so that you can track damage to your LIFE FORCE and tally the damage you inflict

upon your opponents.

CREATING YOUR CHARACTER

Included with this epic, interactive fantasy adventure is a CHARACTER LOG sheet. It is highly recommended you make photocopies of it for gameplay. (CHARACTER LOG sheets are also available for downloading and printing on our Facebook page, under the files tab at **Savage Realms Gamebooks**).

YOUR NAME
In the space provided, write your character's NAME.

YOUR LIFE FORCE (LF SCORE)
Not simply just a measure of your health, it is also a measure of your overall fortitude, stamina, and resilience. Your default LF score is always **25**, and any damage you sustain, whether it be from opponents, traps, or whatever, is subtracted from this number. (Use a separate sheet of paper to track any damage you might take during the course of your adventure).

CHARACTER CLASS
In this gamebook, you play the role of a FIGHTER ADEPT.

YOUR COMBAT SKILL SCORE (CSS)
This encompasses both your attack and defensive abilities when in combat. To determine your Combat Skill Score or CSS, roll a 1d6 and record that number in the space provided. If your roll is a 3 or LESS, then your default CSS is automatically a **3**.

SKILL AND ATTRIBUTE SCORES

In addition to your Combat Skill Score, you also have three other skills as well as six attributes:

Your SKILLS:

STEALTH
(This affects your ability to sneak, hide, silently take out opponents, and even blend into a crowd).

LOCK PICKING
(This affects your ability to unlock and open doors, chests, and locks).

PICKPOCKETING
(This skill affects your ability to remove items from someone's person or even plant something on them without being detected).

Your ATTRIBUTES:

INTELLECT
(This attribute may come into play when solving problems and puzzles).

STRENGTH
(This attribute comes into play when you need to complete certain physical tasks).

AGILITY
(This attribute is a measure of your ability and speed when running or fleeing, but could also come into play when dodging attacks or reacting).

CHARISMA
(This affects your ability to bribe, persuade, intimidate, barter, and even lie).

RESISTANCE
(This affects your ability to resist certain lesser spells, as well as poisons, venom, and toxins).

LUCK
(Although it is neither a skill nor an attribute, you can never have too much LUCK on your side).

Using your allotted budget of **18 points**, distribute those points between your skills and attributes now. Each skill and attribute must have a minimum of **1 point** assigned to them, but cannot, at any time in the game, ever have more than **5**. (Write these numbers next to their corresponding skill or attribute now on your CHARACTER LOG sheet).

PLEASE NOTE that as the game progresses, you will have opportunities to increase the scores of both your skills and your attributes, but those scores can never exceed **5**, which is the maximum you can have for each one.

YOUR PURSE AND YOUR INVENTORY
Throughout the game, you will find various items that can be used during the course of your adventure. Gold pieces and gold coins are added to your PURSE. Everything else that you find is recorded in your INVENTORY. Any items, including money, that is spent, consumed, sold or is stolen must be removed from your PURSE and INVENTORY.

You begin your adventure with EIGHT items — a double-edged longsword, chainmail armor, a bedroll with a blanket, provisions (food), TWO HEALTH potions, and a wound dressing kit. Add these items to your INVENTORY now.

ENCOUNTERS
This is where you can keep track of all the various monsters and enemies you have faced and defeated throughout your adventure.

COMBAT

The combat in this gamebook is a simple, two-dice (2d6) attack/defend system. Each combat round begins with you rolling a 1d6 and then adding it to your Combat Skill Score. The other 1d6 is rolled for your opponent and then added to their Combat Skill Score (represented in the text as Combat). Whoever has the highest total between you and your opponent is the party that "hits." A 1d6 is then rolled to see how much damage is inflicted. A tie, where both of your totals are the same, means that neither of you hit.

This continues until you or the opposing side has been eliminated!

MULTIPLE OPPONENTS
Although in real-life combat scenarios multiple opponents would most likely attack simultaneously, in this adventure, they are fought one at a time.

HEALTH POTIONS
HEALTH potions can be used at any time to restore lost LF points, except when you are in combat. Each HEALTH potion can be used ONE TIME to restore 5 points. You are also free to use as many of them as you wish at any time, but your LIFE FORCE can never ever exceed its original default of **25**.

DYING
If you are killed in combat or die because of a failed

check or a choice you made, your adventure is over and you must return to the beginning of this book and restart your quest.

USING YOUR SKILLS AND ATTRIBUTES

Throughout the course of this story, you will be introduced to unique scenarios that may call upon you to use a specific skill or attribute. Whenever this happens, you will be prompted to do a check by rolling a 1d6. If your roll is AT or UNDER your CURRENT SCORE for the skill or attribute that is being checked, you have successfully passed that check. If, however, your roll exceeds your current score, then your check has failed.

SKILL AND ATTRIBUTE INCREASES

In real life, we learn from our failures and mistakes. For this reason, skill and attribute increases in this book are awarded for FAILURES rather than successes. This not only simulates learning, but prevents power creep and the cliche' "success-breeds-success" dynamic. Of course, if that failed check results in your untimely demise, then you will obviously NOT be awarded an increase. As stated previously, those scores can never exceed **5**, which is the maximum you can have for each one.

Now that you have a firm grasp of the mechanics...

THE BACKGROUND AND LORE

THE LICH LORD'S CURSE
The northeastern Kingdom of Olomar had at one time been a mecca of trade and commerce, but a terrible curse on the land, coupled with the ravages of war and a great famine have transformed much of this once prosperous nation into a desolate wasteland. Now, overrun by the undead and savage beasts and men alike, only a few scattered villages dare to call this god-forsaken land their home.

THE LABYRINTH
Perhaps the most famous, if not notorious of all landmarks in the Kingdom of Olomar is the mysterious Legorian Labyrinth. Built directly into the base of a gigantic plateau, its origin and creation date back several millennia when it was constructed by an ancient elven race called the Legorians. Its exact purpose and intent remain a mystery to this day.

THE LICH LORD
Once a powerful, elven magician skilled in the art of necromancy, the wizard, Sineus, sought to defy death and gain eternal life through divination and the dark arts. Little did he know, that in doing so, he would suffer a fate far worse than death — immortalized as one of the undead and doomed forever to haunt the stygian depths of the Legorian Labyrinth!

Gather your wits, muster your courage, and steel your nerves, for your quest begins now...

Welcome to the World of Ataraxia!

1

'A fool's quest,' they declared, shaking their heads in disbelief. 'Reckless and foolhardy,' said others, 'and one that will surely claim your life.'

In any event, you have never been one to shy away from a challenge, and in this case, the lure of adventure and the promise of a great treasure are just too tempting!

You have already traveled a great distance from afar, braving harsh terrain and even the elements, whilst beset by bandits and beasts at every turn. As you reflect on these things, you realize that for you, the journey has only just begun.

The road ahead takes you through a stretch of land that is barren and almost devoid of vegetation. Huge boulders are strewn across the landscape and the path before you is now nothing but a sea of crumbling rock and sand, so much so that it is becoming more and more difficult for you and your mount to even stay the course. Up ahead, you can see the Faalmund Plateau rising up from the harsh desert floor in stark contrast to the beautiful, Ataraxian sky.

With every step and with each passing moment, the way before you is becoming even more demanding and treacherous, but eventually, you fight your way to the base of the flat-top mountain until you are standing at last before the massive gates of the Legorian Labyrinth. Hewn from solid rock, the elven gates are overgrown with vegetation and covered in runes from a long-forgotten race. The gates are sealed tight and though you search diligently, you are unable to find any means of opening them. There is little recourse now but to find another way in...

Turn to 494

2

The liquid is surprisingly sweet and quite refreshing as you quickly down the entire glass container. You place the empty decanter back on the tray and wait for several moments, but find that you do not feel any different than you did before drinking the elixir.

The imp-like creature bows and then turns and heads back into the open doorway. It returns moments later, this time, holding a large hand mirror.

Holding it up, you are startled to see an old and decrepit person staring back at you. Clearly, the years and life itself have not been kind to this aged and frail individual. It is at that moment that you look down at your hands and realize that the old person in the mirror is actually you!

(Unfortunately, the decanter was filled with an AGING potion and the effects are PERMANENT. You must now subtract 5 points from your LIFE FORCE, and from this point forward will never be able to have an LF score that is higher than **20**. The effects of this potion, however, CAN BE REVERSED, but only by drinking a POTION OF RESTORATION).

Turn to 426

3

You have stopped at the base of a dead tree to rest when suddenly, you are startled by the voice of a woman.

"I really wish that it did not have to come to this, but I am afraid I have no other choice," says the woman.

Looking up, you see a beautiful, elven maiden standing some distance from you. In her hands, she holds a mage's staff, which is pointed directly at you.

"I'm not quite sure I understand," you say, as you slowly rise to your feet.

"I am sorry... truly I am, but there is no other way! I cannot allow you to continue any further!" replies the woman, as she brings her staff back and launches a ball of fire at you...

(At this time, please perform an Agility check. If your check fails, you have been struck by the fireball and must roll a 1d6 to determine how much DAMAGE you have sustained. Also, make sure to add 1 point to your Agility score for failing).

ELVEN SORCERESS   Life Force 25   Combat 5

(When you have brought the sorceress' LIFE FORCE down to 15, DO NOT continue fighting her, but instead, **proceed to 390**).

4

With a loud, snake-like hiss, the lizardman immediately launches an offensive, aggressively lunging at you with its broad-headed spear...

(Don't forget that you can now utilize Laurick in battle as well. Simply roll an additional 1d6 for the wood elf along with your roll. Laurick has an LF score of 25 and a Combat Skill Score of 3).

LIZARDMAN SENTRY   Life Force 29   Combat 3

Did you kill the lizardman? If so, **turn to 496**

5

(At this time, please remove EVERYTHING from your PURSE and INVENTORY, your weapon included, with the exception of your chainmail armor).

You awaken with a start, still lost in the lingering haze from a restless and tormented sleep. As your eyes gradually adjust to the dim light of your surroundings, you realize that you are in a strange and unfamiliar place. A quick visual scan of your environment tells you everything in an instant. You are in what appears to be some sort of holding cell — a prisoner no doubt within the dark and dank confines of some unknown and foul-smelling dungeon. Rough-hewn brick and mortar-daubed walls greet you on all sides and other than the one single, wooden door with a small, barred window at eye-level, there is no other means in or out of your place of confinement.

Even more disturbing are the nagging questions now flooding your mind. 'How did you get here?' and, 'Where exactly is HERE?'

Groggy and still somewhat disoriented, you make your way over to the door and much to your surprise, find that it is ajar. The door groans reluctantly as you swing it open upon its rusty hinges and step out into the corridor beyond...

Turn to 256

6

Up ahead, you can hear the loud roars of a large, predatory cat — probably an adult lion, with its deep-throated cries reverberating throughout the tunnel system. Although the ferocious beast is still not within your line of sight, you know you are close and begin to approach more cautiously, weapon in hand.

Rounding a sharp bend in the tunnel, you step out into an enormous cavern, and what you see next makes your heart race and literally causes you to tremble in fear.

Sitting at the far end of the cavern is a creature with the bushy mane and body of a lion, but with the hideous face of a man! Giant, bat-like wings sprout from its muscular shoulders, with each one of its four powerful paws sporting razor-sharp talons. In lieu of a lion's tail is the heavy, segmented tail of a scorpion, terminating in a large, venomous barb.

You quickly realize that the creature you are seeing is a manticore! As a child, you thought the manticore was just a ghost story — tales told by night to frighten the children — but the flesh-and-blood creature standing before you is anything but a child's fairy tale! Upon noticing you, the manticore lets out a blood-curdling roar and charges full speed towards you...

MANTICORE   Life Force 35   Combat 4

If you defeat the manticore, **turn to 80**

If, however, it is you who is killed, **go to 307**

7

With a glowing orb illuminating the way, you and Avril-Lyn guardedly make your way down the stairwell to the level below and make an unexpected discovery at the bottom — a heavy, metal door with a small, barred window!

"Thank the Ancients!" comes the voice of a man from the other side of the door. "Long have I prayed for the gods to grant me succor and you have come at last! There's a key hanging on the far wall right next to the stairs..."

Moved by the prisoner's plight, you grab the key from its hook on the wall and are about to unlock the door to the holding cell when Avril-Lyn quickly stops you.

"Wait!" says the sorceress, the apprehension quite noticeable in her voice. "This door, the bars, even its hinges... all of them have been made out of silver! This prison might have been created just especially for whoever or whatever is in there right now."

"Please..." pleads the voice. "Do not abandon me here to die in this godforsaken place alone!"

If you decide to release the prisoner, **turn to 449**

If you think it would probably be best to leave the man to his fate and carry on instead, **go to 169**

8

"Well done, adventurer! Bravo!" declares the halfling, smiling and clapping his hands together. "Kudos for finding that which was hidden in plain sight! Well then, a wager is a wager and I am most certainly a halfling of my word."

The halfling snaps his fingers and you suddenly find yourself standing on the other side of the gorge. Looking across to the other side, you discover that Tomlin Underhill, along with his table and chairs, has vanished...

Turn to 339

9

The corridor abruptly comes to an end and you find yourself standing at the foot of a crumbling staircase. So deteriorated are many of its stairs, that at times you struggle just to maintain your footing as you ascend — the stone breaking apart and giving way beneath your feet with each precarious step.

Eventually, you reach the summit of the staircase and discover a corridor that picks right up where the one at the bottom left off...

Turn to 199

10

After safely clearing the last pendulum, you take a brief rest and then continue down the corridor...

Turn to 463

11

Almost immediately, after rotating the last turn-stone, a barrage of darts spews forth from multiple hidden apertures, with some of them hitting you.

(To determine how much DAMAGE you sustained, roll a 1d6 and subtract this amount from your LIFE FORCE now).

You have obviously chosen the wrong combination of symbols!

Please return to 87

12

(At this time, please perform a Stealth check).

If your check is successful, **turn to 199**

If your check failed, add 1 point to your Stealth score and then **go to 107**

13

Moving cautiously from one building to another and utilizing each one as cover, you circumnavigate the plaza and the mysterious object, eventually finding your way out of the city and back into the forest...

Turn to 296

14

At daybreak's first light, you set out once more, and after navigating the treacherous swamp for a good part of the morning, you eventually find yourself following the muddy banks of a slow-moving river. A foul smell emanates from its disgusting waters, filling the air and your nostrils with its putrid stench.

Suddenly, a slimy tentacle covered with suction cups breaches the water near you, sweeping you off of your feet and nearly causing you to tumble into the river. In an instant, you are back on your feet, your weapon readied, and not a moment too soon!

Rising out of the murky depths of the river is a terrifying monstrosity that you thought only existed in stories told by parents to frighten disobedient children who were playing too close to the river. They called it the Lurker, warning the little ones that it was lurking just below the surface of the water and waiting to devour them. Even as you are watching in horrified disbelief, the creature grabs onto the trunk and branches of a nearby cypress with its tentacles, dragging itself out of the river and onto the muddy shore.

You retreat further back onto the drier ground and away from the river, but much to your astonishment, the monstrous beast appears to be just as equally mobile on land as it is in the water. Surprisingly fast on land, the creature uses the cypress trees to maneuver its gigantic body across the swamp floor towards you — its hideous, tooth-filled maw snapping open and shut as it anticipates the taste of your flesh.

Relentless in its pursuit of you, it appears you will have no choice but to engage this fearsome creature in battle...

LURKER   Life Force 50   Combat 4

If you defeat the lurker, **turn to 408**

If the lurker defeats you, **go to 275**

15

You are making your way down the corridor when quite suddenly and unexpectedly, you encounter a monster...

(Roll a 1d6 to determine which monster from the table below you will have to face).

1	DIRE RAT	Life Force 5	Combat 1
2	RABID WARTHOG	Life Force 12	Combat 1
3	LESSER MUMMY	Life Force 14	Combat 2
4	GIANT PRAYING MANTIS	Life Force 15	Combat 2
5	ORC	Life Force 20	Combat 3
6	UNDEAD OGRE	Life Force 27	Combat 3

(You can also exercise the option of trying to flee by performing an Agility check).

If you are able to successfully flee, **turn to 183**

If not, add 1 point to your Agility score and prepare to face the monster in battle...

WANDERING MONSTER	Life Force ?	Combat ?

If you defeat the wandering monster, **go to 183**

16

The baboon attacks with the ferocity of a cornered animal, but in the end, is unable to contend with your skills as a warrior.

A search of the fallen adventurer's half-eaten body nets you 25 gold pieces. You also discover a partially-buried chest, which adds another 50 gold pieces and two HEALTH potions to your total loot.

(Add these items to your PURSE and INVENTORY now) and then **proceed to 139**

17

Unable to withstand the surprising strength of your attack against her, the sorceress backpedals, and then, with a wave of her hand, disappears...

Turn to 181

18

The corridor terminates at a heavy, wooden door with a small, barred window at eye-level. Looking through the bars, you see what appears to be a chamber on the other side. Directly in front of you and in the center of the room is a podium fashioned from solid rock with a large scroll sitting on top of it. There is also another heavy, wooden door on the opposite side of the chamber.

Opening the door, you cautiously approach the podium, and, picking up the tattered scroll, carefully unroll it. There is an incantation written upon it and although the writing is quite faded, it is still legible enough to read...

If you decide to read what is written in the scroll out loud, **turn to 172**

If you choose instead to exit the room via the door on the far side of the chamber, **go to 403**

19

The spider shudders as you deliver the final death-dealing blow between its multiple eyes. Inside of the chest is a HEALTH potion and a RESURRECTION elixir...

(HEALTH potions can be used at any time to restore lost LF points, except when you are in combat. Each HEALTH potion can be used ONE TIME to restore 5 points. You are also free to use as many of them as you wish at any time, but your LIFE FORCE can never ever exceed its original default of **25**. RESURRECTION elixirs enable you to rejoin the battle after being killed, without having to start over at the beginning of the book).

(Add these items, including the torch you found, to your INVENTORY now).

Turn to 305

20

Before you is a wide passageway, but it is the large, bluish-green crystals naturally occurring on both the walls, floor, and ceiling of the passage that gives you pause, for a strange and unearthly glow emanates from each one, brightly illuminating the path ahead.

Straight away, you and the sorceress set out and it is not long before you come to a two-way junction, with the passage you have been following bending slightly to the left, and another one branching off to the right.

"Any thoughts on which way we should go?" you ask.

"I'd say that either one is probably as good a choice as any at this point," Avril-Lyn replies nonchalantly.

If you decide to take the passage on the left, **turn to 175**

If you choose the passage on the right, **go to 384**

21

After a time, the passage begins to make a noticeable swing to the right, gradually curving to the left to the point of almost doubling back on itself. A sharp right, followed again by another right-hand turn finds you in a wide hallway with a high ceiling and walls constructed from large, rough-hewn blocks of stone. The hallway is well-lit by a series of consecutive torches on both sides, and as you make your way forward, what you see next makes you momentarily question your sanity.

Crawling on the ceiling and making her way upside down towards you is what looks like a beautiful, young maiden. Almost immediately, you find yourself strangely enthralled by her great beauty, even smitten as you gaze longingly into her eyes. But whatever hold she has upon you quickly vanishes as two large, batlike wings slowly unfold from her back and her face becomes contorted as her jaws dislocate like a python to reveal two rows of razor-sharp fangs.

Dropping down from the ceiling a short distance away, the vampire lands softly on her feet, and then, with a growl-like hiss and talons bared, lunges for you...

VAMPIRE   Life Force 30   Combat 4

If you kill the vampire, **turn to 176**

If, however, you are the one who is defeated, **go to 470**

22

Unable to withstand the surprising strength of your attack against her, the sorceress backpedals, and then, with a wave of her hand, disappears...

Turn to 431

23

You quietly and cautiously open the door, and, peering inside, see an orc seated at a wooden table drinking a bottle of what is obviously strong liquor. The creature is clearly intoxicated, so much so that it is having a heated discourse with itself, mumbling, and yelling at itself in the first person. This goes on for many minutes, with the orc finally passing out and planting face-first on the table, spilling the bottle of liquor everywhere.

There could be something useful or even valuable on the orc's person...

If you decide to pickpocket the orc, **turn to 394**

If you would rather exit the room and move on to the next door, **go to 303**

24

The passage eventually finds its end, culminating at a large, wooden door that has been reinforced with steel bands. Pressing your ear to the door, you hear the rhythmic percussion of waves gently breaking upon what must be the shore. Throwing open the door and stepping outside, you are immediately greeted by the brilliant splendor of a white sand beach, scintillating like a million tiny diamonds in the Ataraxian sun.

To your left, an unscalable wall of rock rises high above you as you follow the narrow strip of shoreline hugging its base. It is not long before you stumble upon the entrance to a cave. Peering into the dimly lit grotto, you are disturbed by the scene before you.

Milling around in the knee-deep water are several, enormous clams, each one using their large, muscle-like foot to move blindly about. You also spot what appears to be a partially submerged chest in the very back of the cave...

If you decide to find out what is in the chest, **turn to 312**

If you choose to press on instead, **go to 173**

25

The wooded path you have been following suddenly splits into a two-way fork, with one trail veering slightly left before continuing straight ahead and the other branching off sharply to the right...

If you decide to head left, **turn to 125**

If your decision is to go right, **go to 395**

26

Sometime later, you and Avril-Lyn come to a door on the right-hand side of the passage, and, hearing nothing when you press your ear to the wood, cautiously push the door inward and open.

At first glance, the room beyond appears to be empty, but as you are turning to leave, you spot what appears to be a small flask lying on its side in the farmost corner. Retrieving the flask from the floor, you hear the sound of liquid moving around inside of it as you pick it up and examine it...

If you decide to drink the contents of the flask, **turn to 174**

If you decide that it is not worth the risk, **go to 253**

27

The corridor opens up into a large, cavern-like room. As you step into the chamber, your ears are met with the industrial roar of heavy equipment in operation. Ancient machinery, coupled with strange technology, fills the room, testifying to the advanced race that created it. Could it be possible that these machines are remnants of the lost Legorian civilization?

A quick sweep of the room is rewarded with the discovery of a HEALTH potion lying on the ground next to one of the pieces of machinery.

(HEALTH potions can be used at any time to restore lost LF points, except when you are in combat. Each HEALTH potion can be used ONE TIME to restore 5 points. You are also free to use as many of them as you wish at any time, but your LIFE FORCE can never ever exceed its original default of **25**).

(Add the HEALTH potion to your INVENTORY now).

A passageway hidden from view behind some equipment affords you an exit from the room...

Turn to 132

28

You approach the chest cautiously, mindful of the possibility of traps. The chest looks to be quite old, but is otherwise ordinary in its appearance. The wood on it has begun to deteriorate in places and the metal bands and latch are completely encrusted with rust, testifying to its great antiquity.

You are about to flip the latch and open the chest when suddenly, the lid springs open, revealing not treasure, but an enormous mouth filled with dagger-like teeth and what appears to be a tongue.

You realize, too late, what you thought to be a chest is none other than a creature known as a changeling. Because they are quite slow and unable to move with any kind of speed whatsoever, changelings will quite often mimic inanimate objects in order to lure and capture unwary and unsuspecting prey.

Before you can even react, its tongue has already wrapped itself tightly around your wrist and is trying to pull you into its mouth...

(At this time, please perform a Strength check).

If you successfully free yourself, **turn to 409**

If, however, you are unable to break free, **go to 248**

29

A search of the necromancer's body, as well as a quick sweep of the room itself, nets you 5 gold pieces and an unusually large opal.

(Add these items to your PURSE and INVENTORY now) and then exit the room **by going to 199**

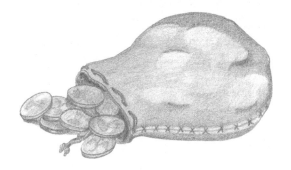

30

The tunnel leads into a high-ceilinged, cavern-like chamber with rocks strewn about its floor. In the center of the room is the statue of a minotaur perched upon a stone pedestal. From where you are standing, there appears to be some kind of inscription on the base of the pedestal, but you are just too far away to make out what it says.

There is also another tunnel leading out of the room to your immediate right...

If you choose to investigate the statue, **turn to 119**

If you prefer to leave the room via the tunnel on your right, **go to 219**

31

Kneeling down beside the base of the gigantic tree, you are surprised to discover many more of the very same talismans strategically placed in abundance around the opening. Cautiously making your way in, you discover that the ground within has been partially excavated and the inside of the tree hollowed out to create a small chamber of sorts.

Exhausted, you lay out your bedroll, and moments later, fall into a deep and dreamless sleep, remaining so until morning...

Turn to 441

32

You step off of the pressure plate, and right away, the chamber comes to a grinding halt as the door swings open to reveal a dimly-lit passage...

Turn to 420

33

With the giant totally preoccupied, you are able to creep silently up to it and attack.

Much to your surprise, the giant stops weeping, and, suddenly aware of your presence, quickly leaps to its feet. Too late you realize that the creature now towering above you is no ordinary giant at all, but is composed entirely out of solid rock. It is a stone golem, and unfortunately, your weapon is completely ineffective against it!

Also unfortunate for you is that the stone golem immediately seizes you and with brute force savagely throws you against the cavern wall. The impact is the equivalent of you falling from a great height, literally causing your body to burst open, spilling your intestines and your vital organs all over the floor of the cavern.

Why this stone golem was crying will forever remain a mystery...

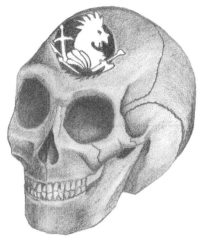

34

Almost immediately, you come upon two more doors, one on the left-hand wall of the corridor and the other directly across from it on the right-hand side.

Making ready with your weapon, you grab onto the handle of the door nearest you with your free hand...

(At this time, please roll a 1d6).

If your roll is an ODD number, **turn to 348**

If your roll is an EVEN number, **go to 257**

35

With the rapidity of thought itself, you instantly find yourself standing before the massive and fortified gates of the castle stronghold's gatehouse. A surreal, almost phantasmagorical mist completely envelops the ground with a thick, low-lying veil of white, while above, a rough, woolen blanket of mottled gray now hides any traces of the Ataraxian sun.

One of the heavy, wooden gates has been left ajar, and you are relieved to find that there is just enough space to squeeze through sideways. You are in what is obviously the inner courtyard, and it, too, has been overrun by the same supernatural mist.

Suddenly, without any warning whatsoever, the doors of the keep are thrown wide open with such force and violence, that both of them come off of their hinges and topple to the ground!

Emerging from the keep, and bounding down the wide staircase on all fours like a giant ape, is a horrifying creature that makes anything and everything you have ever encountered pale in comparison. Standing nearly one-and-a-half times your height, you are shocked to discover it has literally been constructed from the corpses of both men and beasts that have been sewn together to create its composite form!

Within moments, the quivering mass of cadaverous gray flesh is upon you...

FLESH GOLEM   Life Force 45   Combat 4

If you defeat the flesh golem, **turn to 329**

36

Still shuffling towards you, Umra falls to his knees, eventually toppling to the ground as he expires. You watch as his body begins to crumble and deteriorate, until all that remains of the Resplendent One is a pile of sand and some tattered strips of cloth. Reaching down, you retrieve the golden, bejeweled crown that once adorned the mummy's brow as well as the gold necklace once encircling his neck. You shake the sand from them, but they, too, soon disintegrate in your hands.

Making your way onto the dais, you notice what appears to be an earthen firepot in the shape of a human skull sitting on the floor next to Umra's sarcophagus. As soon as you pick it up, the skull instantaneously begins to emit an unearthly glow from within its eye sockets, kindling an eerie green flame on top of it.

(You have unwittingly discovered The Fire of Faeren-Galle, a legendary and epic, enchanted weapon that will consume every enemy with its strange fire, regardless of how many there are if they are standing within the vicinity of the one holding it. You can now use this weapon in a future battle to simultaneously and immediately dispatch multiple enemies with LF scores of 25 or less or on a more powerful enemy whose LIFE FORCE has been reduced to 25 or less. After its one-time use, The Fire of Faeren-Galle's flame is extinguished and the weapon must be REMOVED from your INVENTORY).

You also discover 50 gold pieces and a HEALTH potion inside of Umra's sarcophagus.

(Add these items to your PURSE and INVENTORY now).

A further search of the tomb and its contents, as well as a quick sweep of the smaller sarcophagi, yields nothing worth taking.

Turn to 105

37

Upon seeing you, the hobgoblins are instantly on their feet with their weapons drawn and immediately advance towards you...

HOBGOBLIN   Life Force 27   Combat 3
HOBGOBLIN   Life Force 26   Combat 3

If you defeat the hobgoblins, **turn to 103**

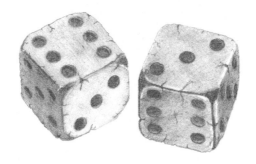

38

You have only traveled for a short time when quite unexpectedly, you stumble upon what is perhaps one of the most bizarre scenes you have ever laid eyes on. Kneeling in the sand is a half-naked, old man, who, much to your amazement, is completely focused and hard at work on building a sandcastle of all things! Though you try to get his attention by calling out to him several times, the man seems to be completely oblivious to your presence and continues to work diligently on his creation.

Realizing that this man has either lost his mind or is under some kind of powerful enchantment, you resume your trek along the shoreline...

Turn to 293

39

Upon seeing you, the goblinoids are instantly on their feet with their weapons drawn...

GOBLINOID   Life Force 26   Combat 3
GOBLINOID   Life Force 24   Combat 3
GOBLINOID   Life Force 23   Combat 3

If you defeat the goblinoids, **turn to 192**

40

You have only traveled but a short while when you stumble upon what is perhaps the most bizarre thing you have ever laid eyes on. Buried up to the top of their necks in the sand and facing each other are two men, but what makes this already unusual scenario even odder is the fact that they are arguing loudly about a woman!

"For the last time already, Larrs, she told me she didn't have a husband!" says one of the men. "And there was nothing to indicate that she was married or even spoken for! So how could I have possibly known that she was someone's wife, much less your wife? I didn't even know that you had gotten yourself married!"

"You knew full well that she was my wife, Jarred, but that certainly didn't stop you from sleeping with her, did it, you wretched, good-for-nothing, snake bastard?" shouts the other man.

"Maybe if you were even half the skryll that I am, your wife wouldn't have been unfaithful to you!" replies the one called Jarred.

What happens next could not have been any more unexpected, for even as you are watching in utter astonishment, spider-like legs unfold from the bottom of Larrs' bodiless head as he lunges viciously for Jarred. The two heads begin grappling with each other and rolling around in the sand, all the while still quarreling amongst themselves.

Shaking your head in utter disbelief, you continue on your way...

Turn to 498

41

The passage twists and turns before ending at a large, wooden door set within an ornately carved archway. The doorway opens into a wide hallway, but it is what your eyes immediately see that gives cause for alarm.

Leaning with their backs against the walls on both sides of the hallway are the skeletal remains of several persons — their jaws hanging wide open as if they perished in mid-scream. A thick, heavy layer of dust covers both the floor and the skeletons, with the absence of any footprints in the dust being a strong indicator that no one has come through here in quite some time.

With no recourse but to stay the path ahead, you enter the corridor, the soft footfalls of your boots upon the dusty floor extremely perceptible in the palpable, tomb-like silence surrounding you.

You have just passed the first of them when suddenly and quite unexpectedly, the skeleton leans forward, grabbing onto your leg with one of its boney hands. As you quickly turn and free yourself, simultaneously the others begin to stir, as if awakened from a deep slumber. One by one, each of them begins to crawl towards you, dragging their lower extremities across the dust-laden floor, their gaping maws unable to disengage and close.

Perhaps there is a way to get past them without having to fight them...

(Continued on overleaf)

(At this time, please perform an Agility check).

If you successfully evade the skeletons and are able to flee the hallway, **turn to 235**

Otherwise, prepare to engage them in battle. Add 1 point now to your Agility score for failing your check and then **go to 455**

42

Knowing that cats are, more often than not, the familiars of witches and warlocks and that it is highly unlikely that someone's pet would be simply wandering around a dungeon, you decide to go in for a closer look.

"Here, kitty, kitty, kitty," you say as you slowly approach. "Nice, kitty..."

It hisses and lashes out at you with its claws before quickly slinking off to one of the farmost corners of the room.

Suddenly, the cat begins to convulse violently, and then, right before your very eyes, begins to contort and change, its body literally transforming. Moments later, you find yourself staring at a faceless monstrosity straight out of your worst nightmares. With the exception of its tooth-filled mouth and a couple of stubby horn-like growths, what should be its face is completely devoid of any other features, including eyes and a nose. Its body is thin and sinewy, with elongated arms and legs, and hands and feet that seem to be largely disproportionate.

You realize that the thing standing before you is a metamorph. Metamorphs are able to take on the appearance of the last person or creature they devoured and use this ability to lure their next victim to their untimely demise.

(Continued on overleaf)

With its claws and teeth bared, the metamorph begins advancing across the room towards you...

METAMORPH   Life Force 20   Combat 3

If you defeat the metamorph, **turn to 166**

43

With the water now quite cloudy from all of the small pieces of rotting tissue floating in it, you conduct a quick search of the troglodytes' corpses and between them, find a combined booty of 15 gold pieces, which you quickly drop into your satchel before carrying on.

(Add these to your PURSE now) and then **turn to 115**

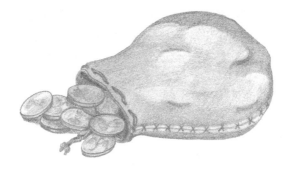

44

With the daylight quickly waning, you decide that the first order of business should be to find shelter to ride out the approaching storm and rapidly descending night. A short, but fortuitous hike leads you to the discovery of a small cave — and not a moment too soon, for even as you are lighting your torch, a heavy rain begins to fall.

The opening of the cave is just large enough for you to enter, and as you are slipping in, you notice hundreds of small talismans suspended by strings of varying lengths all around the entrance.

Once inside, a casual search of the cave rewards you with a small quantity of smoked fish and dried fruit, as well as a HEALTH potion. You also find a kit used for dressing wounds and a bedroll consisting of some bedding and a thin blanket.

(Add these items, including the bedroll, to your INVENTORY now) and then **turn to 201**

45

Another door almost immediately presents itself on the right, introducing you to what appears to be, for all intents and purposes, a cloakroom — for hanging by hooks from every wall are the hooded, mustard-colored robes worn by Arachnae's followers.

Quickly donning the garments of the Faithful, you and Avril-Lyn exit the cloakroom...

Turn to 259

46

You hear the lock mechanism disengage and the lid of the chest springs open, revealing 10 gold pieces, a HEALTH potion, and an ancient, bejeweled, ornamental dagger. Upon closer examination, you realize that the dagger has been forged from silver.

(HEALTH potions can be used at any time to restore lost LF points, except when you are in combat. Each HEALTH potion can be used ONE TIME to restore 5 points. You are also free to use as many of them as you wish at any time, but your LIFE FORCE can never ever exceed its original default of **25**).

(Add these items to your PURSE and INVENTORY now).

You can still search the pile of bones. If this is your choice, **turn to 221**

If you decide to leave the room, **go to 484**

47

Within seconds, the giant wasps surround you and begin to attack...

GIANT WASP	Life Force 5	Combat 2
GIANT WASP	Life Force 5	Combat 2
GIANT WASP	Life Force 4	Combat 2
GIANT WASP	Life Force 4	Combat 2

If you defeat the wasps, **turn to 61**

If, however, it is you who are killed, **go to 165**

48

The corridor runs straight for about a hundred paces and eventually begins to slope downwards before twisting and turning upon itself. It is here that the corridor abruptly ends, blocked from any further travel by a gigantic boulder that seems oddly out of place.

The heavy smell of rotten eggs fills the air and you immediately find it extremely difficult to breathe. Panic begins to ensue as your breathing becomes more and more irregular and labored. Completely disoriented, you inadvertently stumble face-first into the boulder. Reeling in pain from the impact and gasping for air, you instinctively reach out to brace yourself from falling and discover a cleverly hidden lever that causes the boulder to swing aside when you pull it. Fresh air suddenly rushes into the corridor from the room just beyond, and as you collapse to your knees, your grateful lungs drink deeply of it...

Turn to 157

49

At long last, the weary trek upstream is over as you finally reach the river's source. Up ahead, you can see the mighty headwaters, and just beyond, a colossal waterfall fed by what must be a ginormous underground spring. At the base of the waterfall is a gigantic crystal clear pool. As you approach the waterfall, you can just make out the outline of what could be a cave or even a tunnel just beyond its curtain of cascading water.

Suddenly, a figure slowly emerges from behind the wall of water. At first, you think it is just a cyclops because of its one enormous eye, but then, as it is uncovered by the waterfall, you discover that from the waist down it actually has the body of a huge horse. Its massive body is extremely well-muscled and in its hand, it holds a humongous spear.

It is a cyclotaur and upon seeing you, the gargantuan brute draws its spear back and launches it towards you with tremendous force!

(At this time, please perform a Luck check. If successful, the cyclotaur's throw either missed its mark or you were miraculously somehow able to dodge it. If, however, your check failed, you have been struck by the spear and must now roll 2d6 to determine how much DAMAGE you have sustained. Subtract this from your LIFE FORCE now. Any damage you receive will be retained until you use a Health potion. If you are still alive, add 1 point to your Luck score for failing).

(Continued on overleaf of illustration)

After throwing its spear, the monstrous beast does not waste any time, immediately galloping straight for you...

CYCLOTAUR   Life Force 40   Combat 4

If you defeat the cyclotaur, **turn to 102**

If, however, the cyclotaur kills you, **go to 415**

50

Unable to break free from the powerful sorcery of the siren's song, you continue to wade farther out and deeper into the murky depths of the lake. Water fills your lungs as your head slips beneath the water's surface, and though you are drowning, you are too enthralled by the siren's song to even care. And as the last remnants of oxygen escape from your lungs, the siren is already dragging your lifeless body back to its lair so that it can feed...

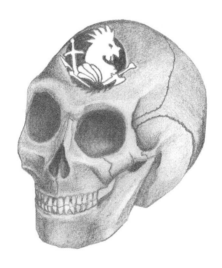

51

Finding nothing of any use or value when you search its body, you exit the room via the door the thrall came in and discover another flight of stairs going up. Unlike the previous stairwell, this one is well-lit and is a straight shot to the top.

Yet another door finds you in a short corridor — this one taking you to what was obviously the barracks used for housing the guards at one time. A somewhat smaller chamber coming directly off of the living quarters probably more than likely served as a weapons cache as well as an armory.

A quick sweep of both the barracks and the armory proves fruitless...

Turn to 476

52

After a time, you notice that the passage has gradually begun to swing to the left, eventually taking you in a large circle and leading you back to the junction where you originally started...

Please go back to 385

53

You have not gone far when suddenly, the floor beneath you gives way, sending you flying down a greased chute at high speed. At the bottom is a chamber filled with sharpened pikes, as well as the skeletal remains of an unlucky few. With no way of stopping or even slowing down, you slide uncontrollably right into the middle of this deathtrap!

(How lucky are you? Find out now by performing a Luck check. If your check is successful, then you escape with only minor scratches and wounded pride. If, however, your check failed, you have been seriously injured. Add 1 point to your Luck score for failing, and then roll 2d6 to determine how much DAMAGE you have sustained. Subtract this amount from your LIFE FORCE now. Any damage you receive will be retained until you use a Health potion).

On the far side of the chamber is a tunnel that leads back to the original passage you were following...

Turn to 425

54

The man crumples to the floor dead, once again becoming the pile of rags you saw when you first entered the room. A quick search of his person gives you an easy 10 gold pieces, which you add to your satchel before exiting the room...

(Add the gold to your PURSE now) and then **go back to 214**

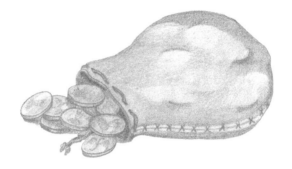

55

The tauregg is an incredibly formidable opponent, but in the aftermath, your skillful prowess proves too much for the savage beast. Eventually, it expires from the severity of the wounds you have inflicted upon it — its magnificent and terrible form collapsing at your feet.

Also dead is your skeletal companion, Mateo, the last remaining crew member of the ship, The Serpent's Wake, and although you knew him for only a short period of time, you find yourself filled with a profound sense of grief at his unexpected loss.

And so, it is with a heavy heart that you press on...

Turn to 478

56

Rounding a sharp bend, the passage suddenly culminates at the edge of a massive cavern, and for a brief moment, both you and Mateo find yourselves transfixed and filled with wonder by the breathtaking sight before you.

Large, pink crystal formations adorn the floor and ceiling of the cavern in perfect disarray — their translucent beauty sharply contrasted against the harsh backdrop of stone, stalactites, and stalagmites, and at the same time, boldly reflected within the small, shallow pools of water throughout.

Picking your way through, you eventually discover a narrow fissure that transitions into a wide corridor...

Turn to 148

57

Stopping to rest at the base of a gigantic tree, you have barely even sat down when suddenly, a headless cadaver that is also missing its arms falls from above, hitting the ground hard not far from where you are sitting. Terrified, you leap to your feet, simultaneously readying your weapon as you hurriedly back away from the tree.

Looking up, you are shocked to discover an enormous praying mantis perched in the leafy canopy above — its raptorial, front limbs still clutching a human arm, which it voraciously devours with its mandibles.

In another instant, the humongous insect has leaped to the ground and is now advancing hungrily towards you...

GIANT PRAYING MANTIS   Life Force 25   Combat 3

If you defeat the mantid, **turn to 361**

58

58

You have stopped beside a large boulder to rest when suddenly, you are startled by the voice of a woman.

"I really wish that it did not have to come to this, but I am afraid that I have no other choice," says the woman. "Stand up... slowly, and do not make any sudden moves!"

Rising to your feet, you see a beautiful elven maiden standing some distance from you. In her hands, she holds a mage's staff, which is pointed directly at you.

"I'm not quite sure I understand," you say, as you slowly rise to your feet.

"I am sorry... truly I am, but there is no other way! I cannot allow you to continue any further!" replies the woman, as she brings her staff back and launches a ball of fire at you...

(At this time, please perform an Agility check. If your check fails, you have been struck by the fireball and must roll a 1d6 to determine how much DAMAGE you have sustained. Also, make sure to add 1 point to your Agility score for failing).

ELVEN SORCERESS   Life Force 25   Combat 5

(When you have brought the sorceress' LIFE FORCE down to 15, DO NOT continue fighting her, but instead, **proceed to 255**).

59

It is not long before the tunnel you are following leads you to another chamber — this one oval in shape and quite spacious. Peering into the room, you see several bioluminescent orbs floating lazily about. Their aerial dance is almost hypnotic and you are immediately captivated by their translucent beauty.

Without even thinking, you step into the room and the orbs surround you and begin emitting a high-pitched but barely audible hum. Suddenly, you find yourself completely overwhelmed with feelings of hopelessness, gloom, and depression, so much so that you fall to your knees and begin to weep uncontrollably...

(You have been bewitched by several MELANCHOLY ORBS. At this time, please perform a Resistance check).

If you successfully resist the melancholy orbs, **turn to 200**

If, however, the orbs' hold on you is too strong, **go to 145**

60

You touch the S, I, X, T, and Y in their appropriate order, with each one lighting up in response as you do so. There is a loud rumble as the massive stone door swings open and grants you and Avril-Lyn passage...

Turn to 20

61

Completely surrounded by the deadly flying insects, a tenacious battle ensues, with you fighting for your very survival while your opponents vie to make you their next source of food. One by one they fall, until finally, the last of the giant wasps lie dead at your feet.

Thoroughly exhausted, you collapse against a nearby rock formation to recover. Your time of rest, however, is short-lived, for you have barely even sat down before you are having to leap back to your feet again.

Emerging from the entrance to the hive is none other than the matriarch insect, herself — the wasp queen! Upon seeing you and noticing some of her subjects are dead, she quickly launches herself into the air, immediately mounting an airborne offensive against you...

GIANT WASP QUEEN   Life Force 25   Combat 3

If you kill the wasp queen, **turn to 471**

If the wasp queen kills you, **go to 287**

62

In a split-second moment of hesitation, you grossly miscalculate your window of opportunity and the portcullis literally splits you in twain from crown to foot!

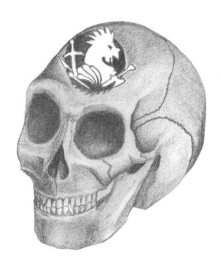

63

As impressive and grandiose as the chamber before, the hallway boasts more of the same fine white marble, only this time, with bold and beautiful reliefs and intricate patterns set into the polished stone and overlaid with gold. Ancient tapestries run from the floor to the ceiling, only adding to the massive corridor's magnificence, while masterfully carved statues of elvenkind and heroic beasts grace both sides of the hallway.

The foyer terminates at a set of beautifully hand-crafted, double doors. You are about to swing them open to see what is beyond them when suddenly, you are startled by a voice behind you.

"Salutations, bold and fearless adventurer..."

With a swiftness that only comes from being a seasoned warrior, you quickly whirl around to face the author of the voice, simultaneously bringing your weapon to combat readiness.

Standing some distance away from you is an extremely short and repulsive-looking creature with flattened facial features, a sloped forehead, large pointed ears, and a short beard. It is dressed in fine, exquisite clothing and is also holding what appears to be a leather travel bag of some sort.

"Declare your intentions, goblin!" you say emphatically.

"Apologies, good and noble one... I can assure you, I am unarmed and mean no ill will towards you," the goblin replies.

"Then what business is it that you have with me, goblin?" you ask, your patience quickly diminishing by the moment.

"Begging your pardon, but perhaps it might be better if I showed you," the goblin says, eagerly clapping its hands together while giving you an awkward, toothy smile.

Picking up its small, well-worn travel bag by the handle with both hands, the goblin gives it a hard shake and instantly, it transforms into a large vendor's booth, with the goblin somehow standing behind a counter inside of it. Affixed just above the creature, and with words scrawled in big, uneven letters is a huge wooden sign that reads: GRAZU'S WORLD-FAMOUS EMPORIUM.

"Welcome to Grazu's World-Famous Emporium!" the goblin exclaims, beaming proudly.

"World-famous, huh? How is it then that in all of my travels I have never heard tell of you?" you ask matter-of-factly.

"Allow me kindly, if you will, to introduce myself," the goblin continues, completely ignoring your quip. "I am Grazu, a lowly and unassuming merchant who has navigated the far reaches of the universe to bring you the best of the best and the finest of all the realms have to offer..."

"Lowly, indeed," you mumble under your breath, still fixated on the gigantic sign above the goblin.

It is here Grazu pauses for a brief moment just for effect.

"What do you say? Surely, there is something that I must have for a person of your, uh... tastes..."

"OK, goblin," you reply, "I will look at your wares, but be forewarned, I will not tolerate any trickery on your part."

"But of course," Grazu says, with a nod and a nonchalant wave of one of its arms.

Walking over to the goblin's booth, you begin to peruse the menu of items available for purchase. Knowing full well that the Lich Lord will be unlike any other opponent you have faced thus far, you casually scan the list, looking for any items that might help you...

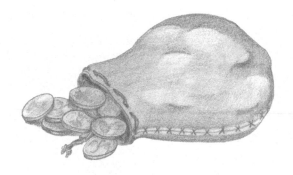

GRAZU'S WORLD-FAMOUS EMPORIUM

ITEM:	PRICE:
TROLL STOOL	5 GP
WOLFSBANE	5 GP
GARDEN GNOME	5 GP
SET OF LOCKPICKS	5 GP
RUSTY DAGGER	5 GP
MIC STAND	5 GP
DWARVEN NESTING DOLLS	10 GP
POTENT POISON AGAINST THE UNDEAD*	10 GP
SILVER BULLETS	10 GP
MAGE'S ROBE	10 GP
INVISIBLE POTION OF INVISIBILITY	10 GP
ELVEN CHESS BOARD	15 GP
RESTORATION POTION**	20 GP
HEALTH POTION***	25 GP
RESURRECTION ELIXIR (Limit One)****	50 GP
TOILET PAPER	100 GP
HALFLING BATTERING RAM	150 GP
GOLD NECKLACE W/DIAMONDS & RUBIES	200 GP
DRAGON TEETH	500 GP
BALLISTA	900 GP
OUIJA BOARD	SOLD OUT
UNICORN HORN	SOLD OUT
HENSON M5000 PULSE PLASMA RIFLE	SOLD OUT

*   Causes 5 points of instantaneous damage to the undead

**   Reverses the effects of an AGING potion

***   Restores 5 points to your LIFE FORCE

**** Enables you to rejoin the battle after being killed without having to start over at the beginning of the book

(This is also your opportunity to sell any items you may have acquired during your quest thus far and then use the gold pieces obtained to purchase any of the items listed in Grazu's inventory. What follows is a list of those particular items and what Grazu, the Goblin Merchant, will purchase them for should you decide to sell them. Be sure, after selling them, to revisit the menu of items for sale).

TORCH	5 GP
DECOMPOSING HUMAN FOOT	5 GP
BEAR CLAW	5 GP
SILVER, BEJEWELED DAGGER	5 GP
SKELETON KEY	10 GP
HEALTH POTION	10 GP
UNUSUALLY LARGE OPAL	10 GP
GOLD RING	10 GP
GOLD COIN	10 GP
RESURRECTION ELIXIR	20 GP
SENTINEL'S POWER CORE	25 GP
GIANT, NEARLY FLAWLESS RUBY	25 GP
GOLD NECKLACE	25 GP
MINOTAUR HORN (EACH)	25 GP

(Be sure to adjust your PURSE and INVENTORY accordingly after you have finished buying and selling).

After completing your transaction with Grazu, you waste no time and head straight for the double doors leading to the throne room, and ultimately, the final showdown with the Lich Lord...

Turn to 98

64

The door introduces you to what was probably, in all likelihood, a servant's access tunnel and you soon find yourself standing in a room that must have been the servant's quarters. Telltale trundles filled with straw bedding immediately confirm this and aside from them and a few, insignificant items, there is little else in the room.

Turn to 499

65

Unable to withstand the surprising strength of your attack against her, the sorceress backpedals, and then, with a wave of her hand, disappears...

Turn to 161

66

It is during the hottest part of the day that you and Mateo happen upon a small, ramshackle building that probably served as a fishing hut at one time. Approaching the dilapidated structure with caution, you peer in and find that, with the exception of a wooden bench and some old fishing nets hanging on the walls, the place is completely empty.

Suddenly, Mateo lets out a blood-curdling scream. Quickly turning around while simultaneously drawing your weapon, you are horrified to discover a giant sea serpent clutching Mateo's limp and bloodied body in its powerful jaws. Before you even have time to react, the monstrous creature slithers back into the water with Mateo still in its mouth and in an instant is gone.

Grieving the tragic and unexpected loss of your newfound friend, it is with a heavy heart that you press on...

Turn to 462

67

Rolling onto its side, you watch as the behemoth fish sinks slowly to the bottom, its gills still fluttering as it is quickly lost in a blood-red mist...

Turn to 306

68

With even the very shadows fleeing the encroaching darkness, you and Mateo hole up for the night inside the tight confines of a small cave. Inside, you discover many more of the very same talismans as before — all of them strategically placed in abundance around the opening of the entrance itself.

An uneventful night eventually retreats at daylight's coming, and at first light, you and Mateo immediately set out...

Turn to 215

69

Up ahead, you can make out the latticed grille of an iron portcullis blocking the path forward. Standing next to the heavy grating and clutching a weighty, long-bladed spear is a reptilian-like creature with scaly armor plating and a broad, sweeping tail.

It is quite obvious that this reptilianoid has been posted at this checkpoint as a sentry. Perhaps there is a chance you could offer it a bribe and persuade it to let you pass.

Gripping his sword in readiness, Laurick gives you a nod, letting you know he is ready to follow your lead, whatever it is you decide...

If you decide to offer the lizardman a bribe, **turn to 117**

If you choose to fight your way past instead, **go to 4**

70

"Who are you?" you ask, simultaneously readying your weapon as you guardedly step into the chamber.

"I am Althaeus," replies the old man, still hovering motionlessly in midair. "I am the Oracle of Old, known to some as the Chronicler, the Librarian, the Keeper of Knowledge, and the Cataloger of Secrets..."

It is here that Althaeus pauses for a brief moment, and then, as if able to read your very thoughts, says, "Your mind is troubled by many questions, but you may find the answers to those questions even more troubling. Suffice it is to say that it is neither my place nor purpose to grant you the answers that you seek."

"But do not despair, my child," he continues, "for Greater Purpose yet awaits you. You need only to forsake the cares, pursuits, and pleasures of this life, and with me as your mentor and spiritual guide, Infinite Knowledge of the Secret Things shall awaken within you..."

If you decide to accept Althaeus' offer for Infinite Knowledge, **turn to 137**

If you choose to leave and continue down the passage instead, **go to 354**

71

So powerful and strong is the dryad's enchantment over you, that eventually, the memories of your past and even your present begin to fade, becoming nothing more than just the blur of some distant and long-forgotten dream.

If you were able to pull back the curtain of illusion, you would discover that there is no forest nor table laden with food and drink. You would also undoubtedly see that you are actually standing in an empty chamber surrounded by the skeletons of other adventurers who fell prey to the dryad's bewitchment. They, too, thought they were feasting and making merry with a beautiful, young maiden, completely oblivious to the fact they were actually withering away from dehydration.

If only you did not have such a weak mind!

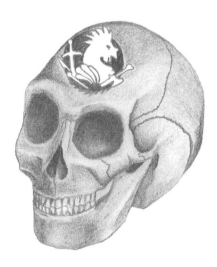

72

Brutally savage and viciously unrelenting, the werewolf unleashes a fierce onslaught of claws and teeth, coupled with its preternatural strength and speed. In the end, however, the fearsome creature is unable to contend with the precision and ferocity of your attacks and counter-attacks.

(During your battle with the lycanthrope, were you at any time wounded? If so, do not read any further, but instead, **turn to 357**).

Using the key, you open the chest and among its many useless contents discover a HEALTH potion as well as 20 gold pieces. You also do a quick sweep of the room and find what appears to be part of an old map just laying on the floor amongst all of the empty bottles.

(Add these items to your PURSE and INVENTORY now), and then **proceed to 167**

73

Opening the door, you are startled to discover what appears to be a severed, human hand decomposing on the floor in one corner of the room. On one of its fingers is a large, gold ring...

If you decide to retrieve the ring from the severed hand, **turn to 460**

If you have not already investigated what lies beyond the first door, **go to 294**

You can also check out the second door if you wish and have not already done so. If this is your choice, **proceed to 114**

If you would rather forego the remaining doors entirely and continue down the corridor, then **turn to 199**

74

After traveling for a great while, the landscape begins to make a dramatic change, with the dismal and depressing swamp eventually reverting back to a tidal, saltwater marsh, and from there, a white, sand-covered beach.

Almost immediately, you find yourself confronted with the decision on whether or not to continue following the shoreline or to make your way up a narrow, steep-walled gorge leading inland up and away from the beach...

If you decide to stay on the beach, **turn to 423**

If you decide to head inland via the ravine instead, **go to 243**

75

You must have nodded off, because you are suddenly jolted awake by the impact of your body being thrown roughly about. Even as you are coming to your senses and scrambling to reach for your weapon, it is at that moment you come to the realization that you are still inside the hollowed-out trunk and that something outside is literally rocking the tree back and forth!

Crawling towards the entrance, you find yourself being buffeted against the tree's interior as you struggle to even stay on your hands and knees so that you can keep moving forward. Tumbling out of the opening onto the ground, you are on your feet in an instant with your weapon ready, but are definitely not prepared for what it is that you see next.

Standing on top of the fallen tree above you is a creature that is both woman and something else entirely — her snake-like jaws dislocating to reveal two rows of razor-sharp fangs as she opens and closes her hideous mouth. With a growl-like hiss, two large, batlike wings slowly unfold from her back as she immediately launches herself at you...

VAMPIRE   Life Force 30   Combat 4

If you kill the vampire, **turn to 270**

If, however, the vampire kills you, **go to 486**

76

After traveling for some time, you hear the distinct sounds of moving water coming from up ahead. The tunnel ends abruptly and you step out into a massive cavern extending in both directions as far as the eye can see. Stalactites and stalagmites are scattered about the floor and ceiling in perfect disarray and a small, but powerful river courses through the middle of the cavern.

Making your way to the water's edge, you discover the current is much too swift and strong for you to cross...

If you decide to make your way upstream, **turn to 150**

If you would rather head downstream instead, **go to 399**

77

Picking up an old, rusty broadsword from the ground, you begin calling out loudly, at the same time, banging on one of the temple's supporting columns with the sword. Slipping the shield onto your arm and readying your weapon, you position yourself some distance away with your back to the entrance and wait.

Using the highly-polished surface of the shield as your eyes, you watch as, moments later, the medusa emerges from her temple lair — her loathsome, living serpentine locks writhing upon her head as she drags her hideous, snake-like body over the debris and fallen rubble. Dagger-like talons and two rows of razor-sharp teeth complete the terrifying picture now mirrored in the shield before you.

Unable to pinpoint your exact whereabouts, the medusa begins to frantically search for you, quickly darting in between and around the statues of her many hapless victims with her scaly coils in tow. Even as you are watching in awestruck horror, the medusa wraps herself around the stone figure of an orc, and then, in a fit of rage, crushes it, sending pieces of it flying everywhere.

With your hand firmly upon your weapon, you brace yourself for the inevitable as the medusa unknowingly slithers towards your position. Closing your eyes firmly, you wait until she is nearly upon you, and then, with the shield raised, quickly pivot around to face her. There is the abrupt sound of rock cracking and splintering loudly, and then, silence. Slowly lowering your shield, you open your eyes to find that the reptilian hybrid-monstrosity is no more — turned into solid stone by her own horrifying reflection!

It is at that moment that you notice strange, rune-like markings all around the outer edge of the shield itself, as well as the word "Ovon-Yar." As impossible as it may seem, it suddenly dawns on you that, whether by destiny or just plain dumb luck, you have unwittingly found the fabled Shield of Ovon-Yar, a mythical weapon of incredible power!

(The Shield of Ovon-Yar is an epic, enchanted weapon that is able to capture the power and essence of certain types of monsters — in this case, the medusa's ability to turn living creatures into stone. The shield may be used ONE TIME on a SINGLE or even MULTIPLE opponents, regardless of what their LF scores may be. You can now use this weapon in a future battle to turn your opponent(s) to stone, but once used, the shield is powerless until it has been recharged with the power and essence of another monster).

A quick sweep of the medusa's temple lair leads to the discovery of a chest containing 20 gold pieces, a HEALTH potion, two gold rings, and a skull compass.

(Add these items, including the shield, to your PURSE and INVENTORY now) and then **proceed to 483**

78

Right away, you notice that the corridor is becoming visibly wider and higher, eventually transitioning into a massive cavern. Here, you see the same glowing fungus as before, only now it is splashed intermittently across a landscape of gigantic mushrooms and enormous toadstools.

The cavern seems to extend as far as the eye can see and it is almost surreal as you begin your trek through this strange and wondrous forest of fungi.

You have not gone far when all of a sudden, you hear a strange clicking noise coming from up ahead and just to the right. The same noise also begins to come from the left as well, followed by more of the same from behind you. Readying your weapon, it is not long before you are introduced to the authors of the mysterious clicking sounds.

Scuttling towards you on their many legs are several giant centipedes and it is more than obvious that they view you as their next potential food source...

GIANT CENTIPEDE	Life Force 13	Combat 2
GIANT CENTIPEDE	Life Force 12	Combat 2
GIANT CENTIPEDE	Life Force 11	Combat 2
GIANT CENTIPEDE	Life Force 11	Combat 2

If you kill the centipedes, **turn to 468**

79

Rounding a sharp bend, you are very much dismayed to find the way forward has been effectively blocked by a massive pile of rubble due to the ceiling having collapsed, forcing you to turn back...

Turn to 193

80

In the ensuing battle, you quickly find your metal and skill as a warrior tested as the manticore unleashes a vicious onslaught of claws and teeth in combination with its deadly stinger. The manticore is a formidable opponent, but in the aftermath, your prowess proves to be too much for the savage creature. Eventually, it expires from the severity of the wounds you have dealt it — its magnificent and terrible form collapsing at your feet.

This encounter has taken its toll on you as well, and so, after taking a much-needed time of rest so that you can eat and dress your wounds, you decide to do a quick sweep of the cavern. Your search produces a booty of 75 gold pieces and a HEALTH potion, which you immediately place in your satchel.

(Add these items to your PURSE and INVENTORY now) and then exit the manticore's lair **by turning to 153**

81

Considerably larger than any of the previous passages thus far, you are astonished to discover that the entire ceiling is one tangled and twisted mass of intertwined tree roots. A steady profusion of water drips from them, collecting in small, shallow pools throughout — probably due to heavy rainfall completely saturating the ground above.

Lying face down and partially submerged in one of the puddles is the grisly and decomposing remains of a large ogre...

Searching the ogre's body could potentially yield items of use or value. If this is your choice, **turn to 217**

If you would rather carry on instead, **go to 325**

82

Within moments, the bones of the undead lie scattered all around you. Sifting through their remains, you discover a gold ring, but nothing else of any use or value.

After a brief rest and a meager meal in your stomachs, you and Mateo immediately resume your trek through the primeval forest...

(Add the ring to your INVENTORY now) and then **proceed to 467**

83

The hallway you find yourself in is much larger than the ones previously and noticeably darker. Four doorless rooms line the right-hand side of the hall.

Searching these rooms could potentially yield items of use or even value...

If you decide to continue on without searching the rooms, **turn to 305**

If you would like to search the rooms, **go to 184**

84

The stench of decaying flesh lies heavily in the air as you make your way forward. Nearing a bend in the corridor, you hear what sounds like something or someone scratching, followed by a series of low, guttural growls. Creeping quietly forward, you peer around the corner and what you see fills you with absolute fear and dread.

Just around the bend is a gigantic bear, but it is immediately obvious that something is terribly amiss with it. One side of the creature has been completely laid bare, so much so that you can clearly see its ribs and all of its putrefying organs inside. Even more terrifying is the fact that half of the bear's face is nothing but skull and bone, stripped clean of any fur and flesh, with an empty eye socket completing the ghastly and gruesome picture before you.

The bear raises its hideous snout and begins to sniff the air, turning quickly in your direction. Your scent has obviously given you away, and upon detecting you, the savage beast immediately charges full speed towards your position...

UNDEAD BEAR   Life Force 35   Combat 4

If you defeat the undead bear, **turn to 109**

85

You are moving forward at a steady, but somewhat cautious pace when the silence is suddenly pierced by a series of high-pitched squeaks coming from farther on up.

The passage unexpectedly widens, but what you see next is something that gives you fearful pause, for coming around the bend just ahead of you is literally the largest mouse you have ever seen! Under normal circumstances, a mouse would never be a threat, but in your current diminutive state, the gigantic rodent you now face is all but an apex predator! At its shoulder, the gigantic rodent is easily as tall as you, and as its hungry eyes discover you, it breaks into a full-on charge straight for you...

GIANT MOUSE   Life Force 28   Combat 2

If you defeat the giant mouse, **turn to 346**

86

You find yourself in a small, empty room, with a single wooden door being the only other means of entry other than the culvert you just came out of.

You quietly and cautiously open the door, but only just a crack. Immediately, your ears are confronted with what sounds like a woman chanting loudly. Opening the door just a little more so that you can assess the situation, you are stunned to see a dark-cowled figure in a long, black robe. She is standing over what is clearly a dead body resting on a table and shouting incantations over it. Even as you are watching, the corpse on the table begins to stir, gradually sitting up and sliding off the table onto its feet.

There is a corridor just to your right, and with the lady necromancer and her undead construct's attention diverted, perhaps you can make for it without being seen…

(At this time, please perform a Stealth check).

If you successfully sneak past them, **turn to 149**

If, however, you are detected, add 1 point to your Stealth score and prepare for battle **by going to 469**

87

Kneeling and positioning yourself onto the ladder, you begin the slow descent to the rocky outcropping below — the flimsy, makeshift ladder twisting and turning as you make your way down one rung at a time.

Moments later, you find yourself standing before the opening of a small cave. You are about to light your torch and enter, but realize that the passageway beyond is already lit. A strange and unearthly glow emanates from the walls, illuminating the path before you. Upon closer examination, you realize it seems to be radiating from the fungus that is growing unchecked throughout the entire tunnel system.

The passage abruptly terminates before the latticed grille of a large, iron portcullis that runs from the floor to the ceiling. On both sides of the portcullis are two upright, rectangular-shaped stones — each one having four symbols representing the elements, with a different symbol on each of its four sides. A more casual inspection reveals that each one is actually a turn-stone and can be rotated so that you can choose which symbol is front-facing. It suddenly dawns on you that the mechanism for opening the portcullis must have something to do with the turn-stones, but with so many possible combinations, which one is the correct one?

A careful sweep of the area turns up no other obvious means of opening the gate, but you do find four small pieces of folded parchment tucked away inside a hidden cranny in the wall.

Unfolding them, you read the faded writing on each one out loud...

On the first piece of parchment is the following phrase:

Windswept whispers of ancient lore

The second piece of parchment has this:

Forged in fire and bound by light

The third one reads simply:

Earthen born by the darkest night

And the fourth:

Washed in rivers of waters pure

Rereading each piece of parchment again, you realize that hidden within these four cryptic messages are the very clues needed to solve the turn-stone puzzle. The question is, in what order should each one of these phrases be so that the turn-stones themselves can be arranged in their proper sequence?

(Continued on overleaf)

87 Continued

(The puzzle's solution can be found on the last two pages of this book).

If your guess is AIR, EARTH, FIRE, WATER, **turn to 389**

If your guess is WATER, AIR, EARTH, FIRE, **go to 260**

If your guess is EARTH, FIRE, WATER, AIR, **proceed to 412**

If your guess is FIRE, EARTH, AIR, WATER, **turn to 11**

88

Unlike the previous passage you were in, this one curves, meandering back and forth, until finally, it opens into a wide, rectangular chamber that is extremely well-lit...

Turn to 214

89

After plodding along for what seems like hours, the dreary monotony of the landscape is finally broken by the outline of a structure just visible through the trees up ahead.

Stepping out from the treeline, you find yourself standing in a large clearing. Before you is an old, dilapidated, shack-of-a-house, and with the rapidly falling blackness of evening so close at hand, you quickly resolve in your mind that it would be best to stay here through the night.

Making your way towards the ramshackle building, you are immediately taken aback by what you discover. Hundreds of talismans suspended by strings of varying lengths adorn the cottage on all sides — especially around the doors and windows!

A quick glance through one of the windows assures you that the cottage is empty. Once inside, you immediately bar the door, with a quick search of the premises rewarding you with a wheel of cheese and a HEALTH potion. You also find a kit used for dressing wounds, as well as a bedroll consisting of some bedding and a thin blanket.

(Add these items, including the bedroll, to your INVENTORY now) and then **turn to 419**

90

Grabbing your lifeless body with one of its massive hands, the hill giant throws you across its shoulder and lumbers off in the direction it came from. Not only will you become its next meal, but this hill giant gets to add another skull to the collection around its neck!

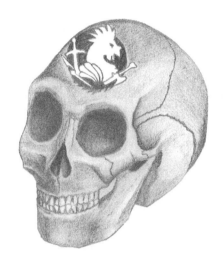

91

Just ahead, you notice another hallway branching off, and almost immediately, find your nostrils assailed by the fetid stench of death and decay. Readying your weapon, you cautiously make your way in, all the while gagging as the smell only intensifies with every step forward.

What awaits you at the corridor's end is something more horrifying than anything you could ever have imagined. Once a chapel of worship, it is now a veritable graveyard — its floor literally covered by the bones and putrefying remains of countless creatures!

You are on the very verge of vomiting, when suddenly, villainous laughter echoes throughout the chamber. It is quickly followed by a deep but eloquent voice, saying, "To who or what do I owe such an unexpected pleasure? It is not every day that a fly wanders so willingly into the spider's web!"

Looking up, you immediately make a frightening discovery, for there, hanging upside down from the rafters high above, is a gigantic, batlike creature. It is also at that moment that you are confronted by another terrifying realization — that this very same creature is the one who is speaking to you!

"Your determination and bravado are to be commended..." says the giant bat, as it looks down upon you from on high. "They are commendable, but still foolish nonetheless! In any event, coming here was a grave miscalculation on your part, and I can assure you, this intrusion will not go unpunished!"

Unfurling its powerful wings to their full span, the winged monstrosity drops down from the ceiling, sending skulls and bones flying in all directions as it lands on its feet in front of you. In that same instant, a startling transformation takes place as the fiendish creature reverts back to its vampiric, humanoid self, leaving no doubt whatsoever as to the identity of the person now standing before you.

"And now, foolish fly… you will die!" declares TitusMirror, his jaws dramatically dislocating to expose two rows of dagger-like fangs…

VAMPIRE SOVEREIGN   Life Force 45   Combat 6

If you defeat the Vampire Sovereign, **turn to 319**

92

"As much as it grieves me to tell you this, I am sorry to say that your answer is incorrect," replies the halfling. "Although your answer is indeed the missing number in the sequence, it is NOT the HIDDEN number, and therefore, not the solution to the puzzle! That being said, unfortunately, we do have an agreement and I am afraid that it is time to settle."

(Your INVENTORY up to this point should look like the following, this, of course, being contingent on whether or not you have used up all of your HEALTH potions:

1   Smoked fish and dried fruit
2   Large, uncut diamond
3   Half of your gold pieces
4   Health Potion
5   Blade of Alakara
6   All of your gold pieces

Roll a 1d6 and the number that it lands on will determine what item(s) from above you MUST give to the halfling. If you do not have any HEALTH potions left or have already used the Blade of Alakara, then simply leave those items off of the list and roll until one of the other remaining items is forfeited. If your roll is a 4, even though you might have more than one HEALTH potion, you only have to give Tomlin ONE. If your roll is a 3 or a 6, unfortunately, you MUST give the entire amount of gold pieces specified to the halfling.

Subtract the item/items given to the halfling from your INVENTORY now).

92 Continued

"Well met, traveler!" declares the halfling, as he places the item(s) inside his leather satchel. "And just so there are no hard feelings between us, I have decided that I am going to help you anyway!"

The halfling snaps his fingers and you suddenly find yourself standing on the other side of the gorge. Looking across to the other side, you discover that Tomlin Underhill, along with his table and chairs, has vanished...

Turn to 339

93

Approaching the reptilian gatekeeper, you offer it 10 gold pieces to open the portcullis and allow you passage...

(At this time, please perform a Charisma check).

If you successfully gain passage, **turn to 289**

If you are unsuccessful, add 1 point to your Charisma score and then **go to 355**

94

As soon as the man is in close proximity to you, you quickly dispatch him. There is a look of terror mixed with surprise on the man's face as he falls to his knees, his hands clutching at the mortal wound in his chest.

"Ogre..." the man says in a barely audible whisper as he gasps for air, and then, slowly raising his arm, motions in the direction from whence he came before collapsing to the ground dead.

You look towards where he was pointing and see an enormous ogre in the distance sprinting at full speed towards you. Too late, and regretfully so, you realize the man was not trying to attack you at all, but was trying to warn you about the savage creature that was pursuing him.

In only moments, the formidable brute is upon you, brandishing its crudely-fashioned battle-axe as it advances towards you...

OGRE   Life Force 32   Combat 3

If you kill the ogre, **turn to 448**

If the ogre defeats you, **go to 240**

95

The brood of hatchlings are no match for your skill and prowess, and within moments, their scaly, reptilian bodies lie strewn across the ground before you. Knowing full well that their mother could return at any given moment, you decide to do a quick search of the nest.

Right away, your eyes are drawn to the metallic glint of something half-buried in the dirt. Kneeling down, you uncover what appears to be some sort of dagger-like weapon, but what a strange and extraordinary one it is! With the exception of its finely-crafted blade, the entirety of this unusual weapon seems to be composed literally out of small leafy, tree saplings! Upon closer examination of the blade itself, you discover strange, rune-like markings up and down the blade on both sides, as well as the word "Alakara." Could it be? You quickly realize that, against impossible odds, you have somehow accidentally found the fabled Blade of Alakara, a mythical, one-time-use weapon of incredible power!

(The Blade of Alakara, otherwise known as The Wood Nymph's Blade, is an epic, enchanted weapon that may be used only ONE TIME and only on a SINGLE opponent with an LF score of 25 or less, or on a more powerful enemy whose LIFE FORCE has been reduced to 25 or less. You can now use this weapon in a future battle. Even the most casual strike will bring instantaneous death to your opponent, causing them to transform permanently, right where they stand, into a tree! The weapon will then disintegrate after its one-time use and must be REMOVED from your

INVENTORY).

Rather than risking a potential encounter with an angry mother dragon, you decide the best course of action is to find your way back to where the original path forked and this time head left...

Turn to 125

96

You open the door and discover a completely empty room.

Please go back to 214

97

The hyena leaps to its feet and begins to bark and growl loudly, waking its sleeping master, who immediately grabs his battle-axe and begins advancing towards you...

BARBARIAN   Life Force 25   Combat 3
HYENA   Life Force 13   Combat 2

If you defeat both of them, **turn to 191**

98

A magnificent antechamber awaits you on the other side as you shove open the double doors, cautiously entering what was probably once a transitionary vestibule between the previous hallway and the throne room of the ancient Legorian Kings.

The floor is completely engulfed by a low-lying, almost spectral mist and there is a perceptible difference in the temperature, the room being noticeably colder by several degrees. The air here is also thick and you can literally feel a very dark and palpable heaviness all around you.

Directly in front of you is another set of double doors, both even more spectacular in their beauty and craftsmanship than the ones you just came through. Making your way to them, you take several deep breaths and find yourself momentarily lost in morbid reflection at the looming challenge just beyond.

Once again you breathe in deeply, and then quietly and cautiously opening the double doors, enter the throne room...

Turn to 209

99

You have not gone far when you unexpectedly run into a roaming monster...

(Roll a 1d6 to determine which monster from the table below you will have to face).

1	POISONOUS SNAKE	Life Force 2	Combat 1
2	SKELETON	Life Force 6	Combat 2
3	GIANT BEETLE	Life Force 8	Combat 2
4	HALF-ORC	Life Force 25	Combat 3
5	BANDIT	Life Force 25	Combat 3
6	SABRE-TOOTHED LION	Life Force 29	Combat 3

(You can also exercise the option of trying to flee by performing an Agility check).

If you are able to successfully flee, **turn to 155**

If not, add 1 point to your Agility score and prepare to face the monster in battle...

WANDERING MONSTER	Life Force ?	Combat ?

If you defeat the wandering monster, **go to 155**

100

You step off of the pressure plate and right away, the chamber comes to a grinding halt as the door swings open to reveal nothing but a wall...

Please return to 300 and roll again

101

The orc is so inebriated that it is completely unaware as you search its person. On the creature's belt, you find a smelly, leather pouch reeking of rot and decay. Inside of it, is a decomposing, human foot and 10 gold pieces.

(Add the gold to your PURSE now. You may also take the severed, decomposing foot if you wish as well and add it to your INVENTORY).

A search of the room reveals nothing else of interest, use, or even value, so you return to the main chamber outside...

Please go back to 214

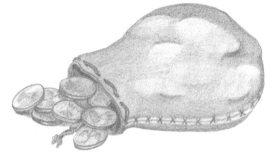

102

The cyclopean centaur collapses in a cloud of dust before you. Making your way up to the waterfall, you step through the wall of pouring water and discover a large cave within, which is no doubt the lair of this savage beast. Inside, you find a chest containing 50 gold pieces and a strange battle horn carved from the tusk of some kind of beast. There is an inscription etched into the side of it, but in a language you are unable to decipher, and as you turn it over in your hands, you also notice some elvish symbols as well. It is then that you come to the realization that you are holding the fabled elven weapon, El-Ladra's Horn of Adrenaline — a mythical, one-time-use weapon of incredible power!

(Blowing El-Ladra's Horn of Adrenaline causes all of your enemies, regardless of how many there are to turn to dust when they hear it. It may be used ONE TIME on a SINGLE or even MULTIPLE opponents, regardless of what their LF scores may be. You can now use this weapon in a future battle. After being used, the Horn's power is completely depleted and cannot be recharged until the first full moon of the Raothromm Elven Harvest).

(Add these items to your PURSE and INVENTORY now).

In the back of the cave, you discover a tunnel...

Turn to 199

103

Unable to contend with your ferocity and skill as a warrior in close-quarters combat, you quickly dispatch the intoxicated hobgoblins.

A search of their persons, as well as the room itself, nets you 25 gold pieces, a pair of six-sided dice, and the unusual gamebook, all of which you secure in your satchel before heading down the corridor...

(Add these items to your PURSE and INVENTORY now) and then **proceed to 334**

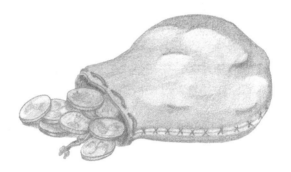

104

The tunnel at first swings far to the left, but then quickly deviates back to the right, before finally becoming a straight shot forward.

You have not gone far when suddenly, your eyes are immediately drawn to the form of something awkwardly stumbling down the corridor in your direction. It is still too far away to make it out in any great detail, but whatever it is, the sickening smell of putrefaction grows stronger in your nostrils as it gets closer.

Staggering towards you is a thing that was clearly once human, its nearly skeletal remains in such a state of advanced decomposition, that it is now impossible to tell whether it was once a man or a woman. Hollow and empty eye sockets stare blankly at you, while what is left of its flesh is barely clinging onto its bones.

Blind, but somehow able to sense your presence, the undead monstrosity comes at you with outstretched, spade-clawed hands...

REANIMATED CORPSE   Life Force 10   Combat 2

If you kill the reanimated corpse, **turn to 430**

105

You are making your way down the corridor when quite suddenly and unexpectedly, you encounter another monster...

(Roll a 1d6 to determine which monster from the table below you will have to face).

1	UNDEAD RAVEN	Life Force 1	Combat 1
2	GIANT LAND LEECH	Life Force 5	Combat 1
3	RABID CHIMPANZEE	Life Force 13	Combat 2
4	CRAZED GNOME	Life Force 15	Combat 2
5	CAVEMAN	Life Force 25	Combat 3
6	STRANGE CREATURE	Life Force 30	Combat 3

(You can also exercise the option of trying to flee by performing an Agility check).

If you are able to successfully flee, **turn to 495**

If not, add 1 point to your Agility score and prepare to face the monster in battle...

WANDERING MONSTER   Life Force ?   Combat ?

If you defeat the wandering monster, **go to 495**

106

Even as you are delivering the final, death-dealing blow, the spider begins to visibly shudder, ichor spraying everywhere as it collapses in a motionless heap before you.

Within moments, the wood nymph and her winged mount are free. You watch as she hurriedly clambers onto the dragonfly's back and in an instant is borne away and quickly lost from view.

A casual search of the desiccated corpses strewn about the spider's lair brings you a total of 25 gold pieces and a HEALTH potion.

(Add these items to your PURSE and INVENTORY now).

After a brief rest, you retrace your steps, eventually finding your way through the relentless underbrush and back to the path where you were before...

Turn to 302

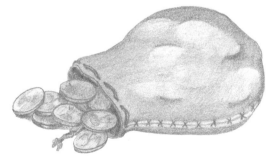

107

Hoping to avoid any kind of confrontation with the giant reptile, you quietly and carefully begin to make your way forward through the water-soaked cavern.

You have not even walked five paces before the snake raises itself out of the water and is swinging its head in your direction. Suddenly aware of your presence, it recoils backward in surprise, momentarily disoriented by your unexpected appearance.

Even as you are readying your weapon, the monstrous serpent is already moving in for the kill...

GIANT SNAKE   Life Force 27   Combat 3

If you kill the snake, **turn to 239**

If, however, you are the one that dies, **go to 311**

108

Try as you might, you are never able to overtake the light, which seems to vanish every time you even get close — only to reappear again in the distance far from you.

Suddenly, you are unable to move your feet and almost immediately, the horrifying realization sweeps over you that you are also sinking as well. In your pursuit of the mysterious light, you must have unknowingly wandered out into the bog! Desperation quickly turns into full-blown panic as you struggle to free yourself from the shifting mud that is rapidly pulling you down, until eventually, you are overcome by exhaustion.

The will-o-wisp once more materializes before you, so close this time that if your hands and arms were not already pinned underneath the muck, you could easily reach out and touch it. It is literally the last thing you see as your head slips slowly beneath the surface...

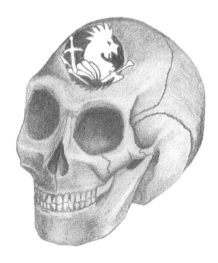

109

Although quite formidable, the horrific creature eventually slumps to the cold stone floor, overcome by the brutal onslaught of your attacks. Even so, the undead bear has taken quite a toll on you as well. After resting for a spell and dressing your wounds, you continue your trek down the corridor...

Turn to 464

110

The corridor snakes its way back and forth blindly before abruptly coming to a dead end.

Suddenly, you hear a loud rumble behind you and watch in stunned disbelief as the ceiling literally collapses and a torrent of falling rock and debris completely engulfs the passageway behind you. When the dust finally settles, your worst fears come to fruition as you realize you and Avril-Lyn are now hopelessly trapped and that it is only a matter of time before your oxygen supply is depleted!

"Well, there's definitely no way we're moving that pile of rocks," you say. "What do we do now?"

"Looks like we're just going to have to find another way out," answers the sorceress wryly. "Fortunately, it just so happens I have a spell for such an occasion as this."

Avril-Lyn utters an incantation, and much to your complete surprise and utter amazement, you and all of your personal effects begin to shrink! Mere moments later, you and your elven companion are little more than insects compared to your former selves, and the passage that was previously just wide enough for two to walk side-by-side now rises high above you on all sides like a massive cavern.

While you are mulling over what your next move should be, you notice the dark opening of a crack at the base of one of the walls. Avril-Lyn once again uses her magic to conjure forth a glowing orb, and with the way before you now brightly illuminated, you and the sorceress enter the fissure...

Turn to 85

111

With the giant's attention wholly wrapped up in its emotional breakdown, you have no problem whatsoever slipping past it unseen and into the tunnel on the far side of the cavern...

Turn to 199

112

Continuing its gradual slope upwards, the ravine soon finds its end, with you and Mateo emerging at the very edge of a large, grassy meadow. It is what you see on the other side that fills you with absolute fear and dread.

Moving silently along at a slow gait through the tall grass on the far side of the field is a fearsome monstrosity that could have easily stepped right out of your worst nightmare. Its head and torso are those of a massive gorilla, but with four powerful arms instead of two, while from the waist down, its body is that of a large, adult male lion.

For several moments, it sniffs the air and then looks in your direction. Spotting you and your companion, the terrifying creature lets out a blood-curdling roar, and after pounding on its chest with its fists, bounds full speed across the meadow towards you...

TAUREGG   Life Force 40   Combat 4

(Don't forget that you can now utilize Mateo in battle as well. Simply roll an additional 1d6 for the sailor along with your roll. Skeleton Mateo has an LF score of 15 and a Combat Skill Score of 2).

If you defeat the tauregg, **turn to 55**

If, however, you are killed by the tauregg, **go to 283**

113

"I am a recent convert to the Faith," you reply.

(At this time, please perform a Charisma check).

If your check is successful, **turn to 284**

If, however, your check is unsuccessful, add 1 point to your Charisma score and prepare to engage the cultists **by going to 480**

114

Other than what appears to be some straw bedding in one corner and a small, clay pot containing 15 gold pieces, the room is otherwise empty.

(Add the gold pieces to your PURSE now).

If you have not already investigated the first door, **turn to 294**

If you choose to open the third and very last door, **go to 73**

If you would rather forego the doors and continue onward down the corridor instead, **proceed to 199**

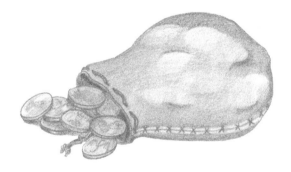

115

After running relatively straight for the next several minutes, the passage begins to make a noticeable shift upwards, until the only direction you and Avril-Lyn can swim moving forward is up.

Soon thereafter, you unexpectedly find yourselves breaking the surface of the water. You are floating at the bottom of a large pit, and as you are treading water and trying to get some sense of your surroundings visually, you notice what appear to be hand and footholds carved into the rock face of one side of the pit. Paddling over to where they are, you use the lower ones to pull yourself out of the water and then quickly ascend to the top and out of the pit.

Directly adjacent to the pit is the opening to a passage, affording you an exit...

Turn to 315

116

You find yourself in a small, foyer-like area with a broad hallway running in both directions to the left and to the right. Several bed chambers, with their doors wide open, adjoin the hallway on the opposite side, but the heavy layer of dust on the floor and furniture, as well as the absence of any footprints, tells you no one has been inside any of them in quite some time...

Turn to 91

117

Approaching the reptilian gatekeeper, you offer it 10 gold pieces to open the portcullis and allow you passage...

(At this time, please perform a Charisma check).

If you successfully gain passage, **turn to 245**

If, however, you are unsuccessful, add 1 point to your Charisma score and then **go to 4**

118

"Well," says the sorceress, "there doesn't appear to be any traps of any kind in there..."

If you have not already done so and would like Avril-Lyn to cast a *detect life* spell, **turn to 332**

If you would rather investigate the room yourself, **go to 428**

Perhaps Avril-Lyn was right when she suggested you head back to the three-way junction. If this is what you would like to do now, **proceed to 264**

119

The inscription appears to be an incantation of some kind and without even thinking about it, you read each word out loud...

INVOCAR DATOR VITAE MINOTAURUS

Suddenly, the statue begins to crack all over, the hard, stony exterior crumbling away to reveal flesh and bone just beneath. You quickly retreat to a spot some distance away, too late realizing you have unwittingly brought the minotaur to life by reciting the spell written on the base below it.

The minotaur bellows loudly as it steps down off of its stone pedestal, and then, pawing at the dirt with one of its large hooves, charges angrily towards you...

MINOTAUR   Life Force 32   Combat 3

If you defeat the minotaur, **turn to 424**

120

A quick, but thorough search of the room and its contents yields nothing of any real use or value. Cautiously exiting the room, you and your elven companion continue down the corridor...

Turn to 34

121

Using a hand to tell Avril-Lyn to stay put, you cautiously make your way into the hallway. Suddenly, one of the stones in the floor sinks noticeably beneath the weight of your foot. You hear a sharp *click*, and without warning, oil begins spewing down from small apertures in the ceiling above, completely drenching you. Before you can even react, the oil is ignited by a nearby torch, causing you to burst into flames. The pain is excruciating and unlike anything you have ever experienced! Mere moments later, you collapse to the floor, quickly succumbing to the shock induced by being burned alive...

122

Rounding a sharp bend, you unexpectedly come face-to-face with a monster...

(Roll a 1d6 to determine which monster from the table below you will have to face).

1	VENOMOUS LIZARD	Life Force 3	Combat 1
2	GIANT WASP DRONE	Life Force 8	Combat 2
3	TWO-HEADED BOAR	Life Force 12	Combat 2
4	UNDEAD HOBGOBLIN	Life Force 14	Combat 3
5	GOBLINOID	Life Force 24	Combat 3
6	SHAMBLER	Life Force 27	Combat 3

You can also exercise the option of trying to flee by performing an Agility check).

If you are able to successfully flee, **turn to 367**

If not, add 1 point to your Agility score and prepare to face the monster in battle...

WANDERING MONSTER   Life Force ?   Combat ?

If you defeat the wandering monster, **turn to 367**

123

"Well done, adventurer! Bravo!" declares the halfling, smiling and clapping his hands together. "Well then, a wager is a wager and I am most certainly a halfling of my word."

The halfling snaps his fingers and you suddenly find yourself standing at the top of the cliff, staring out at an endless expanse of ocean merging with the sky. Cautiously making your way to the edge of the precipice and looking down, you discover that Tomlin Underhill, along with his table and chairs, has vanished...

Turn to 368

124

The door introduces you to a long and narrow corridor that eventually finds its end at yet another door — this one much larger than the previous two. With your weapon in hand and ready for whatever might await you on the other side, you open the door.

Dazzling sunlight immediately floods in and for more than a moment, you are temporarily blinded by the unexpected and sudden brightness as you step through the open doorway and outside...

Turn to 298

125

You are moving at a steady pace and have not traveled long when quite suddenly, you find the way forward has been cut off. Blocking the path entirely before you is the gigantic, freshly-killed carcass of some unknown, behemoth beast. Its body has been savagely mauled, with huge chunks of meat viciously torn from it and its side sliced and laid open by what must have been the enormous claws of some apex predator. But it is the telltale scorch marks and the massive patches of burnt flesh that not only complete the gruesome picture before you, but also reveal that this was the bloodthirsty and brutal act of a dragon!

With a veritable wall of thorns and thick brambles on both sides of the path preventing you from going around the carcass, you determine that, in order to continue moving forward, you will have to make your way up and over the creature's body. You quickly discover that scaling the fallen beast is easier said than done, its blood making for an extremely slippery slope as you attempt to reach what would be its back.

Eventually, you make it to the top, but what you see on the other side and waiting just below fills you with utter dismay...

Turn to 290

126

The corridor abruptly terminates and you find yourself standing before a large, wooden door. Cautiously opening it, you are almost immediately overwhelmed by the stench of decaying flesh. It is then that you make an alarming discovery.

At the far end of the room is a large wooden table and sitting in the middle of it is a severed head! The head is so decomposed you cannot tell if it belonged to a man or to a woman. There also appears to be something in its mouth, which could potentially be something of value or even use to you.

You can also see a door on the other side of the room...

If you would like to take a closer look at the severed head, **turn to 437**

If you would rather leave through the door on the opposite side of the room, **go to 244**

127

Defeated and still clinging to life, you watch in abject helplessness as Glorandol, Eloshann, and Maegyddo complete their ritual of unbinding, permanently freeing themselves from their prison, at the same time, opening a gateway connecting Ataraxia to the Realms Beyond. Legorian Sentinels and other amalgamations born of their technomancy begin to pour out, one after another, until, like a plague of locusts, the Red Plains of Duhar are covered by the Legorian Kings' horrific, hell-spawned army...

The fate of Ataraxia is now sealed!

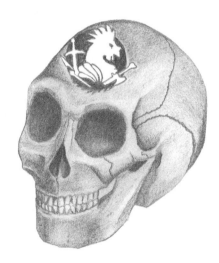

128

The passage quickly finds its resolution at a large, oaken door with the representation of a spider carved into its surface.

"The Temple of Arachnae..." says the sorceress, confirming what was already going through your mind. "We will have to proceed with much greater caution from here on out!"

Pressing your ear purposefully against it, you listen intently for several moments but hear nothing. Trying the handle, you discover that it is unlocked and step cautiously into the corridor just beyond...

Turn to 276

129

More than a little troubled by your encounter with the mysterious woman, you set out once more. A short while later, you round a bend, only to discover that the way forward has been cut off by a wide gorge running in both directions. Cautiously making your way to its edge, you peer down into its rocky depths and can just make out the remnants of a bridge resting at the bottom.

Discouraged but undaunted, you turn to head back and are startled to see a table and chairs where there were none before, and much to your amazement, a halfling seated at the table as well! He is wearing an appallingly bright, multi-colored tunic with matching trousers and there is a leather satchel sitting on the ground beside his chair.

"Greetings, adventurer!" declares the halfling. "It certainly is a lovely day for a leisurely stroll through the woods, wouldn't you say? Ah, but where are my manners? Tomlin Underhill at your service! It would seem that this chasm has put you at somewhat of an impasse. Perhaps I can be of some assistance with that!"

"Alright then," you reply. "You have my ears, halfling. What exactly are you proposing?"

Motioning for you to have a seat in one of the empty chairs, the halfling removes a good-sized scroll from his leather satchel, and then, carefully unrolling it, spreads it out on the table before you.

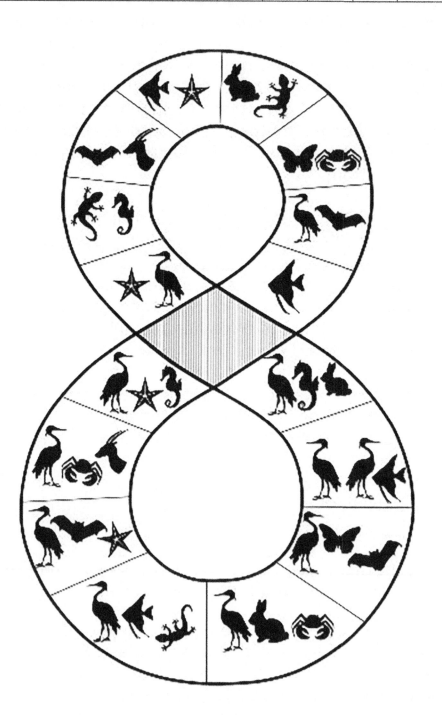

"What you are seeing here is a puzzle," Tomlin explains. "In fact, this very puzzle just so happens to be one of my own creations! The terms are simple. Solve this puzzle by finding the hidden number and I will get you to the other side of that chasm. If, however, you are unable to solve the puzzle, then I get to take one item from your satchel."

With little else in the way of alternatives, you reluctantly accept the halfling's offer.

Taking a much closer look, you see what appears to be a symbol in the shape of a figure eight beautifully inked onto the scroll. It is divided into seventeen sections, and with the exception of the one in the very middle, each section has the silhouette of one or more animals inside of them. Just above the figure eight is a horizontal table with ten different animal silhouettes, along with what is obviously their assigned numeric values...

(Find the hidden number. That number is not only the puzzle's SOLUTION, but is also the MAGIC NUMBER and the section that you must turn to in this book in order to continue! PLEASE NOTE: There is only ONE CORRECT ANSWER to this puzzle! The puzzle's solution can be found on the last two pages of this book).

Did you find the hidden number? If so, then **go to that section number now**. If, however, you are unable to solve the puzzle, then **turn to 443**

130

Waiting for you at the bottom is a massive door made entirely out of stone. Carved in relief into its face are the following letters:

```
C O T N K A E G P S
I Q M X P E R H Z J
U C P S Y L A O V K
F W N D O H Q B T X
R M G P E Z S K Y C
```

You also notice a tablet affixed to the wall on the left-hand side of the door. This, too, is also made out of stone and inscribed into it is what appears to be, at first glance, a riddle of some sort:

From the fifth take its seventh
From the second take its first
From the fourth take its tenth
From the first take its third
From the third take its fifth

Puzzled, you immediately turn your attention back to the characters on the door and are surprised to find that each individual letter lights up when touched. Touching each one in succession, you quickly discover that only 5 letters at a time can be lit. Could it be possible that what you are looking at here is the means by which this obviously enchanted door is opened?

Intrigued, you decide to examine the tablet again, only this time much more closely...

(The solution to this puzzle is not only the COMBINATION that unlocks and opens this door, but is also the NUMBER OF THE SECTION you must turn to next in order to continue. The puzzle's solution can be found on the last two pages of this book).

Did you find the correct sequence of letters to open the door? If so, **turn to that section now.** If not, then unfortunately, your adventure ends here.

131

You are making great progress when suddenly and quite unexpectedly, you round a bend and come face-to-face with another fearsome denizen of the forest...

(Roll a 1d6 to determine which monster from the table below you will have to face).

1	GIANT MOSQUITO	Life Force 4	Combat 1
2	TWO-HEADED VIPER	Life Force 5	Combat 1
3	REVENANT	Life Force 15	Combat 2
4	BLACK BEAR	Life Force 27	Combat 3
5	WOLF-WERE	Life Force 30	Combat 4
6	SASQUATCH	Life Force 32	Combat 4

(You can also exercise the option of trying to flee by performing an Agility check).

If you are able to successfully flee, **turn to 68**

If not, add 1 point to your Agility score and prepare to face the monster in battle...

(Don't forget that you can now utilize Mateo in battle as well. Simply roll an additional 1d6 for the sailor along with your roll. Mateo has an LF score of 25 and a Combat Skill Score of 3).

WANDERING MONSTER   Life Force ?   Combat ?

If you defeat the random, wandering monster, **turn to 68**

132

You are making your way down the corridor when quite suddenly and unexpectedly, you encounter a roaming monster...

(Roll a 1d6 to determine which monster from the table below you will have to face).

1	FERAL CAT	Life Force 5	Combat 1
2	GIANT BAT	Life Force 7	Combat 1
3	HARPY	Life Force 12	Combat 2
4	UNDEAD ELF	Life Force 13	Combat 2
5	DIRE WOLF	Life Force 18	Combat 2
6	BUGBEAR	Life Force 25	Combat 3

(You can also exercise the option of trying to flee by performing an Agility check).

If you are able to successfully flee, **turn to 481**

If not, add 1 point to your Agility score and prepare to face the monster in battle...

WANDERING MONSTER   Life Force ?   Combat ?

If you defeat the wandering monster, **turn to 481**

133

You have just started paddling your way down towards the gaping maw of the passage below you when suddenly, something of considerable size emerges from it! Clearly an apex predatory fish of some kind, its large, dragon-like head is split by an enormous, crescent-shaped mouth filled from top to bottom with sharp, translucent teeth. A luminous, fleshy lobe dangles in front of its face from a filament-like spine protruding just behind its head.

Upon seeing you, the monstrous fish swiftly changes direction, hurtling straight for you with its jaws agape...

GIANT ANGLER FISH   Life Force 40   Combat 4

(Because movement underwater can be much more restrictive, subtract 1 each time you roll. Be sure to do the same for each one of Avril-Lyn's rolls as well).

If you defeat the giant angler fish, **turn to 67**

134

Avril-Lyn utters an incantation and mere moments later, you and your elven companion are little more than insects compared to your former selves — the passage suddenly a massive cavern rising high above you on all sides.

With the impact of the portcullises striking the floor now almost ear-shattering, you hurriedly make your way to the first one, noting the timing as it comes crashing down and just as quickly rises and falls again.

Seizing the opportunity, you and the sorceress make your move, breaking into a full-on sprint as the latticed grille is raised upward. You repeat this process successfully with the second and last portcullises as well.

Unfortunately, with your attention completely fixated on getting past the portcullises, you fail to notice the giant centipede stalking you. Under normal circumstances, you could easily crush this myriapod underfoot, but now, in your current diminutive state, this multi-legged monstrosity is all but an apex predator. Before you are even aware of its presence and can react, the centipede has already wrapped itself around you. Stinger-like appendages called forcipules inject a powerful and fast-acting venom into your body.

Within moments, your lifeless corpse is being devoured head-first...

135

Within moments, the lock mechanism has disengaged, causing the lid of the chest to spring open. Inside, you find 30 gold pieces, a HEALTH potion, and the tooth of a large shark, all of which you quickly add to your satchel as you are exiting the cave...

(Add these items to your PURSE and INVENTORY) and then **proceed to 40**

136

Unable to withstand the savagery of your skilled attacks, the two-headed monstrosity topples to the ground, nearly crushing you in the process.

Strapped to the troll's back by the very same chains it was wielding is a large, wooden chest, inside of which, you discover 75 gold pieces, a HEALTH potion, and a strange hand mirror with the name "Maeroketh" etched into the handle. As you turn the mirror over in your hands and examine it more closely, you quickly realize that somehow, against impossible odds, you have accidentally found the fabled Mirror of Maeroketh — a mythical, one-time use weapon of incredible power!

(The Mirror of Maeroketh or Gorgon's Hand Mirror, is an epic, enchanted weapon that can turn your opponents into stone, regardless of how many there are. You can now use this weapon ONE TIME in a future battle to simultaneously and immediately dispatch a SINGLE or even MULTIPLE opponents, regardless of what their LF scores may be. After its one-time use, however, the Mirror's power will be completely depleted, causing it to disintegrate, and must be removed from your INVENTORY).

(Add these items to your PURSE and INVENTORY now) and then **turn to 488**

137

"You have chosen rightly," says the old man, slowly descending from his perch in midair and alighting onto his feet. He motions for you to sit at a small table that you had not noticed before and hands you a small decanter containing some sort of purple, pudding-like substance. "You must drink this first in order to begin your Awakening."

Taking a deep breath, you reluctantly down the contents of the decanter. Within moments, you are horrified to find that you are completely paralyzed!

"Your choice, as rewarding as it shall be, is not without sacrifice," the Oracle of Old says in a calm, but hardly reassuring voice.

Utterly helpless and unable to move, you watch in absolute horror as Althaeus pulls out his dagger and making his way over to you, reaches into your mouth and removes your tongue in a single motion.

"True Enlightenment demands great sacrifices, my child," declares the old man. "An unfettered mind can never truly traverse the interplanetary and cosmic planes with an unbridled tongue that is not in check..."

138

Almost instantaneously, the sudden movement of you entering the chamber causes the bulbous heads of the fungi to erupt violently, filling the room with a cloud of crimson spores. Unable to breathe and desperately clutching your throat as you gasp for air, you stagger forward, eventually collapsing face-first into a bed of fungi as the world around you and your thoughts fade into a scarlet oblivion...

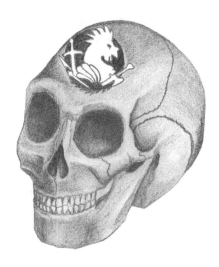

139

Suddenly, the passageway you have been following drops off on the right-hand side and you now find yourself walking next to a ravine. The way ahead becomes more and more treacherous by the minute and you realize the passage itself has begun to take on a steep decline.

Struggling to retain your footing, you feel yourself sliding uncontrollably down the path toward the chasm's edge...

(How lucky are you? Find out now by performing a Luck check. If your check is successful, you miraculously escape going over the edge of the ravine, instead coming to rest at the bottom of the decline. If, however, you are unsuccessful, you have fallen into the ravine. Add 1 point to your Luck score and then roll 2d6 to determine how much DAMAGE you sustained from the fall. Subtract this amount from your LIFE FORCE now. Any damage you receive will be retained until you use a HEALTH potion).

Turn to 380

140

Not being much of a water person anyway, you decide to continue hiking downstream on foot. You have not traveled far when suddenly, you see something making its way out of the water onto the land not far from where you are standing. Scuttling towards you is the largest mud crab you have ever seen, standing fully as tall as you and snapping its chelae.

In just a few short moments, the creature is upon you, giving you no choice but to engage it in combat...

GIANT MUD CRAB   Life Force 32   Combat 3

If you kill the crab, continue your trek downstream **by going to 392**

141
Guardedly peering into the room, you notice that, just like the room on the other side of the hallway, there are several bunk beds on the opposite wall, two of which have occupants who are fast asleep and snoring quite loudly.

In the farmost corner from where you are standing, is what appears to be a large trunk...

If you decide to sneak into the room and find out what is inside the trunk, **turn to 220**

If you would rather continue down the hallway instead, **go to 45**

142

Setting out immediately at daybreak, you have not ventured far before coming to a sudden fork in the path...

If you decide to head left, **turn to 324**

If you choose the path going right instead, **go to 57**

143

The corridor goes on for what seems like forever, with no doorways or tunnels branching off to break its monotonous run. Finally, it opens up into a good-sized chamber. There is a large chest sitting on the floor in the center of the room.

On the far side of the chamber is another tunnel opening...

If you would like to investigate the chest, **turn to 28**

If you decide to leave the room and continue on your way instead, **go to 388**

144

The door introduces you to a massive, torchlit chamber with holding cells on both sides. Blood-splattered walls and a crimson floor speak of countless atrocities and the air is completely saturated with the reek of fecal matter mixed with blood and carrion. With the exception of some rats, the room appears to be otherwise vacant.

Silently congratulating yourself on your good fortune thus far, you are emerging from the stairwell, when the door on the far side of the chamber unexpectedly opens and a thrall steps into the chamber.

Drained of life by the vampire to which they are now devoted, thralls are basically undead servants who will literally fight to the death to protect their evil masters. And this one is no exception, for upon seeing you, the thrall draws its sword and immediately charges towards you like some wild beast...

THRALL   Life Force 25   Combat 3

If you defeat the thrall, **turn to 51**

145

Feelings of abandonment and failure, intermingled with grief and despair, sweep over you like sand overrun by the ocean's tide. Filled with guilt, shame, and self-loathing, you quickly descend into the pit of debilitating fear and crushing madness, doomed to be a prisoner forever of your own emotional insecurities...

146

Having spent the greater part of the day in the oppressive heat, you stop briefly to rest, eat, and rehydrate. Sitting down on the sand, you watch the steady procession of small waves breaking upon the shore with a soft hiss. Tiny crabs dance clumsily across the clean, white sand and the air is filled with the smell of brine and seaweed.

Scanning the beach ahead, you catch sight of something that makes you second guess whether you might be dreaming or are actually still awake, for making its way towards you is the translucent and ghostly form of a sailor.

"Tell me, spirit, what is it that you seek?" you ask, as the apparition stops within a few paces of where you are standing.

"Name's Mateo," replies the spirit. "I became a castaway here when the ship I was first mate on ran aground."

"And what of the rest of your crew?" you ask.

"Includin' the Captain and meself, twas fifty of us aboard the Serpent's Wake," the spectre recounts. "I can remember that day like it was only yesterday. The sea was a dead calm and there was no wind — not even so much as a whisper in our sails. We'd been driftin' fer days, ya see, and then all of a sudden, the ship began to move like it had a life of its own. It was like somethin' had taken o'er the Serpent's Wake and was now controlling it! Brought us here, it did! Brought us to this infernal island of death! Fifty of us landed on this accursed rock! Fifty men strong we were, but this island demanded sacrifice and sacrifice it took! The first night we lost ten good men when the vampires came. Some nights the vampires didn't come at all and some nights we were able to fight them off. One by one, we were slaughtered like human cattle and those the vampires didn't take, the island did. Of the Serpent's Wake crew, only I am left to tell the tale..."

"I will ask you again, spirit. What is it that you seek from me?" you ask.

The phantom is silent for many moments, and then, without warning, draws his cutlass and aggressively lunges at you...

MATEO'S GHOST   Life Force 15   Combat 3

If you defeat Mateo's ghost, **turn to 378**

147

As you approach the first of the smaller sarcophagi, you hear what sounds like wind howling and reverberating throughout the tomb. Your hair begins to move as if being ruffled by a strong breeze.

Suddenly, the sound of crumbling rock fills the chamber, but as you look around, you quickly realize that what you are actually hearing is the lids on some of the smaller sarcophagi moving. You make ready your weapon and watch as, one by one, the lids slide off and come crashing to the ground. Out of each sarcophagus steps a shriveled and desiccated corpse. Hollow, empty eye sockets stare back at you as they shamble towards you, swinging their sickle-like khopeshes...

THE CHILDREN OF UMRA, THE RESPLENDENT
LESSER MUMMY   Life Force 13   Combat 2
LESSER MUMMY   Life Force 12   Combat 2
LESSER MUMMY   Life Force 11   Combat 2

If you defeat the Children of Umra, **turn to 406**

148

The corridor runs straight for several hundred paces before being joined by another corridor on the left. A torch flickers at the entrance to a room next to where the two corridors meet.

Carefully and quietly approaching the doorway, you peer into the room and are surprised to find a man passed out on the floor still holding a half-empty bottle of ale. The heavy smell of strong liquor fills the room and the floor is literally strewn with empty bottles. There is also a small, wooden chest in the farmost corner...

If you decide to sneak into the room and see what is inside the chest, **turn to 342**

If you would rather press on instead, **go to 167**

149

Her attention wholly fixated upon the dark ritual she is performing, the lady necromancer is unaware of your coming and going, as you successfully make your way across the room and into the nearby corridor without being detected...

Turn to 199

150

Following the shoreline, you make your way upstream. Suddenly, you find yourself falling flat on your face and being dragged toward the water. Instinctively, your hand is already on your weapon and striking the tentacle wrapped tightly around your ankle. Its grip relaxes, and in an instant, you are back on your feet, your weapon readied.

Rising out of the murky depths of the river and advancing towards you through the water is an enormous creature resembling not only an octopus, but having the features of a squid as well!

You retreat further back onto much drier ground, thinking there is no way it can reach you, but much to your surprise, it uses its tentacles to drag itself onto the rocky beach and continues to come for you. Despite being out of the water, the creature is surprisingly fast on land, its appendages snaking ever closer to you as it snaps its parrot-like beak in eager anticipation of your flesh.

It appears you have no choice but to engage this fearsome monster in combat...

KRAKEN   Life Force 50   Combat 4

If you defeat the kraken, **turn to 444**

151

Your intuition and better judgment tell you that something is not quite right here and that leaving the relative safety of the cottage in the middle of the night might be a foolish and rash move. Your instincts, in this instance, prove to be all too correct.

Stopping a short distance from your window, the young maiden quickly realizes that you have no intention of coming out and rises to her feet. Suddenly, she is no longer in pain. It is then, by the radiant light of the harvest moon above that you are able to see the woman for what she truly is!

White fangs glisten in the platinum moonlight as she opens her mouth, her jaws dislocating like those of a python as she lets out a growl-like hiss. Two large, bat-like wings unfold from her back, and in an instant, the vampire is gone.

The rest of the night passes without incident, but you are unable to get any kind of restful sleep...

Turn to 14

152

"You are the same three spirits who appeared after I defeated the Lich Lord," you say, addressing the ghostly entities standing before you. "You took his staff and now have rescued me from certain death. Why?"

"I am Glorandol and this is Eloshann and Maegyddo," replies the spectre in the middle, speaking in an ancient and unknown tongue that you should not be able to understand and yet somehow do. "Many, many millennia ago, we three kings ruled as One. Ours was a kingdom of love, peace, and prosperity, and one abounding in the wisdom and knowledge of the Ancient Ones. A mecca of peace and academic pursuits, the glorious Kingdom of Legoria existed as such for many, many thousands of years, untouched by the sins of war and undefiled by the greed and lust that so characterizes humankind."

"But that would all change when four, extremely powerful sorcerers would unite to overthrow us and all that Legoria represented, seeking for themselves that which we had created for good, that they might use it for their dark intents and evil purposes. Our collective, intellectual minds, the greatest the world of Ataraxia has ever seen, gave us unparalleled advances in the sciences, birthing many untold technological wonders. It was this technology that they sought to make their own and in a twist of ironic fate, that very same technology would also bring about the total annihilation of our people, as well as the end of Legorian civilization itself."

"The sorcerers forced us to watch as they mercilessly

slaughtered every last one of our people. Then, using their combined dark magic and three, incredibly powerful artifacts, they banished us to the Realms Beyond, sending us to a perpetual prison without walls, where we are neither alive nor truly dead."

"When you defeated the Lich Lord, we knew that in you we had found our champion and the one that could free us from the chains of eternal exile..."

"I'm not sure I understand," you say.

This time, it is the one called Eloshann who speaks. "In the very same way that the sorcerers were able to use those three artifacts to banish and bind us, so, too, when they are again reunited, those same artifacts also have the power to release us..."

"These artifacts... how could one even possibly know where to begin looking for them?" you ask, somewhat intrigued.

"Of the two remaining artifacts, we know that one of them is here on this island and the other somewhere deep within the endless Warrens of Wvanderfell," answers Maegyddo. "Both are guarded by a fearsome and formidable monster."

"Didn't you say there were three artifacts?" you interject. "Why now are there only two?"

"Because one of the three has already been recovered," Glorandol says in a matter-of-fact voice.

"The Lich Lord's staff..." you reply.

The three spectral kings nod their heads in affirmation.

"So then, this... place... this island and my being here... none of this is by any means a coincidence, is it?" you say.

"It would seem that fate has bound you to this island, but to what end and for what purpose, of that we cannot say for certain," says Maegyddo.

"So why not simply recover the artifacts yourselves?" you ask.

"Our powers are limited beyond the veil of our torment," replies Eloshann. "There is also a powerful magic that not only binds the artifacts to the monsters that guard them, but also restrains us from even coming anywhere near them. Unfortunately, that same enchantment also prevents any and all from leaving this island..."

"Of course..." you mumble under your breath.

"Find the castle," Glorandol adds. "It is there that the master of this island dwells — an ancient and powerful evil unlike anything you have ever faced and whose origin predates perhaps even history itself — the Vampire Sovereign and blood sire of the vampire race, TitusMirror! But finding the castle will be far from easy, for each day at sundown, the castle disappears, only to reappear again in a different place on the island. Unspeakable horrors await you, but it is there that you will find the artifact, and quite possibly, your freedom. May the gods give you strength and grant

you success."

And then, just as suddenly and mysteriously as the apparitions appeared, they are gone.

Grieving the tragic and unexpected loss of your new friend, it is with a heavy heart that you press on...

Turn to 3

153

The course you are following runs straight for a time and then abruptly shifts directions, heading sharply to the right before finally terminating at an oddly-shaped chamber with uneven walls. In the center of the room is an iron grate covering up a dark, slimy manhole in the floor. The aperture is just large enough for an adult of your size, and peering through the bars of the grate, you spot what appears to be the metal rungs of a ladder affixed to the wall within.

With there being no other means of egress from the room other than the way you came in, you lift the grate from its position, and, leaning it against the wall, begin a careful descent one rung at a time into the dark unknown...

Turn to 360

154

Kneeling in the center of a triangle that has been drawn onto the floor in the middle of the room is the hooded figure of a man. He appears to be in a trance-like state, his eyes completely white as he launches into a ritualistic chant in an unknown tongue. It is then that the utterly unimaginable occurs!

Even as you and Avril-Lyn are watching in terrified amazement, the cultist abruptly stops chanting and after a few successions of "Arachnae be praised" becomes silent. Almost immediately, several large, spindly legs begin to aggressively wiggle their way out of the man's mouth. These are rapidly followed by two pedipalps, a pair of chelicerae, a cephalothorax, and an abdomen as a large spider bursts from the Faithful One's mouth. In another instant, the arachnid has bitten its former host, its neurotoxic venom affecting him almost immediately. And then, in the ensuing moments, the spider begins to feed on him.

Drawing your weapon, you quickly dispatch the vile creature and then make haste from the chamber by way of the door on the opposite side...

Turn to 300

155

Eventually, you come to a three-way junction. The passageway on the right has been overrun by some sort of creeping, sickly-looking vegetation that literally covers the walls, floor, and even the ceiling. The passage on the left seems to be a straight shot for as far as you can see...

If you choose the tunnel on the left, **turn to 454**

If you decide to take the tunnel on the right, **go to 230**

156

You have not traveled far down the corridor when suddenly, you stumble upon the chaotic scene of an old man in a filthy robe trying to fight off some imps with a stick. He is bleeding from numerous small wounds and it is immediately evident he is growing weary with exhaustion from batting at the creatures flying above and around him.

Making ready with your weapon, you decide to come to his aid, calling out to attract the creatures' attention. Upon seeing you, the imps promptly abandon the old man and begin making their way rapidly towards you...

IMP	Life Force 3	Combat 1
IMP	Life Force 2	Combat 1
IMP	Life Force 2	Combat 1
IMP	Life Force 1	Combat 1

If you defeat the imps, **turn to 436**

157
Rising to your feet, you discover that you are in a large, octangular chamber. At its center is a pillar-like pedestal with what appears to be a purple, velvet pillow resting on top of it. Directly opposite of you and on the other side of the chamber is another corridor.

Intrigued by the pedestal and pillow, you move in for a closer look. Sitting on top of the pillow is a ring, and as you approach, it is as if the ring is speaking your name, in quiet whispers beckoning for you to master its forgotten secrets...

If you decide to put the ring on, **turn to 372**

If you would rather press on instead, **go to 237**

158

The door connects you to a wide, circular tunnel, and straight away, the passage begins to take on a noticeable, downward slope, eventually finding its resolution at the threshold of an open doorway. Guardedly approaching, you discover a large chamber that is almost completely engulfed by spider webs. Just beyond, is what appears to be the opening to another passage.

Suddenly, there is considerable movement in one of the farmost corners of the room, causing you and Avril-Lyn to retreat backward several steps. What emerges from the chaotic tangle of silken threads is without a doubt one of the most horrific things you have ever encountered.

There are five of them — each one having the torso, arms, and head of a very young child, but from the waist down, the thorax, abdomen, and spindly legs of a spider.

You brace yourself as the multi-legged monstrosities hungrily advance...

ARACHNAE'S OFFSPRING

SPIDERLING	Life Force 17	Combat 3
SPIDERLING	Life Force 17	Combat 3
SPIDERLING	Life Force 16	Combat 3
SPIDERLING	Life Force 16	Combat 3
SPIDERLING	Life Force 15	Combat 3

If you defeat them, **turn to 322**

159

Barbaric and savage in every way, the troll-gre attacks with the ferocity of an animal that has been cornered and is fighting for its life. In the end, however, it is you who ultimately prevails. The troll-gre, bleeding profusely, eventually expires from the severity of its wounds, collapsing to the ground like a felled tree before you.

Searching its corpse, you discover a coin purse containing 15 gold pieces, a large, uncut diamond, and a HEALTH potion.

(Add these items to your PURSE and INVENTORY now) and then **proceed to 25**

160

You and the sorceress make short work of them. A quick search of the room, as well as both of the cultists, proves unfruitful, and much to your dismay, the trunk is also empty.

Before vacating the chamber, you and Avril-Lyn quickly move the bodies of the dead acolytes back to their respective beds so that it will appear they are sleeping...

Turn to 45

161

More than a little troubled by your encounter with the mysterious woman, you set out once more. Directly ahead and extending as far as the eye can see is a broad chaparral consisting of mostly scrub oak, bushes, and a few small trees. In the far-off distance, you spot what might possibly be a range of small mountains, and it is towards these, the only visible landmark, that you head.

A meandering maze confronts you at every turn and you quickly realize that without the mountains as your reference and guide, one could easily become disoriented and even lost in this labyrinth of brush and shrubbery.

You unexpectedly find yourself standing in a small glade and what you see next literally sends shivers down your spine...

Turn to 371

162

Making your way over to the chest, you discover that it is locked, and when you carefully examine it are unable to find any obvious or hidden means of unlocking it.

It appears you have no choice but to try and pick the lock...

(At this time, please perform a Lock Picking check).

If you successfully pick the lock on the chest, **turn to 46**

(If you are unsuccessful, add 1 point to your Lock Picking score and then choose one of the options below).

If you decide to search the pile of bones, **go to 221**

You can also leave the room **by going to 484**

163

Emerging from the treeline at the far side of the clearing is a fearsome monstrosity that could have easily stepped right out of a child's worst nightmare. Its head and torso are those of a massive gorilla, but with four powerful arms instead of two, while from the waist down, its body is that of a large, adult male lion.

For several moments, the terrifying creature sniffs the air, and then, with a blood-curdling roar, disappears back into the forest.

More than just a little shaken by the near encounter, you cross the stream and cautiously make your way into the clearing, eventually finding the path where it picks up again on the opposite side...

Turn to 238

164

You step off of the pressure plate, and right away, the chamber comes to a grinding halt as the door swings open and several spiders easily the size of a large watermelon emerge from the space beyond...

SPIDER HATCHLING   Life Force 7   Combat 3
SPIDER HATCHLING   Life Force 6   Combat 3
SPIDER HATCHLING   Life Force 6   Combat 3
SPIDER HATCHLING   Life Force 6   Combat 3
SPIDER HATCHLING   Life Force 5   Combat 3
SPIDER HATCHLING   Life Force 5   Combat 3

If you defeat the hatchlings, **return to 300 and roll again**

165

Though you fight bravely, the flying insects are just too many in number, eventually surrounding you and each one, in turn, stinging you. The effects of the wasps' venom are almost instantaneous as you begin to experience dizziness and nausea and start to vomit. Within moments, anaphylactic shock sets in and you find yourself struggling to breathe. The wasps, however, are relentless and continue to sting you, injecting more of their deadly toxin into your body.

It is not long before you succumb, and even as you are collapsing to the cavern floor, the wasps immediately drag you into their nest where your body will become food to be shared with the entire colony...

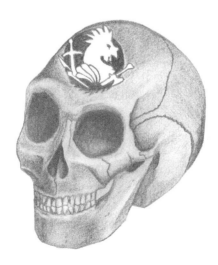

166

Finding nothing on the metamorph's body, you quickly exit the room and carry on...

Turn to 199

167

Pressing on, you and Mateo follow the dimly lit passage until it finds its end at a large, metal door. Gripping his sword in readiness, Mateo gives you a nod as you grasp the handle and swing the door open.

The blinding splendor of the sun immediately welcomes you as you step outside. Laid out before you is a harsh and barren landscape of sand and rock and one completely devoid of any vegetation. Just ahead, you can clearly see what appears to be the rotting carcass of some gargantuan creature — the heavy smell of its putrefaction carried to your nostrils by a gentle breeze. A rough, but well-used path meanders its way up a boulder-strewn pass just beyond.

It is towards these two points of reference that you and Mateo immediately head...

Turn to 351

168

Drifting in and out of consciousness, you eventually come to. You are completely naked and lying on top of a metal table that sits unusually close to the floor. You try to sit up and are shocked to discover that, with the only exception being your eyes, you are unable to move.

Suddenly, two strange creatures appear on either side of you. Their skin is a pale gray in color, but perhaps what is most startling about them is their big, black, almond-shaped eyes and their large, bulbous heads that seem oddly disproportionate in relation to their long, slender bodies.

Communicating with each other with short clicks and popping noises, one of them leaves your field of vision and returns with what appears to be some sort of blade-like instrument. Holding it directly over your sternum, you watch in horror as the blade begins to glow with a white-hot light. You try desperately to scream, but no sound emerges, and although you cannot feel a thing, you are still fully conscious as your chest is cut open and every one of your organs exposed...

169

169

Pressing on, you have not ventured far when the passage makes an abrupt swing to the left. It is here that the way forward becomes significantly smaller and more narrow. Worse still, the tunnel begins to dip down and is now partially submerged underwater — no doubt caused by massive flooding within this particular area.

Deciding the best course of action is to keep moving forward, you slowly and cautiously step down into the crystal-clear, knee-deep water with Avril-Lyn close behind you. It soon becomes apparent as you plod along that, although gradual, the water is definitely getting deeper. By this time, the water level has reached your waist and with the ceiling rapidly getting closer and closer with each passing moment, you quickly realize at this rate, the passageway will soon be beneath the water entirely. It is not long before you find yourselves standing neck-deep with the ceiling now just barely above your heads.

"Looks like we're going for a swim," says Avril-Lyn wryly. "Fortunately, it just so happens I have a spell for such an occasion as this..."

The sorceress utters an incantation, and much to your complete surprise and utter amazement, gills instantly appear on both sides of your neck and on Avril-Lyn's as well! Slipping beneath the surface of the water, you marvel as the filaments within your newly-formed gills immediately begin extracting the dissolved oxygen from the water, enabling you to breathe with ease as you resume your path forward... **Turn to 489**

170

Up ahead, you can make out the latticed grille of an iron portcullis blocking the path forward. Standing next to the heavy grating and clutching a weighty, long-bladed spear, is a reptilian-like creature with scaly armor plating and a broad, sweeping tail.

It is quite obvious that this reptilianoid has been posted at this checkpoint as a sentry. Perhaps there is a chance you could offer it a bribe and persuade it to let you pass...

If you decide to offer the lizardman a bribe, **turn to 93**

If you choose to fight your way past instead, **go to 355**

171

Suddenly, you hear the sound of hooves rapidly approaching, and looking up, see a crazed centaur with a large spear charging madly through the underbrush towards you. Upon seeing you, the centaur slows to a halt, and drawing back its spear, launches it at you with tremendous force.

(At this time, please perform a Luck check. If successful, the centaur's throw either missed its mark or you were miraculously somehow able to dodge it. If, however, your check fails, you have been struck by the spear and must now roll 2d6 to determine how much DAMAGE you have sustained. Subtract this from your LIFE FORCE now. Any damage you receive will be retained until you use a Health potion. If you are still alive, add 1 point to your Luck score for failing. Any damage you receive will be retained until you use a Health potion).

After throwing its spear, the brute beast immediately gallops straight for you...

CENTAUR   Life Force 32   Combat 4

If you defeat the centaur, **turn to 374**

172

You recite the incantation aloud:

PARVUS DIMINUTIVE MUNTI PETIT

Almost immediately, you begin to experience a sensation that is akin to falling rapidly through the air. Looking up, you see the podium towering high above you and realize that you were never actually falling, but shrinking! In fact, you are no more than a few centimetres tall — a mere insect compared to your former self...

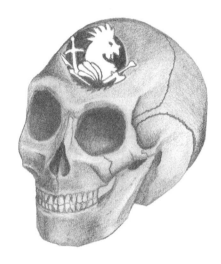

173

Knowing full well that taking unnecessary risks would be extremely foolhardy, you elect to move on — the amber sun visiting its lukewarm rays upon you as you march along. Waves of turquoise turn into white blankets of froth as they gently kiss the sand beneath your boots, while above and all around you, flocks of seagulls effortlessly hug the unseen currents of the salt-filled, ocean air.

After a time, the barrier cliff to your left begins to give way, eventually transitioning into a series of gigantic boulders...

Turn to 356

174

Removing the stopper, you quickly down the contents of the flask in a single swig...

(At this time, please roll 2d6).

If you roll a 2, **turn to 363**

If you roll a 3 or a 4, **go to 207**

If your roll is a 5 or a 6, **proceed to 414**

If you roll a 7 or an 8, **turn to 341**

If you roll a 9 or a 10, **go to 288**

If your roll is an 11 or a 12, **proceed to 452**

175

The passage carries on straight for a considerable distance before finally making a sharp bank to the right. Readying your weapon, you guardedly approach the bend, and, cautiously peering around it, are very much dismayed by what you see lying in wait.

Not even fifteen paces from your position is an amorphous, blob-like mass of flesh literally covered with eyes and eyestalks as well as numerous mouths filled with dagger-sharp teeth. No doubt the aftermath of sorcery gone afoul, you watch in horrified fascination as it partly oozes and partly drags its disgusting form across the passage floor.

Quickly realizing the only way forward is to confront this terrifying monster in combat, you step out in full view. Upon seeing you, the hideous aberration immediately launches its tentacle-like pseudopods at you...

(At this time, please perform an Agility check. If your check is successful, then you either dodged the pseudopods or they missed. If, however, your check failed, you have been struck by them. Add 1 point to your Agility score for failing and then roll a 1d6 to determine how much DAMAGE you have sustained. Subtract this amount from your LIFE FORCE now. Any damage you receive will be retained until you use a Health potion).

Surprisingly agile, the fiendish creature rapidly slides

(Continued on overleaf of illustration)

its way towards you, its hideous, tooth-filled maws snapping open and shut in hungry anticipation...

(You may now utilize Avril-Lyn in combat. Simply roll an additional 1d6 for the sorceress along with your own roll. Avril-Lyn has a LIFE FORCE of 25 and a Combat Skill Score of 5).

NAMELESS ABOMINATION   Life Force 35   Combat 4

If you defeat this monstrosity, **turn to 386**

If, however, you are killed, **go to 292**

176

With an ear-shattering shriek, the vampire falls to her knees, and then, throwing her hands up into the air, begins to crumble, disintegrating until all that remains of her is a pile of dust and the garments she was wearing.

With a quick search of the vampire's garments turning up nothing, you carry on, discovering an intersecting corridor at the far end of the hallway...

Turn to 318

177

Grabbing the handbell, you give it a quick shake, its light tinkling ring amazingly loud and reverberating throughout the chamber.

Suddenly, a small door materializes out of nowhere in front of you and right next to the table. Almost immediately, the door swings open and out walks a hideous, imp-like creature balancing a large serving tray on its shoulder and one hand. On the serving tray is what appears to be some sort of decanter filled with a greenish-blue liquid, along with another sign that reads: DRINK ME!

If you decide to drink the potion, **turn to 2**

If you think it would be best to leave through the door on the opposite side of the room instead, **go to 426**

178

"You are the same three spirits who appeared after I defeated the Lich Lord," you say, addressing the ghostly entities standing before you. "You took his staff and now have rescued me from certain death. Why?"

"I am Glorandol and this is Eloshann and Maegyddo," replies the spectre in the middle, speaking in an ancient and unknown tongue that you should not be able to understand and yet somehow do. "Many, many millennia ago, we three kings ruled as One. Ours was a kingdom of love, peace, and prosperity, and one abounding in the wisdom and knowledge of the Ancient Ones. A mecca of peace and academic pursuits, the glorious Kingdom of Legoria existed as such for many, many thousands of years, untouched by the sins of war and undefiled by the greed and lust that so characterizes humankind."

"But that would all change when four, extremely powerful sorcerers would unite to overthrow us and all that Legoria represented, seeking for themselves that which we had created for good, that they might use it for their dark intents and evil purposes. Our collective, intellectual minds, the greatest the world of Ataraxia has ever seen, gave us unparalleled advances in the sciences, birthing many untold technological wonders. It was this technology that they sought to make their own and in a twist of ironic fate, that very same technology would also bring about the total annihilation of our people, as well as the end of Legorian civilization itself."

"The sorcerers forced us to watch as they mercilessly

slaughtered every last one of our people. Then, using their combined dark magic and three, incredibly powerful artifacts, they banished us to the Realms Beyond, sending us to a perpetual prison without walls, where we are neither alive nor truly dead."

"When you defeated the Lich Lord, we knew that in you we had found our champion and the one that could free us from the chains of eternal exile..."

"I'm not sure I understand," you say.

This time, it is the one called Eloshann who speaks. "In the very same way that the sorcerers were able to use those three artifacts to banish and bind us, so, too, when they are again reunited, those same artifacts also have the power to release us..."

"These artifacts... how could one even possibly know where to begin looking for them?" you ask, somewhat intrigued.

"Of the two remaining artifacts, we know that one of them is here on this island and the other somewhere deep within the endless Warrens of Wvanderfell," answers Maegyddo. "Both are guarded by a fearsome and formidable monster."

"Didn't you say there were three artifacts?" you interject. "Why now are there only two?"

"Because one of the three has already been recovered," Glorandol says in a matter-of-fact voice.

"The Lich Lord's staff..." you reply.

The three spectral kings nod their heads in affirmation.

"So then, this... place... this island and my being here... none of this is by any means a coincidence, is it?" you say.

"It would seem that fate has bound you to this island, but to what end and for what purpose, of that we cannot say for certain," says Maegyddo.

"So why not simply recover the artifacts yourselves?" you ask.

"Our powers are limited beyond the veil of our torment," replies Eloshann. "There is also a powerful magic that not only binds the artifacts to the monsters that guard them, but also restrains us from even coming anywhere near them. Unfortunately, that same enchantment also prevents any and all from leaving this island..."

"Of course..." you mumble under your breath.

"Find the castle," Glorandol adds. "It is there that the master of this island dwells — an ancient and powerful evil unlike anything you have ever faced and whose origin predates perhaps even history itself — the Vampire Sovereign and blood sire of the vampire race, TitusMirror! But finding the castle will be far from easy, for each day at sundown, the castle disappears, only to reappear again in a different place on the island. Unspeakable horrors await you, but it is there that you will find the artifact, and quite possibly, your freedom. May the gods give you strength and grant

178 Continued

you success."

And then, just as suddenly and mysteriously as the apparitions appeared, they are gone.

After recovering your weapon and all of your belongings, you hastily withdraw from the village and head back into the swamp...

Turn to 74

179

Beyond the door is a dimly lit tunnel, illuminated by only a few, randomly placed torches. The corridor continues for some time and then makes a sharp turn before abruptly junctioning into two more tunnels.

The tunnel on the right terminates at a large wooden door. With the utmost caution and your weapon readied, you open the door and suddenly find yourself stepping out into the dazzling sunlight, and for more than a moment, you are blinded by the sudden brightness of your new surroundings.

You are in a forest, but your mind tells you this cannot possibly be real, and yet, all of your senses, including touch, cannot deny the evidence that is all around you. You can hear the sounds of birds calling loudly as well as the noisy hum of busy insects. The grassy sward beneath your feet is the most brilliant shade of green you have ever seen and gargantuan trees tower above you, their huge limbs stretching out in all directions to create a thick, leafy canopy. Beautiful and exotic flowers of different sizes, shapes, and colors literally paint the landscape as far as the eye can see, while giant toadstools and mushrooms only add to the mystery of this fairy-tale garden...

If you decide to explore the forest, **turn to 413**

If you think it would be best to leave and take the left tunnel instead, **go to 122**

180

More than a little troubled by your encounter with the mysterious woman, you set out once more. Directly ahead and extending as far as the eye can see is a broad chaparral consisting of mostly scrub oak, bushes, and a few small trees. In the far-off distance, you spot what might possibly be a range of small mountains, and it is towards these, the only visible landmark, that you head.

A meandering maze confronts you at every turn and you quickly realize that without the mountains as your reference and guide, one could easily become disoriented and even lost in this labyrinth of brush and shrubbery.

You unexpectedly find yourself standing in a small glade and what you see next literally sends shivers down your spine...

Turn to 234

181

More than a little troubled by your encounter with the mysterious woman, you set out once more. Like a cruel and unyielding mistress, the sun ruthlessly beats down upon you as you hike across the broken land, and with not even a wisp of a cloud to diffuse the devastating heat, you find yourself forced to rehydrate frequently.

You are progressing up a short, but somewhat steep and rocky incline when much to your surprise, you suddenly hear the sound of a woman singing. Making your way to the crest of the hill, it is what you see when you reach the top that makes you begin to question the very testimony of your ears and eyes.

Dancing on a low, table-like rock just ahead is a beautiful, young maiden — her eyes tightly closed as she sings an ancient song in an unknown tongue. Her every movement is sensual and almost hypnotic and you quickly find yourself strangely bewitched by her beauty and instantly captivated by her mysterious allure.

Snapping back to your senses, you call out to her, but the woman has already crumbled into a pile of sand...

Turn to 490

182

The undead are quickly decimated by your and Mateo's attacks and within moments, what is left of their rotting corpses are literally strewn across the beach all around you. A quick search of their putrefying remains nabs you 20 gold pieces and a gold tooth.

(Add these items to your PURSE and INVENTORY) and then **proceed to 66**

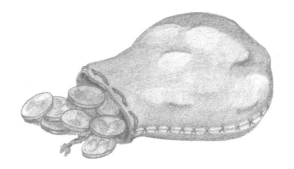

183

The tunnel eventually veers sharply to the left before finally culminating at a long flight of stairs leading upward. You ascend them and find yourself standing in a wide hallway that is extremely well-lit. At the far end of the hallway is a wooden door, which you quietly and cautiously open. The door introduces you to a spacious cavern, but it is what you see and hear next that immediately fills you with apprehension.

Swarming busily around a gigantic hive are several giant wasps — each one fully as large as a medium-sized dog! Even as you watch, others are also coming in and out through an opening in the ceiling high above.

With the wasps' attention wholly focused on what they are doing, perhaps you might be able to slip by them unseen...

If you decide to sneak past them, **turn to 405**

If you choose to fight them instead, **go to 47**

184

A search of the first three rooms reveals nothing of use or of any value. Moving on to the fourth and final room, the largest of the four, you peer inside and are alarmed to discover that the entire room is completely covered by spider webs. A gigantic spider lies in wait in the farmost corner of the room — the desiccated corpses of its many victims scattered throughout its web. Sitting just behind the spider is a small, wooden chest.

Attacking the spider head-on could be a rash and foolish move, but perhaps there is something nearby that could give you more of an advantage when facing the spider...

If you decide to attack the spider, **turn to 477**

If you decide to search the area, **go to 282**

If you think it would be best not to face the spider at all and to move on instead, **proceed to 305**

185

Suddenly, without any warning whatsoever, the doors of the keep are thrown wide open with such force and violence, that both of them come off of their hinges and topple to the ground.

Emerging from the keep and bounding down the staircase on all fours like a giant ape is a horrifying creature that makes anything and everything that you have ever encountered pale in comparison. Standing nearly one-and-a-half times your height, you are shocked to discover that it has literally been constructed from the corpses of both men and beasts that have been sewn together to create its composite form!

Within moments, the quivering, grayish mass of cadaverous flesh is upon you...

FLESH GOLEM   Life Force 45   Combat 4

If you defeat the flesh golem, **turn to 329**

186

Bleeding profusely from its many wounds, the hill giant's breathing becomes more and more labored, until finally, it stumbles forward, and gasping for one last breath, collapses to the floor.

Searching its body, you discover a large satchel hidden beneath the animal skins it is wearing. Inside of the satchel, you find 50 gold pieces, a HEALTH potion, and a sword with strange markings up and down the blade on both sides. You quickly realize that you have accidentally found one of the fabled DeathBringer Blades — a mythical, one-time-use weapon of incredible power!

(DeathBringer Blades are epic, enchanted weapons that may be used only ONE TIME and only on a single opponent with an LF score of 25 or less, or on a more powerful enemy whose LIFE FORCE has been reduced to 25 or less. You can now use this weapon in a future battle. Even the most casual strike will cause instantaneous death to your opponent. The sword will disintegrate after it has been used and must be REMOVED from your INVENTORY).

(Add these items to your PURSE and INVENTORY now) and then **proceed to 271**

187

Sliding down the side of the bloody carcass, you land firmly on your feet with your weapon ready for combat. The carnivorous bird is momentarily caught off guard and initially retreats, but then, shrieking and hissing loudly, slowly advances towards you, clawing at the ground with its lethal, razor-sharp talons...

GIANT FLIGHTLESS BIRD   Life Force 29   Combat 3

If you defeat the giant, flightless bird, **turn to 228**

188

Against your better judgment, you decide to find out exactly what this man's intentions might be.

"An ogre!" yells the man, as he approaches within earshot. "An ogre!"

Before you are even aware of what is happening, you watch as the man stops in mid-stride, a look of sheer horror and absolute shock spreading across his face as he collapses face-first to the ground. Buried deep in the man's back is a crudely fashioned battle-axe, thrown with surprisingly deadly accuracy.

Sprinting towards you and rapidly closing in is a terrifying creature of formidable size and stature. Slowing down to a steady gait, the ogre quickly retrieves its weapon from the man's body and then resumes its mad charge towards you.

Within moments, it is upon you, leaving you little alternative but to fight to the death...

OGRE   Life Force 32   Combat 3

If you kill the ogre, **turn to 448**

If, however, the ogre defeats you, **go to 240**

189

Drifting in and out of consciousness, you eventually come to. You are lying on your side next to others who are also prisoners with your hands bound securely behind your back and your ankles tied as well. Your head is throbbing badly and you suddenly find yourself feeling nauseous. Groggy and still somewhat disoriented, you lift your head just enough to appraise your situation as well as your surroundings.

You are on a ship, that much is immediately certain, but it is the tell-tale, blood-red sails fluttering in the ocean breeze above that confirm your worst fears — you are being held captive on a pirate ship!

Suddenly, you hear coarse talk and laughter as the crew emerges from below deck, and it is immediately obvious by the looks of them that you have fallen into the hands of a brutal and sadistic bunch. As if to underscore this fact, one of the pirates walks over to you and savagely kicks you.

"Now, now, me mateys, is that any way to treat a guest of the Sea Hag?"

Craning your head, you watch as a bearded man, who is quite obviously the ship's captain, steps into your field of vision and approaches you. His weather-worn face is cruel and his narrow eyes cold and calculating. He is wearing a long, burgundy pirate's coat with dark-colored breeches and a pair of charcoal, knee-high boots. Tucked into his belt is what appears to be some sort of handheld cannon, while on his left hip hangs a cutlass. A black tricorn hat adorns his head and there is a large, lizard-like creature lounging

on his shoulder.

Drawing his cutlass and kneeling down beside you and the other prisoners, the pirate captain stares at you for several moments, and then, rising to his feet, says, "This one here looks like they might be more trouble than what they'll fetch in gold..."

"Whattaya reckon we do then, Captain?" asks one of the crew.

"Cut the prisoner's heart out and then feed what's left to the sharks," replies the Captain.

Suddenly, the ghostly forms of what appear to be three elven kings materialize close by. It is at almost the same instant that a strange fire spews forth from the three spectral beings, immediately turning the pirate captain and his lizard into ash. The fire also completely consumes your restraints.

Leaping quickly to your feet, you discover that all of the remaining pirates have jumped overboard, and with the exception of the spirits standing before you and the other prisoners, there is not a soul to be seen on the ship...

Turn to 450

190

You quietly make your way across the room to the chest and then exit without alerting the room's occupants to your presence. The chest contains two HEALTH potions and 5 gold pieces.

(Add these items to your PURSE and INVENTORY now).

If you would like to see what lies beyond the other door across the hall, **go to 141**

Otherwise, **turn to 45**, to continue down the hall.

191

A quick search of the barbarian grants you a HEALTH potion as well as a small coin purse containing 5 gold pieces...

(HEALTH potions can be used at any time to restore lost LF points, except when you are in combat. Each HEALTH potion can be used ONE TIME to restore 5 points. You are also free to use as many of them as you wish at any time, but your LIFE FORCE can never ever exceed its original default of **25**).

(Add these items to your PURSE and INVENTORY now).

Placing the items in your satchel, you exit the room and continue down the passageway...

Turn to 411

192

You search each one of the goblinoids and find a total of 25 gold pieces, a HEALTH potion, and the broken and rusty blade from an old sword. The weapons of the goblinoids are much too burdensome to lug around so you do not take them.

(Add these items to your PURSE and INVENTORY now) and then **turn to 493**

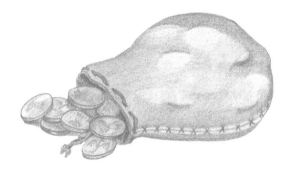

193

Rounding a sharp bend, you unexpectedly and quite suddenly come face-to-face with a monster...

(Roll a 1d6 to determine which monster from the table below you will have to face).

1	SALAMANDER	Life Force 3	Combat 1
2	CAVE SPRITE	Life Force 8	Combat 2
3	RAZORBACK	Life Force 13	Combat 2
4	CAVE LURKER	Life Force 15	Combat 3
5	TROG	Life Force 25	Combat 3
6	DEMOGOBLIN	Life Force 33	Combat 4

(You can also exercise the option of trying to flee by performing an Agility check).

If you are able to successfully flee, **turn to 218**

If not, add 1 point to your Agility score and prepare to face the monster in battle...

WANDERING MONSTER   Life Force ?   Combat ?

If you defeat the random, wandering monster, **turn to 218**

194

The corridor begins to grow noticeably wider and higher, eventually transitioning into a large, subterranean cavern. Jagged rocks and stalagmites rise up from the cavern floor, while high above, stalactites taper down from the ceiling like gigantic icicles.

Not far from where you are standing is a makeshift lean-to that has been fabricated from stones and pieces of driftwood. Thoroughly exhausted, you decide that it would be as good a place as any to get some much-needed rest.

As you make your way towards the crude structure, you are immediately taken aback by what you see. Hundreds of small talismans, each one affixed to strings of varying lengths, adorn the little shack on all sides, especially around the entrance itself.

Once inside, fortune smiles upon you as you discover some smoked fish and some dried fruit, as well as a HEALTH potion. You also find a kit used for dressing wounds and a bedroll consisting of some bedding and a thin blanket. (Add these items, including the bedroll, to your INVENTORY now).

Laying out the bedroll across the cave floor, it is only moments before you are fast asleep. Exactly how long it is that you slept, you have no way of knowing, but when you awake, you find yourself feeling refreshed with renewed vigor. After having some of the smoked fish and dried fruit, you immediately head out...

Turn to 308

195

You decide to attack the snake, which, caught off guard, instantly recoils backward in surprise. For only a moment, the serpent is disoriented, but now fully aware of your presence, poises its head to strike...

GIANT SNAKE   Life Force 27   Combat 3

If you kill the snake, **turn to 239**

If, however, you are the one that dies, **go to 311**

196

Sometime later, you and Mateo come across the massive trunk of a gigantic, fallen oak lying partially across the path. A closer examination, however, quickly leads you to a most unsettling and terrifying conclusion — that this tree did not just fall over! It was definitely and intentionally uprooted, but by what? Even more disturbing is the frightening realization that whatever it was that did this is obviously something of considerable size and immense proportions!

Suddenly, skeletons emerge from the nearby thicket. Each one carries a rusty, bladed weapon, and upon discovering you, immediately begin to advance...

(At this time, please roll a 1d6 to determine how many skeletons you and Mateo will be engaging. If you roll a 1, then you must roll again).

SKELETONS   Life Force 7   Combat 2

(Don't forget that you can now utilize Mateo in battle as well. Simply roll an additional 1d6 for the sailor along with your roll. Mateo has an LF score of 25 and a Combat Skill Score of 3)
.
If you defeat the skeletons, **turn to 82**

197

"Grazu, I was hoping I might ask you about the castle located somewhere on this island," you say.

"The castle you seek is a full day's journey beyond those mountains there," Grazu replies, pointing to a small range of mountains in the far off distance, "but I'm afraid you would never reach it in time before it moved to another place on the island..."

"Surely there must be something in that inventory of yours that could help me get there!" you insist.

Mumbling excitedly to himself, Grazu disappears behind the counter of his vending booth and you hear him rummaging through what might be a crate or even a very large chest. Moments later, the Goblin Merchant returns, holding the most bizarre-looking contraption you have ever laid eyes on.

"This little beauty is called the Atomizer," says the goblin, very much elated.

"Uhh... okay... So, what exactly does it do?" you ask, now more than a little apprehensive.

"The exact science is beyond me," Grazu explains, "but basically, what it does is break something down into tiny little pieces called particles. In this case, that something would be you! Then, after transporting those particles to their new destination, the Atomizer puts them back together again in their original —"

"You'll forgive me, Grazu, if I don't quite share your

enthusiasm," you interject, "but are you sure this is even going to work? I mean, how many times have you actually done this?"

"Well, to be honest..." admits the goblin, with a rather sheepish grin, "I... haven't actually used it on a living creature before..."

Grazu's words are hardly reassuring, and though you have serious reservations, you realize that there is really no other viable means for successfully reaching the castle.

Reluctantly closing your eyes, you soon hear a low, mechanical hum as the device begins to power up. There is the brief and unnatural sensation of tingling throughout your entire body, followed by sudden stabbing pain, and then —

(At this time, please roll a 1d6).

If your roll is an EVEN number, **turn to 35**

If your roll is an ODD number, **go to 401**

198

You try to make a run for it, but the creature lashes out with its long, sticky tongue, sweeping you off of your feet.

You have no choice now but to engage the amphibious monster in combat...

GIANT TOAD   Life Force 30   Combat 3

If you defeat the giant toad, **turn to 89**

199

The corridor eventually leads you to an immense chamber, by far the largest you have been in thus far, with towering walls of fine white marble and a domed ceiling high above.

At the far end of the chamber is a short flight of stairs leading up to a dais, and at the top, what appears to be two, massive, vault-like doors standing side-by-side. Both are nearly three times your height and just about as wide, with a series of giant, interconnecting cogwheels on both sides of them. Other than the way you came in, you can see no other means of egress from the room.

At the foot of the stairs and set into the marbled floor, is a large circle with a system of three rings within it — each one containing various runes and runic symbols. After a closer examination of the rings, you immediately discover that each one can be rotated by hand and turns independently of the others.

Convinced that aligning these runes with their correct corresponding runic symbol is the key to unlocking the doors, you begin examining the puzzle before you more meticulously, but where to begin? There seems to be an endless array of combinations and any wrong one could possibly trigger hidden traps or worse. Even more baffling still is the fact that the runes and runic symbols seem to defy any logical placement or order. By all appearances, they look to be completely random, with no two runes or runic symbols in any of the rings being identical or even remotely resembling another...

(In order to solve this puzzle lock, you will have to have a TOTAL OF THREE successful Intellect checks. If you fail a check, it means you have chosen the wrong combination of runes and have triggered a hidden dart trap. For each failed check, you must roll a 1d6 to determine how much DAMAGE you have sustained. You may roll as many times as necessary until you have either successfully solved the puzzle lock or have been killed by the hidden traps that have been set off! Any damage you receive from triggering a trap will be retained until you use a HEALTH potion. You may also add 1 point to your Intellect score for all of your combined failed checks, but only ONE).

If you successfully solve the runic puzzle, **turn to 246**

200

Powerful emotions rise to the surface, threatening to overcome and completely consume you. You have nearly crossed the breaking point, but then suddenly, you have an unexpected moment of clarity and all of the things you were feeling begin to quickly subside. In that moment, you realize that everything your mind was telling you about yourself and your self-worth is just not true.

One by one, the melancholy orbs leave and drift out of the room, their psychological and emotional hold upon you broken...

Turn to 456

201

You have just spread out the bedroll on the floor and are getting ready to settle in for some much-needed rest and sleep when suddenly, you feel a sharp, stabbing twinge coming from your left thigh. Rolling over and lifting up the blanket, you are horrified to discover the remains of a large spider, which was obviously crushed when you moved...

(You have been bitten by a venomous spider and must now perform a Resistance check).

If your check is successful, **turn to 407**

If, however, your check failed, add 1 point to your Resistance score, and then roll a 1d6 to see how much DAMAGE you sustained from the spider's venom. Any damage you receive will be retained until you use a Health potion. **Go to 407**

202

Suddenly, the entire mound rises up on two legs and begins to move towards you. It is at that moment you realize that the savage creature you now face is a tendril beast! Tendril beasts get their namesake from their long and thin tendril-like appendages, which they use to capture, subdue, and devour their prey. Because their bodies are soft and quite vulnerable, it is not unusual for them to use whatever might be lying around to create a sort of makeshift armour. This, more often than not, is the bones and skeletal remains of their victims!

TENDRIL BEAST   Life Force 31   Combat 3

If you defeat the tendril beast, **turn to 465**

203

The black ooze edges closer and closer, making sucking and slurping noises as it slowly creeps towards you. Standing with your weapon in hand, you watch in horror as a large, subterranean rat ventures too close to the ebony sludge and is dissolved almost instantly.

You quickly realize that your weapon is futile against the black ooze!

Turn to 451

204

Not being much of a water person anyway, you decide to continue hiking downstream on foot. You have not traveled far when suddenly, you see something making its way out of the water onto the land not far from where you are standing. Scuttling towards you is the largest mud crab you have ever seen, standing fully as tall as you and snapping its chelae.

In just a few short moments, the creature is upon you, giving you no choice but to engage it in combat...

GIANT MUD CRAB   Life Force 32   Combat 3

If you kill the crab, continue your trek downstream **by going to 392**

205

The crocodile is relentless, driving you backward with its ruthless arsenal of snapping jaws and powerful, swinging tail.

Suddenly, out of nowhere, you are startled by a series of short, small blasts coming from just behind you. Almost simultaneously, a red mist erupts into the air as the crocodile's head is blown into bits and scattered across the beach. Its headless body stumbles towards you a few more steps and then collapses onto the blood-covered sand.

Stunned by this unexpected turn of events, you momentarily forget about the potential threat from behind and are struck on the back of your head by something hard, causing you to lose consciousness...

Turn to 189

206

Quickly unbarring the door, you rush to the woman's side. It is at that very moment, by the radiant light of the harvest moon above, that you are able to see the woman for what she truly is. Two rows of razor-sharp fangs glisten in the platinum moonlight as she opens her mouth — her jaws dislocating like those of a python. With a growl-like hiss, she rises to her knees as two large, batlike wings slowly unfold from her back, and then immediately lunges for you...

VAMPIRE   Life Force 30   Combat 4

If you kill the vampire, **turn to 313**

If, however, the vampire defeats you, **go to 422**

207

Almost immediately, your mouth and throat begin to burn. This is followed swiftly by severe abdominal pain which causes you to double over and then collapse to the floor in agony. Necrosis is instantaneous as the highly corrosive acid you consumed wreaks massive cellular damage to every part of your body it comes in contact with.

Fortunately, your death is swift!

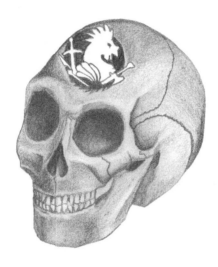

208

The gargoyle proves to be quite formidable in many regards, attacking from both the air and on the ground as well. In the end, however, it just cannot contend with the skill and prowess with which you wield your blade.

Making your way to another set of double doors on the far side, you quickly take leave of the royal garden...

Turn to 116

209

No words will ever accurately convey the horrific scene that now meets your eyes as you enter the throne room. It is a sight so grisly and so ghastly as to make even the bravest of adventurers grow faint of heart. Thousands of human skulls adorn the walls in a grotesque exhibit of the macabre — a mass grave literally put on display in this gruesome chamber of horrors! The very same, knee-deep, supernatural mist swirls about the entire room and a low, ethereal hum only adds to the frightening reality of the moment now before you.

At the far end of the immense and elongated chamber, and rising up and out of the mist like a mountaintop breaching the clouds, is a massive throne composed completely out of skulls. Seated on the throne is the Dark Overlord himself, the Lich Lord, Sineus — his withered hands clutching a staff pulsating with dark and evil magic. You can also see the skeletal remains of his many victims scattered about the dais and stairs before him.

"Foolish mortal!" the Lich Lord sneers from his throne, his voice resonating throughout the chamber. "By your own hand, you have sealed your fate on this day! But your pain will not end with your death, for my wrath will be cruelly exacted upon your soul!"

Erupting into maniacal laughter, the Lich Lord slams the butt end of his staff to the floor, and then, raising it towards the ceiling, launches a devastating blast of energy at you...

(Continued on overleaf)

(With no time to react, you must now roll 2d6 to determine how much DAMAGE you have sustained. Subtract this amount from your LIFE FORCE now).

Almost immediately after his attack, the undead necromancer rises from his throne, and with his staff in hand, descends to meet you head-on...

SINEUS, THE LICH LORD   Life Force 45   Combat 6

If you defeat the Lich Lord, **turn to 402**

210

Turning a sharp bend, you stumble upon the chaotic aftermath of what must have been a recent battle, for scattered throughout the corridor before you are the blood-soaked bodies of several dwarves and probably twice as many orcs. A casual look immediately tells you everything. The dwarves were most likely ambushed by the orcs and in the ensuing confrontation, both sides fell.

Realizing there could be more orcs in the vicinity, you decide to get as far away from the area as possible and leave without searching any of the bodies...

Turn to 99

211

The gold ring comes off with ease, taking nearly all of the rotting skin and flesh on the finger with it in the process.

(Add the ring to your INVENTORY now).

With the room being empty other than what now remains of the severed, putrefying hand, you quickly and quietly exit the room...

If you have not already opened the first door, you may do so **by turning to 294**

You may also investigate what is behind door number two, if you have not already done so, **by going to 114**

If you decide to press on down the corridor instead, foregoing any remaining doors, **proceed to 199**

212

Within moments, the vile, bloodthirsty creatures' bodies lie strewn about the passage. Making your way over to the man who was being attacked by the bats, you discover that he has already succumbed to the massive blood loss caused by his wounds.

A quick search of his person grants you a small coin purse with 5 gold pieces inside.

(Add these to your PURSE now).

Pressing on, you eventually find yourself at a crossroads, with one passage veering sharply to the left and the other bending slightly to the right...

If you decide to go left, **turn to 447**

If you choose the passage on the right instead, **go to 53**

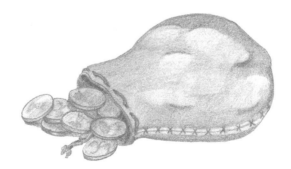

213

"Who are you?" you ask, as you set about freeing the man.

"Name's Mateo," replies the man. "I became a castaway here when the ship I was first mate on ran aground."

"And what of the rest of your crew?" you ask.

"Includin' the Captain and meself, twas fifty of us aboard the Serpent's Wake," Mateo recounts. "I can remember that day like it was only yesterday. The sea was a dead calm and there was no wind — not even so much as a whisper in our sails. We'd been driftin' fer days, ya see, and then all of a sudden, the ship began to move like it had a life of its own. It was like somethin' had taken o'er the Serpent's Wake and was now controlling it! Brought us here, it did! Brought us to this infernal island of death! Fifty of us landed on this accursed rock! Fifty men strong we were, but this island demanded sacrifice and sacrifice it took! The first night we lost ten good men when the vampires came. Some nights the vampires didn't come at all and some nights we were able to fight them off. One by one, we were slaughtered like human cattle and those the vampires didn't take, the island did. Of the Serpent's Wake crew, only I am left to tell the tale..."

Mateo pauses here, a faraway look of reflective thought in his eyes. "Ya saved me life. For that, I am indebted to ya, and if ya'll have me, mate, then me blade is yours..."

With even the very shadows fleeing the encroaching darkness, you and Mateo hole up for the night inside the tight confines of a small cave. Inside, you discover many more of the very same talismans as before — all of them strategically placed in abundance around the opening itself.

An uneventful night eventually retreats at daylight's arrival, and at dawn, you and Mateo immediately set out...

(You may now utilize Mateo in combat. Simply roll an additional 1d6 for the sailor along with your roll. Mateo has an LF score of 25 and a Combat Skill Score of 3).

Turn to 196

214

There are two doors to your left as well as two on the right-hand side. All four are closed and there appears to be no other means of exiting the chamber...

Will you open the first door on the left (**turn to 23**), the second door on the left (**go to 303**), the first door on the right (**turn to 96**), or the second door on the right (**go to 179**)?

215

At long last, the seemingly endless forest finds its end, abruptly giving way to what can only be described as a veritable wasteland of sand and crumbling rock. Harsh, unrelenting, and completely devoid of any vegetation, the barren landscape stretches out in all directions as far as the eye can see, broken only by a few scattered rock formations. In the far-off distance, you spot what might possibly be a range of small mountains and it is towards these, the only visible landmark, that you and Mateo head...

Turn to 429

216

Breaking its hold upon your wrist, you leap backward and off the dais, simultaneously readying your weapon.

Sitting up and climbing out of its sarcophagus, the mummy slowly shuffles towards you with an outstretched arm...

UMRA THE RESPLENDENT   Life Force 35   Combat 5

If you defeat the Resplendent One, **turn to 36**

If, however, Umra kills you, **go to 272**

217

Due to the advanced state of the ogre's decomposition, the pool is now a veritable puddle of slime and ooze, and even as you are kneeling down beside it, the overwhelming combination of both the smell and sight of the rotting corpse causes you to throw up.

Wiping the vomit from your mouth, you do a quick visual scan of your surroundings and are rewarded by the discovery of a spear, which you use to roll the ogre's body over. There is a leather pouch tied to the ogre's belt that you quickly retrieve and then rinse off in one of the other pools. Inside of it, are two HEALTH potions, which you promptly add to the contents of your satchel before pressing on...

(Add these to your INVENTORY now) and then **turn to 325**

218

The passageway soon finds its end at the misshapen entrance of what looks like a small, cavern-like chamber. Peering into the dimly lit chamber, you are appalled to discover the floor is literally strewn from one end to the other with pieces of armor and an array of handheld weapons. There is an exit on the far side of the chamber where the tunnel you have been following seems to pick up again.

Gripping your weapon in readiness, you are about to make your way in when Avril-Lyn stops you.

"Wait!" whispers the sorceress, laying a hand on your shoulder. "Something doesn't feel quite right here. Before you set foot in there, let me cast a spell just to make sure the way ahead is safe..."

If you would rather investigate the room yourself, **turn to 428**

If you decide to have Avril-Lyn cast a *detect life* spell, **go to 332**

If you would like her to cast a *detect traps* spell instead, **proceed to 118**

"We could also head back to the three-way junction," Avril-Lyn suggests. If this is what you would like to do, **turn to 264**

219

The tunnel soon divides in two. You pause for a brief moment to listen at the openings of each one, but both are as silent as a tomb...

If you decide to head down the left tunnel, **turn to 326**

If you choose to make your way down the right-hand tunnel instead, **go to 15**

220

(At this time, please perform a Stealth check).

If your check is successful, **turn to 445**

If, however, it is not, add 1 point to your Stealth score and then **go to 365**

221

You search the pile but find nothing worth taking. As you are turning to leave, you hear a rattling sound and are shocked to discover that some of the bones, along with pieces of armor and clothing, are moving across the floor toward one another, as if drawn together by an unseen force. You quietly watch in fascinated horror as the bones begin to re-assemble themselves.

Within moments, your way to the door is barred by the undead — each one brandishing a rusty weapon as they begin to march menacingly across the room towards you...

SKELETAL WARRIOR   Life Force 10   Combat 2
SKELETAL WARRIOR   Life Force 9   Combat 2
SKELETAL WARRIOR   Life Force 8   Combat 2

If you defeat them, **turn to 362**

222

With the possibility that there might be something you could use on the dead man's person, you resolve to do a quick search of the corpse.

You have knelt down and are about to roll the body over when suddenly, you see movement underneath the cadaver's tunic. Without even thinking, you are instantly back on your feet with your weapon ready. What happens next literally sends chills throughout your entire body.

Spewing forth in all directions from the dead man are hundreds, maybe even thousands, of tiny scorpions. Within moments, they are literally everywhere, but not before you have fled the scene via the corridor on the opposite side of the room...

Turn to 316

223

So inebriated is the man that he is completely unaware as you slip the key off of his belt. It is at that moment that the unthinkable happens! As you are turning, your foot accidentally makes contact with one of the empty bottles, sending it careening loudly across the floor and into the other bottles. Startled from his drunken slumber, the man immediately sits up, and, seeing you, leaps to his feet.

Suddenly, the man begins to transform right before your very eyes, his stature increasing and his frame becoming noticeably larger. Coarse, black hair starts to sprout all over his entire body, and even as you are watching in fearful fascination, the man's jaws elongate into a muzzle-like snout filled with razor-sharp teeth. Exaggerated fingers are soon armed with cruel and deadly claws and human ears quickly become more wolf-like in appearance.

Its metamorphosis complete, you barely have time to ready your weapon as the werewolf attacks...

WEREWOLF   Life Force 30   Combat 4

(Don't forget that you can now utilize Mateo in battle as well. Simply roll an additional 1d6 for the sailor along with your roll. Mateo has an LF score of 25 and a Combat Skill Score of 3).

If you defeat the werewolf, **turn to 72**

224

Making your way up the stairs, you find yourself quietly speculating on why any artist would choose such an unsettling subject matter for expression. But as you continue to come across even more of the same dreadful statues on the stairs, the frightening possibility occurs to you that maybe these are not at all the work of some artist's hands!

Clearly a structure of great antiquity and overrun almost completely by the surrounding vegetation, you are surprised to find that much of the temple is still intact. Here, the gruesome statues are even more numerous than before and you immediately shudder as you come to the terrifying realization that you may have just stumbled upon the lair of a medusa.

Suddenly, your eyes are drawn to the metallic glint of something boldly reflecting the light of the midday sun. Squinting as you make your way towards it, you are astonished to discover a shield that has literally been polished to a mirror-like perfection.

It is then that two wild plans begin to formulate in your mind, but are either one of them worth the incredible risk?

If you decide to enter the temple, **turn to 442**

Perhaps the best strategy here is to lure the medusa from its lair. If this is your choice, **go to 77**

If you decide to head back down to the beach and carry on along the shoreline, **proceed to 483**

225

The passageway dead-ends at a wooden trapdoor set into the cold, stone floor. Lifting it open, you discover what appears to have been a well at one time. A crude, makeshift ladder makes its way down the side of the well until it is eventually consumed by the inky black depths below.

With the only other alternative being to retrace your steps and find another avenue, you decide to press onward and carefully begin your descent. The well is deceptively deep, but eventually, you reach the bottom.

Shrouded in uncanny darkness, you pause to give your eyes a moment to adjust, and then, cautiously feeling around in the dark, discover a door...

Turn to 340

226

The inbred quickly succumbs to your devastating onslaught. A search of its almost inhuman body yields 25 gold pieces and a HEALTH potion.

(Add these to your PURSE and INVENTORY now).

You are about to resume your trek through the inhospitable swamp when without warning, many more of the same disgusting, inbred creatures suddenly appear. Within moments, they have completely surrounded you. You quickly realize that to resist would prove futile and almost certainly fatal.

The swamp folk immediately confiscate everything that is on your person, and then, after binding your hands and feet, one of the larger ones takes his fist and knocks you unconscious...

Turn to 382

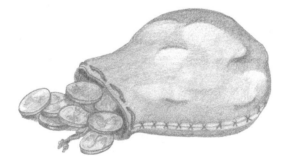

227

A search of the harpies' disgusting carcasses proves to be fruitless. You do, however, discover a small wooden box stashed behind one of the rough-hewn bricks forming the well. Inside of it, you find 75 gold pieces and a HEALTH potion.

(Add these items to your PURSE and INVENTORY now) and then **turn to 18**

228

Suddenly, the unsettling quietude of the forest is interrupted by the desperate cries of a woman calling for help. The cries seem to be coming from somewhere close by, but the harsh undergrowth is so dense in parts as to keep your line of sight from extending very far...

If you determine to help the woman in distress, **turn to 497**

On the other hand, leaving the beaten path might be unwise for a multitude of reasons. Maybe staying the course and not getting involved is the better choice here. If this is your decision, **go to 302**

229

Up ahead, you can see what looks like a doorway opening up on the left. Creeping quietly up to it, you peer into the room.

Seated on a wooden bench against the far wall and fast asleep is a wild-looking, brute of a man clothed in the hides of animals and wearing boots made out of fur. Just within reach and leaning on the bench beside him is a rusty, old battle-axe.

You are about to make your way past him when suddenly, you see something you had not noticed earlier. Lying on the floor a short distance from the man is a large, hyena-like creature, which appears to be sleeping as well.

Preferring not to engage the two of them in combat, you decide the best course of action here is to try and sneak past them...

(At this time, please perform a Stealth check).

If you successfully sneak past them, **turn to 411**

If, however, the hyena discovers you, add 1 point to your Stealth score and then **go to 97**

230

You decide to head down the passage on the right. The odd vegetation is a sickly, gray pallor and is completely devoid of the green pigment normally found in plants.

You have barely crossed over the threshold and entered the passage when suddenly, several gray, leafy tendrils wrap themselves around your legs, causing you to fall flat on your face. Struggling to free yourself, you watch in horror as more of the plant-like shoots begin to slither across your body, wrapping themselves around your torso, neck, and limbs. Unable to move, you desperately try to cry out, but no sound emerges as the tendrils quickly fill your mouth and throat, traveling deep into your lungs and even into your stomach...

231

At first, you are certain you have the upper hand because your opponents are unarmed and crawling on the floor, but you soon discover otherwise. In fact, it is your overconfidence that ultimately proves to be your undoing. Within mere moments, the skeletons have quickly and completely surrounded you, dragging you to the floor and to what is also your tragic and untimely demise...

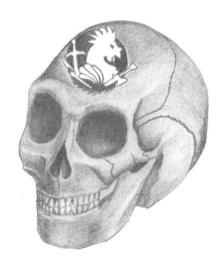

232

232

More than a little troubled by your encounter with the mysterious woman, you set out once more. Like a cruel and unyielding mistress, the sun ruthlessly beats down upon you as you hike across the broken land, and with not even a wisp of a cloud to diffuse the devastating heat, you find yourself forced to rehydrate frequently.

You are progressing up a short, but somewhat steep and rocky incline, when much to your surprise, you suddenly hear the sound of a woman singing. Making your way to the crest of the hill, it is what you see when you reach the top that makes you begin to question the very testimony of your ears and eyes.

Dancing on a low, table-like rock just ahead is a beautiful, young maiden — her eyes tightly closed as she sings an ancient song in an unknown tongue. Her every movement is sensual and almost hypnotic, and you quickly find yourself strangely bewitched by her beauty and instantly captivated by her mysterious allure.

Snapping back to your senses, you call out to her, but the woman has already crumbled into a pile of sand...

Turn to 490

233

Unable to contend with the skill and fury with which you wield your weapon, three of Arachnae's Faithful are soon no more. They are wearing mustard-colored robes with hoods and as you are searching them, you notice that all three have a large, black spider tattooed on their necks just below their right ears. A search of their persons, as well as the rest of the sleeping quarters, yields nothing. The chest, however, contains two HEALTH potions and a drawstring purse containing 5 gold pieces.

(Add these items to your PURSE and INVENTORY now).

Not wanting to draw attention to your presence this early in the game, you and Avril-Lyn quickly pose the dead cultists in their beds so as to present the semblance of sleep...

If you would like to see what lies beyond the other door across the hall, **go to 141**

Otherwise, **turn to 45**, to continue down the hall.

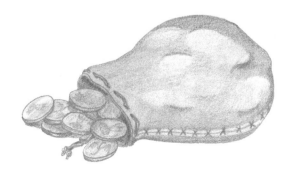

234

Emerging from the thicket is an abomination straight out of your worst nightmares — a multi-legged monstrosity; a hideous amalgamation and what can only be the perversion of a spell gone horribly and terribly wrong. With no apparent rhyme or reason, spindly, insect-like legs of varying sizes and lengths randomly sprout from its severely disfigured mass of a body, while the placement of its head, eyes, and mandibles seem to be nothing more than just an afterthought.

Completely oblivious to your presence, the terrifying creature moves about the clearing for a bit before eventually scuttling back into the underbrush from whence it came...

Turn to 490

235

After walking for a time, the passage you have been following abruptly comes to a dead-end, terminating at a metal culvert just large enough for an adult to enter on their hands and knees. Kneeling next to the opening, you peer inside and down the culvert, which extends as far as the naked eye can see, until it is eventually consumed by the darkness within it.

With the only other course of action being to turn around and retrace your steps, you enter the large conduit — half-crawling and half-shimmying your body forward through a stomach-churning mixture of putrid slime and dead rodents, their bones crunching beneath the weight of your hands and knees.

After pressing forward for a time, you suddenly realize that there is no room for you to even turn around. Should you decide to go back, you would have to back your way out, and with that realization, fear, however irrational it might be, begins to sink its claws into you. Now crawling in pitch dark blackness, you begin to hyperventilate, unable to move as your body becomes paralyzed by the crippling claustrophobia now setting in.

Taking several deep breaths, you somehow come to your senses, and after composing yourself, begin moving forward again. The culvert takes a sharp turn to the right and your spirit is instantly renewed as you see light up ahead coming from the opening at the other end. Moments later, you emerge from the culvert, thankful to be out of its dark confines and able to stand upright... **Turn to 86**

236

"Where are we?" you ask, even as the portal you have just come through is closing behind you.

"We are at the highest point of the place you know as the Faalmund Plateau," replies the mysterious woman.

The Faalmund Plateau... it was beneath this very mountain, in the deepest and darkest recesses of the Legorian Labyrinth, that you defeated the Lich Lord, Sineus!

"Who are you," you ask, "and why did you attack me? "

"My name is Avril-Lyn," replies the elven sorceress. "It was never my intention to harm you, only to frighten you, and that, with the hope you would abandon your crusade to recover the artifact."

"And now, you have asked me to come here with you... Why?" you ask.

"Perhaps it is best if I showed you," says Avril-Lyn as she walks over to a table-like rock formation nearby.

Making your way over to where she is standing, you discover a large bowl-like depression in the rock formation where water has collected to create a small, shallow pool. Avril-Lyn moves both of her hands above the pool in a circular motion, and suddenly, the very events and details she begins to describe are being played out upon the surface of the water for you to see.

"Many millennia ago, there was a kingdom called Legoria ruled by three elven kings — Glorandol, Eloshann, and Maegyddo. The kingdom had expanded and prospered greatly under their reign, but for these three wicked kings, it was not enough. In their all-consuming greed and lust for more, they set their sights not just on the neighboring kingdoms around them, but on the whole of Ataraxia itself!"

"There was just one problem — the people of Legoria had dedicated their entire lives to the pursuit of knowledge and wisdom. They were scholars, not soldiers and were unschooled and untrained in the art of war."

"Knowing they could never hope to achieve the conquest of the world without a powerful army at their beck and call, the diabolical kings committed the unthinkable and the unimaginable — the mass genocide of their own people! Using the dark arts and technomancy, as well as the corpses of those they had slaughtered, Glorandol, Eloshann and Maegyddo would create an army unlike anything the world had ever seen — biomechanical monstrosities and terrible weapons of war that were part machine, and part flesh and bone."

"But unbeknownst to the kings, four sorcerers would come together to stand against them. Channeling each other's magic and using the blood of a phoenix and three powerful artifacts, the sorcerers performed a binding ritual spell, banishing the Legorian Kings and their entire horrific army to the Realms Beyond.

"The cataclysmic fall of Ataraxia had been prevented,

but the sorcerers knew those very same artifacts, along with the blood of a phoenix, could also be used to free the kings from their prison. Such malevolent evil could never be allowed to return to this world, nor the artifacts to fall into the wrong hands."

"The artifacts had to be destroyed, but though the sorcerers tried every conceivable way in which to do so, they could find no means whereby they might destroy them. They realized then that if they could not be destroyed, then the artifacts must be protected at all costs! A blood pact ritual was performed, binding the sorcerers forever to the artifacts until death."

"But binding themselves to the artifacts came with a heavy price. Three of them would become so consumed and so corrupted by the very objects they had vowed to protect that that obsession would eventually drive them mad. In their descent into madness, they would forfeit their goodness, willfully choosing to become the terrible and evil monsters you have faced in order to safeguard the artifacts..."

"Help me understand something," you say. "If these so-called Legorian Kings... this Glorandol... Eloshann and Maegyddo... if they truly are prisoners in the Realms Beyond, how is it that they are now able to come and go as they please?"

"The artifacts are much more than just powerful magical objects," answers the sorceress. "In a very real sense, they are also keys. When the Lich Lord was defeated, his death immediately severed his attachment to the artifact, which was his staff. It also lifted the warding that was on that artifact as well.

When the connection between Sineus and the staff was broken, it was enough to weaken the binding spell that has held the three kings captive and at bay these many thousands of years. With each artifact they possess, their power and strength will only grow."

"How can I be certain any of the things you have shown me and are telling me now are even true?" you ask.

It is here Avril-Lyn pauses, and as she turns away, tears suddenly well up within her beautiful, blue eyes.

"I was there..." she replies after several moments, her voice clearly and genuinely marked with sorrow. "With my own eyes, I witnessed the ruthless slaughter of my people, including my own infant daughter and my husband..."

For more than a moment, you are at a loss for words, stunned by Avril-Lyn's startling revelations.

"If the Legorian Kings successfully acquire the third and final artifact," she continues, "it is only a matter of time before they procure the blood of a phoenix and are able to free themselves. When they do, in their vengeful fury, they will unleash their terrible army of vile monstrosities upon Ataraxia and the world we know will be no more!"

"Please..." says Avril-Lyn, a beseeching expression upon her face. "Help me stop them! Help me recover the final artifact and together we can finish what I should have done a long, long time ago..."

As if to underscore her plea, Avril-Lyn strikes the air with her staff and once again a shimmering portal opens close by. Without waiting for your reply, the sorceress steps into it and is quickly swallowed from view.

You are not far behind her...

Turn to 473

237

Placing the mysterious ring inside your satchel, you promptly exit the chamber and head down the corridor.

(Add the ring to your INVENTORY now).

You have not traveled far when suddenly, you hear the distinct sounds of muffled voices and laughter coming from somewhere up ahead. A wide doorway opens up on the left. Crouching low, you make your way ever so cautiously to its edge and peer into the room just beyond.

Seated at a large, wooden table are two hobgoblins. They are eating and drinking heavily, and appear to be playing some sort of game that, strangely enough, seems to utilize only a book and some dice.

You could fight them, but perhaps the best strategy here would be for you to sneak past them, avoiding a confrontation altogether...

(At this time, please perform a Stealth check).

If you successfully sneak past them, **turn to 438**

If the hobgoblins see you, add 1 point to your Stealth score and then **go to 37**

238

The path now takes you through a dismal stretch of the woods where the trees are either already dead or are in the process of dying. Here, even the existing vegetation that is still alive is a sickly gray pallor and is completely devoid of the green pigment characteristic of most plants.

Suddenly, a thick, leafy tendril shoots out from the underbrush, and before you even have time to react has wrapped itself around your legs and pulled you to the ground. Instinctively, your hand is already on your weapon and striking at the tendril wrapped tightly around your ankles as it drags you roughly across the forest floor. Its grip upon you relaxes, and in an instant you are back on your feet, your weapon ready.

You are standing in a small clearing and are very much alarmed to discover that the entire area is literally strewn from end to end with the bones of men and beasts alike. You also see a cave-like opening on the opposite side of the clearing and quickly realize that this is no doubt the lair of some terrible and ferocious creature, but what?

You are not left to wonder long as a long, tendril-like vine suddenly lashes out at you from within the cave, nearly knocking you down as you struggle to maintain your footing on the bones that are sliding every which way beneath your feet. Emerging from the cave entrance is a terrifying monstrosity that in every respect looks just like a large, leafy plant, but with a gigantic bulbous head and an orifice full of sharp teeth. The plant-like aberration has no eyes that you can see, but

is clearly aware of your position as it moves with incredible speed across the bone-littered landscape towards you. The creature lashes out at you again, this time connecting and successfully wrapping itself around your legs and sweeping you off of your feet. Within moments, its vine-like appendages have completely encircled your body so that you are unable to move or even reach for your weapon as it begins drawing you towards its tooth-filled mouth.

Suddenly, the ghostly forms of what appear to be three elven kings materialize close by. It is at almost the same instant that a strange fire spews forth from the three spectral beings, completely consuming the carnivorous plant and turning it into ash...

Turn to 435

239

The snake rears its massive head one last time and then shudders before crashing to the wet cavern floor — its body continuing to writhe and squirm violently and its tail still madly thrashing about.

A quick search of the cavern reveals a small chest partially submerged in one of the pools. Inside of it, you find 25 gold pieces.

(Add the gold to your PURSE now) and then exit the cavern **by going to 199**

240

Though you fight valiantly, the massive brute proves to be too much for you — the confrontation culminating with your skull being split by the ogre's axe with a single, powerful, downward swing...

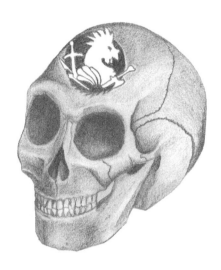

241

With its attention completely focused on its meal, you rush into the cave with the intent of dispatching the sea hag quickly.

It is then that the unfathomable happens! While you are storming in, the toe of your boot catches on a portion of the floor that is uneven, causing you to stumble uncontrollably to the floor.

In an instant, the vile creature is on its feet and is nearly on top of you as you are getting up...

SEA HAG   Life Force 20   Combat 2

If you defeat the sea hag, **turn to 352**

242

It is late afternoon when you unexpectedly stumble upon the remnants of a long and forgotten city from a bygone era. The crumbling ruins have long since been invaded by the forest, and with the exception of a few miniature, boar-like creatures darting in and out of hiding, the place appears to be deserted. An uncanny and unsettling silence hangs heavily over the place, even more so than what you experienced in the forest.

With little alternative but to continue moving forward, you pick your way through what was obviously the city's gates at one time. Before you, and flanked on both sides by the advanced architecture of the ancient and long-dead metropolis, is a broad, paved avenue that seems to run right through the middle of the city. Almost immediately, you are confronted with the uncomfortable sensation that you are being watched. Looking up, you are startled to discover that the rooftops and upper-story windows of every building are literally lined with monkeys. What makes this even more disturbing and unsettling is the fact that every one of them is just sitting there motionless and staring down at you in silence.

A short time later, the avenue finds its end and you find yourself standing at the edge of a large, circular plaza in what seems to be the very heart of the city itself.

Suddenly, a shrill, pulsating hum fills the air and begins to reverberate throughout the city. Quickly finding cover inside a nearby building, you watch in terrified astonishment as a large, saucer-shaped object descends from the sky above, coming to rest in the air just above the plaza. Its appearance is like that of liquified metal and as it hovers in midair, its mirror-like surface reflects the entire panorama of the sky, the city, and even the surrounding forest. Even as you stand there transfixed and wondering what manner of sorcery this is, an opening materializes in the bottom of the floating phenomenon and a flat, disc-like object emerges and gently lands in the plaza.

For several moments you wait, watching intently from your place of hiding, but nothing happens...

If you decide to investigate the strange, disc-like object, **turn to 439**

If you decide to try to find a way out of the city instead, **go to 13**

243

Suddenly, your ears are met with the sounds of crumbling rock coming from above and behind you, followed almost immediately by the thunderous roar of a massive rockslide. Retreating further up into the ravine, you watch in startled disbelief as the entrance to the gorge is swallowed up in an instant by an avalanche of falling stone and debris.

With no other alternative now but to continue following the ravine wherever it leads, you dust yourself off and make your way inland...

Turn to 366

244

You are making your way down the corridor when quite suddenly and unexpectedly, you stumble upon a roaming monster...

(Roll a 1d6 to determine which monster from the table below you will have to face).

1	IMP	Life Force 3	Combat 1
2	GHOULIE	Life Force 4	Combat 1
3	GIANT ANT	Life Force 8	Combat 1
4	HYENA	Life Force 13	Combat 2
5	GOBLINOID	Life Force 20	Combat 3
6	OGRE	Life Force 35	Combat 3

(You can also exercise the option of trying to flee by performing an Agility check).

If you are able to successfully flee, **turn to 83**

If not, add 1 point to your Agility score and prepare to face the monster in battle...

WANDERING MONSTER   Life Force ?   Combat ?

If you defeat the random, wandering monster, **go to 83**

245

Walking over to a series of interconnected cogs, the lizardman begins turning a crank handle, setting the cogwheels in motion and activating an internal winch within the walls.

With a loud rumble, the iron portcullis raises via its attached chains, allowing you and your companion to enter the tunnel beyond...

Subtract 10 gold pieces from your PURSE and then **turn to 387**

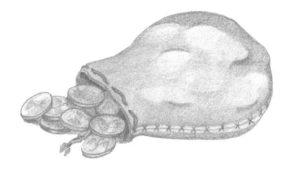

246

Almost instantaneously, you hear the industrial hum of ancient machinery hidden behind the chamber walls coming to life as the gears on both sides of the massive doors begin to turn and the doors start opening. Within moments, both have swung completely open to reveal a monstrous hallway just beyond them.

You are about to make your way up the stairs and onto the dais when suddenly, you hear the heavy footfalls of metal against stone as something extremely large approaches from down the hallway. Whatever it is that is clanking down that corridor towards you is obviously well-armored, and it is a safe bet that it is also armed to the teeth. Once again, you make ready with your weapon, and it is not long before your new adversary introduces itself.

Framed within the opening is a veritable amalgamation of both flesh and bone as well as machinery; a biomechanical juggernaut; a faceless guardian both beautiful and terrifying at the same time — no doubt a remnant of the lost Legorian civilization.

Even as you are marveling at the incredible technology used to engineer such a formidable aberration, you hear the soft purr of internal motors turning as the gatekeeper begins to advance, the floor literally shaking with its every step...

LEGORIAN SENTINEL   Life Force 50   Combat 6

If you defeat the Sentinel, **turn to 400**

If, however, it is you who is defeated, **go to 349**

247

After a time, white sand gives way to more rocky terrain, eventually finding you standing before a vertical rock face. Doing a quick visual study of the cliff's jagged exterior, you immediately notice what appear to be hand and footholds carved right into the rock, starting just to the left of where you are standing and going all the way to the very top.

Reaching for the nearest handhold and getting a firm grip, you pull yourself up until one of your feet is planted firmly on the first foothold and then begin making your way up the sheer face of the precipice. Your progress is extremely slow and every movement physically demanding, but eventually, you reach the summit. Utterly exhausted as you drag yourself up and over the brink at the very top, you collapse onto the ground, your body completely spent...

Turn to 432

248

Try as you might, you just cannot get the changeling to relinquish its grasp upon your wrist, and in an instant, your arm is gone — completely bitten off just above the elbow! You cry out in pain, and it is not long before the severe blood loss causes you to go into shock. Your breathing becomes more and more irregular and labored as you begin to stumble uncontrollably around the room, eventually collapsing onto the hard stone floor.

The changeling stirs, slowly creeping its way across the floor to where you have fallen. Within moments, it has thoroughly devoured you as well as all of your personal effects...

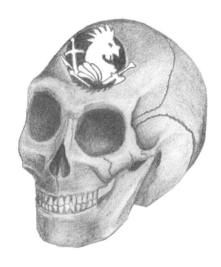

249

The passage quickly finds its resolution at a large, oaken door with the representation of a spider carved into its surface.

"The Temple of Arachnae..." says the sorceress, confirming what was already going through your mind. "We will have to proceed with much greater caution from here on out!"

Pressing your ear purposefully against it, you listen intently for several moments, but hear nothing. Trying the handle, you discover that it is unlocked and both you and Avril-Lyn step cautiously into the corridor just beyond...

Turn to 276

250

With the goblinoids' attention completely diverted, you easily sneak past them without being seen...

Turn to 493

251

The door introduces you to a good-sized chamber, but it is what you see by the light of your torch that immediately gives you pause.

Scattered about the room are several fiendish devices, each one specifically designed with one goal in mind — to inflict physical pain and suffering! In the very center of the room is a table with a wide selection of cruel implements, no doubt meant to exact confession. You also notice various types of restraints firmly anchored to the blood-stained stones of the walls, floor, and ceiling — some of them with the skeletal remains of their last victim lying in a pile beneath them!

Making your way to the far side of the room, you discover another door and a stairway winding upwards...

Turn to 370

252

Instinctively, in the brief instance you are falling, you reach out, miraculously catching hold of the chasm's edge, and then pull yourself to safety.

A quick check reveals that your weapon, satchel, and all the items within it are intact and still on your person.

Turn to 30

253

Almost immediately, you and Avril-Lyn find yourselves descending a short flight of rough-hewn stairs that culminate before a heavy, wooden door. A cautionary listen is greeted only by silence. Weapon in hand, you slowly push the door inward and open. A torchlit, cavernous chamber awaits, along with something else!

Squatting on the far side of the room are two strange, humanoid-like creatures, both of them completely naked and their hairless, muscular bodies so translucent, that you can literally see their skeletons as well as every one of their internal organs beneath their semi-transparent skin and flesh. Right away, you notice the total absence of any eyes, nose, or ears on their heads — just a large, tooth-filled maw where a face would normally be. Disturbingly long fingers only add to the already frightening picture modeled before you.

At your appearance, the grotesque monstrosities rise to their feet and advance, their disgusting mouths emitting slurping and gurgling sounds as they rapidly shuffle across the chamber towards you...

HOLLOW MAN   Life Force 26   Combat 3
HOLLOW MAN   Life Force 25   Combat 3

If you defeat the hollow men, **turn to 487**

254

"You are the same three spirits who appeared after I defeated the Lich Lord," you say, addressing the ghostly entities standing before you. "You took his staff and now have rescued me from certain death. Why?"

"I am Glorandol and this is Eloshann and Maegyddo," replies the spectre in the middle, speaking in an ancient and unknown tongue that you should not be able to understand and yet somehow do. "Many, many millennia ago, we three kings ruled as One. Ours was a kingdom of love, peace, and prosperity, and one abounding in the wisdom and knowledge of the Ancient Ones. A mecca of peace and academic pursuits, the glorious Kingdom of Legoria existed as such for many, many thousands of years, untouched by the sins of war and undefiled by the greed and lust that so characterizes humankind."

"But that would all change when four, extremely powerful sorcerers would unite to overthrow us and all that Legoria represented, seeking for themselves that which we had created for good, that they might use it for their dark intents and evil purposes. Our collective, intellectual minds, the greatest the world of Ataraxia has ever seen, gave us unparalleled advances in the sciences, birthing many untold technological wonders. It was this technology that they sought to make their own and in a twist of ironic fate, that very same technology would also bring about the total annihilation of our people, as well as the end of Legorian civilization itself."

"The sorcerers forced us to watch as they mercilessly

slaughtered every last one of our people. Then, using their combined dark magic and three, incredibly powerful artifacts, they banished us to the Realms Beyond, sending us to a perpetual prison without walls, where we are neither alive nor truly dead."

"When you defeated the Lich Lord, we knew that in you we had found our champion and the one that could free us from the chains of eternal exile..."

"I'm not sure I understand," you say.

This time, it is the one called Eloshann who speaks. "In the very same way that the sorcerers were able to use those three artifacts to banish and bind us, so, too, when they are again reunited, those same artifacts also have the power to release us..."

"These artifacts... how could one even possibly know where to begin looking for them?" you ask, somewhat intrigued.

"Of the two remaining artifacts, we know that one of them is here on this island and the other somewhere deep within the endless Warrens of Wvanderfell," answers Maegyddo. "Both are guarded by a fearsome and formidable monster."

"Didn't you say there were three artifacts?" you interject. "Why now are there only two?"

"Because one of the three has already been recovered," Glorandol says in a matter-of-fact voice.

"The Lich Lord's staff..." you reply.

The three spectral kings nod their heads in affirmation.

"So then, this... place... this island and my being here... none of this is by any means a coincidence, is it?" you say.

"It would seem that fate has bound you to this island, but to what end and for what purpose, of that we cannot say for certain," says Maegyddo.

"So why not simply recover the artifacts yourselves?" you ask.

"Our powers are limited beyond the veil of our torment," replies Eloshann. "There is also a powerful magic that not only binds the artifacts to the monsters that guard them, but also restrains us from even coming anywhere near them. Unfortunately, that same enchantment also prevents any and all from leaving this island..."

"Of course..." you mumble under your breath.

"Find the castle," Glorandol adds. "It is there that the master of this island dwells — an ancient and powerful evil unlike anything you have ever faced and whose origin predates perhaps even history itself — the Vampire Sovereign and blood sire of the vampire race, TitusMirror! But finding the castle will be far from easy, for each day at sundown, the castle disappears, only to reappear again in a different place on the island. Unspeakable horrors await you, but it is there that you will find the artifact, and quite possibly, your freedom. May the gods give you strength and grant

you success."

And then, just as suddenly and mysteriously as the apparitions appeared, they are gone.

Grieving the tragic and unexpected loss of your newfound friend, Mateo, it is with a heavy heart that you press on...

Turn to 418

255

Unable to withstand the surprising strength of your attack against her, the sorceress backpedals, and then, with a wave of her hand, disappears...

Turn to 129

256

You find yourself in a wide corridor, its entire length lined on both sides with the very same holding cells as the one you awoke in. Being completely unarmed, your first instinctive reaction is to be on the lookout for the inevitable arrival of the guards, for they most certainly must have heard your cell door opening. But even after an indefinite amount of time has passed, no one comes, and except for the flickering of the torches randomly placed throughout to dispel the darkness and the occasional squeaky chatter of the rats, the dungeon hall is as silent as a tomb.

A cursory scan of your surroundings helps you to quickly determine your next move, with you immediately making for the flight of stairs at the far end and heading up them.

The stairway spirals upward, terminating at a large, wooden door. Resting your ear against the wood, you listen closely, and, hearing nothing, place your hand on the handle and quietly and cautiously open the door...

Turn to 479

257

Slowly and cautiously opening the door, you peer into the room and quickly realize that you have stumbled upon the sleeping quarters of the Faithful. Several bunk beds, each one built three high, are butted perpendicular against the opposite wall. You also spot a large chest sitting at the foot of the bunk bed farthest from you.

A quick search of the room itself turns up nothing. The chest, however, contains two HEALTH potions and a small coin purse containing 5 gold pieces.

(Add these items to your PURSE and INVENTORY now).

If you would like to see what lies beyond the other door across the hall, **go to 141**

Otherwise, **turn to 45,** to continue down the hall.

258

In an instant, the entire scene around you dissolves and the forest and the table with food are gone, replaced by the hard stone walls and floor of the cold, dimly-lit chamber you now find yourself standing in. The dryad is nowhere to be found, and several skeletons in the room tell you that more than one adventurer fell victim to her enchantment.

You exit the room via the wooden door and head down the other passage...

Turn to 122

259

Just ahead, the corridor finishes at a large, oaken door set within an arched doorway. The door opens into a wide hallway running perpendicular to the one that you have been following. This new corridor continues in both directions before finding its end on both sides at adjoining corridors...

Will you continue left (**turn to 416**) or will you head right (**go to 317**)?

260

Almost immediately after rotating the last turn-stone, a barrage of darts spews forth from multiple hidden apertures, with some of them hitting you.

(To determine how much DAMAGE you sustained, roll a 1d6 and subtract this amount from your LIFE FORCE now).

You have obviously chosen the wrong combination of symbols!

Please return to 87

261

Trudging down the hallway towards you is something you thought only existed in tales told by the campfire at night, but the monster you now see is all too real and anything but just some story. Rumored to be the amalgamation of a spell gone horribly wrong, the terrifying creature before you has the body of a large orc, but its head is that of a wild boar. Two sets of large, formidable-looking tusks protrude from both its upper and lower lips, and in its monstrous hands, it clutches an enormous, two-handed mace.

As soon as it is aware of your presence, the savage brute breaks into a sprint down the hallway towards you...

BORC   Life Force 28   Combat 3

If you defeat the borc, **turn to 393**

262

At long last, the seemingly endless forest finds its end, abruptly giving way to what can only be described as a veritable wasteland of sand and rock. Harsh, unrelenting, and completely devoid of any vegetation, the barren landscape stretches out in all directions as far as the eye can see. In the far-off distance, you spot what might possibly be a range of small mountains, and it is towards these, the only visible landmark, that you head...

Turn to 369

263

You step off of the pressure plate, and right away, the chamber comes to a grinding halt as the door swings open to reveal a giant spider, which hungrily advances toward you...

GIANT SPIDER   Life Force 28   Combat 3

If you defeat the spider, **return to 300 and roll again**

264

Eventually, you and Avril-Lyn find yourselves back at the three-way junction...

If you decide to head down the passage on the left where you can distinctly hear the sound of dripping water, **turn to 81**

If you elect to take the middle passage instead, **go to 110**

265

You pull the lever on the left, and in an instant, the floor beneath you is gone and you have fallen into a pit filled with sharpened pikes!

(At this time, please perform a Luck check. If your check is successful, then you escape the fall without injury. If, however, your check failed, you have been wounded by either the fall itself or by the pikes. Add 1 point to your Luck score for failing, and then roll 2d6 to determine how much DAMAGE you have sustained. Subtract this amount from your LIFE FORCE now. Any damage you receive will be retained until you use a Health potion).

Climbing out of the pit, you pull the other lever on the right...

Turn to 373

266

The passage rises vertically for a short span before eventually leveling off and continuing straight. Spooked by your unexpected arrival, small, octopus-like creatures scatter in all directions before you as you make your way forward and up the passage. Farther on down the tunnel, the same cephalopods are startled into motion again, this time by something else heading your way, and that is when you see them!

Marching towards you and standing out in dramatic contrast against the crystal-clear water are several undead, reptilian monstrosities — their scaly, decomposing bodies wrapped in heavy chains and covered with seaweed-like plants and strange, coral-like growths.

With the only viable option being to meet them head-on in combat, you brace yourself for the ensuing underwater confrontation...

UNDEAD TROGLODYTE	Life Force 15	Combat 3
UNDEAD TROGLODYTE	Life Force 14	Combat 3
UNDEAD TROGLODYTE	Life Force 13	Combat 3
UNDEAD TROGLODYTE	Life Force 13	Combat 3

(Because movement underwater can be much more restrictive, subtract 1 each time you roll. Be sure to do the same for Avril-Lyn and for the undead troglodytes as well).

If you survive this encounter, **turn to 43**

267

You have not gone far when without warning, you see something up ahead that makes you second guess whether you are dreaming or are actually awake.

Surging down the tunnel towards you and numbering in the thousands are throngs of rats! Although you are hopelessly outnumbered, you prepare yourself for the inevitable onslaught rapidly coming your way. Much to your surprise, the rats do not attack, but instead, hurriedly scurry around you as if you are not even there, until moments later, the last of them have disappeared in the direction from whence you came.

Puzzled, you continue down the corridor, but then come to the realization that the rats were fleeing, but from what? You also realize that whatever it is that had the rats spooked is headed straight for you. You ready your weapon, but now proceed with much greater caution.

Your wait is short-lived for you soon discover what it is that the rats were so afraid of — or rather, they discover you!

Scuttling along the floor, walls, and ceiling are several giant ants, who, upon seeing you, quickly scamper towards you.

Unless you want to become their next source of food, it looks like you are going to have to face them in combat...

Resolve this encounter:

GIANT ANT	Life Force 9	Combat 2
GIANT ANT	Life Force 9	Combat 2
GIANT ANT	Life Force 8	Combat 2

If you defeat the ants, **turn to 343**

268

"As much as it may or may not grieve me to tell you this, I am sorry to say that your answer is incorrect," replies the halfling. "That being said, unfortunately, we do have an agreement and I am afraid that it is time to settle."

(If you DID NOT fight the sea hag and loot the chest in her cave, your INVENTORY, up to this point, should look like the following — this, of course, being contingent on whether or not you have used up all of your HEALTH potions:

1   Wheel of cheese
2   Gold tooth
3   Half of your gold pieces
4   Health potion
5   All of your gold pieces

If, however, you DID loot the sea hag's chest, your INVENTORY should look like this, barring you have not used all of your HEALTH potions:

1   Wheel of cheese
2   Gold tooth
3   Half of your gold pieces
4   Health potion
5   The tooth of a large shark
6   All of your gold pieces

Roll a 1d6 and the number it lands on will determine what item(s) from above you MUST give to the halfling. If you do not have any HEALTH potions left because you used all of them, then simply leave them off of the list and roll until one of the other remaining items is forfeited. If your roll is a 4, even though you might have more than one HEALTH potion, you only have to give Tomlin ONE. If your roll is a 3 or a 6, unfortunately, you MUST give the entire amount of gold pieces specified to the halfling. Subtract the item/items given to the halfling from your INVENTORY now).

"Well met, traveler!" declares the halfling, as he places the item(s) inside his leather satchel. "And just so there are no hard feelings between us, I have decided that I am going to help you anyway!"

The halfling snaps his fingers and you suddenly find yourself standing at the top of the cliff, staring out at an endless expanse of ocean merging with the sky. Cautiously making your way to the edge of the precipice and looking down, you discover that Tomlin Underhill, along with his table and chairs, has vanished...

Turn to 368

269

You find yourself in a spacious, rectangular room nearly three times as long and easily twice as high as it is wide. Moth-eaten tapestries and faded banners grace the hard stone walls throughout, testifying to the bygone days of its former glory and splendor. Two extremely long tables, with benches equally as long, run almost two-thirds the length of the chamber. There is a wide aisle between the two of them. At the far end, and looking out over the room from atop a raised platform is the high table where the nobility would have sat.

You are in the Great Hall, this much is now obvious — the Grand Chamber where the king and his esteemed guests would have made merry, wining and dining into the wee hours, whilst women danced, performers performed, and minstrels played and sang. Once a noisy throng resonating in celebration, the room is now but a desolate and empty reminder of what once was.

Just behind the king's table, you notice that there is another set of double doors...

Turn to 457

270

With an ear-shattering shriek, the vampire falls to her knees, and then, throwing her hands up into the air, begins to crumble, disintegrating until all that remains of her is a pile of dust and the garments she was wearing. A search of the vampire's garments proves fruitless.

The rest of the night passes without incident, but you are unable to get any kind of restful sleep...

Turn to 142

271

The passage continues for a time before curving sharply to the right and heading in a different direction. At the bend is a door, which you discover to be locked. Because the lock mechanism is completely rusted, it cannot be picked.

Perhaps the door can be broken down...

If you decide to break the door down, **turn to 398**

If you decide to move on, **go to 59**

272

The mummy proves to be much more formidable than you had anticipated. Grabbing onto your wrist with one of its spade-clawed hands, you watch in absolute horror as your skin begins to shrivel up and your arm starts to wither. You try desperately to reach for the weapon you have dropped with your other hand, but the rest of your body has already started to deteriorate as well. You feel yourself growing weaker and weaker by the moment as your life force ebbs away, until finally, you succumb to the power of Umra, the Resplendent...

273

You instantly find yourself standing in a wide-open sward of crimson extending in all directions as far as the eye can see. You quickly realize that the amulet has transported you to the Red Plains of Duhar, a region uniquely known for its sweeping expanses of blood-red, close-cropped grass. Just ahead and slightly to your left is a low, but large, table-like rock formation. Three figures are standing on top of it, and as you rapidly make your approach with your longsword in hand, the elven kings immediately shift their focus to you. Lying on her side not far from them is the sorceress, Avril-Lyn, but you cannot tell if she is dead or just unconscious.

"Well, well, well..." says Glorandol, clearly surprised to see you. "At first, you were just an amusing annoyance, but now, you are proving to be quite the proverbial thorn in our sides!"

"You may have all three of the artifacts," you reply, "but without the blood of a phoenix you will never complete the unbinding ritual!"

"You fool!" declares Glorandol, a contemptuous look upon his face and his voice rich with arrogance. "Avril-Lyn IS the phoenix, and soon, the kingdoms of Ataraxia will bow defeated before the demonstrative power of our strength and might! Unfortunately, my insolent friend, you will not be alive to see any of it!"

Even as he finishes speaking, a crackling, blue ball of energy leaps from his hand, totally engulfing you in mere seconds, but much to your surprise as well

as the dismay of the elven kings, you are completely unaffected. Once again, the amulet has protected you from certain death!

"Very well then, hero," says Glorandol, smiling smugly as all three of them draw their swords and begin marching steadfastly towards you, "then your fate will be meted out by our blades instead..."

THE LEGORIAN KINGS

GLORANDOL	Life Force 33	Combat 6
ELOSHANN	Life Force 33	Combat 6
MAEGYDDO	Life Force 33	Combat 6

If you defeat the Legorian Kings, **turn to 500**

If, however, it is you who is defeated, **go to 127**

274

Staying low and moving quietly between the various rock formations and stalagmites, you slowly make your way around the giant wasps until you reach an exit on the far side of the cavern...

Turn to 199

275

Although you put up a valiant fight, in the end, you are just no match for the river behemoth, eventually succumbing to the devastating wounds it has inflicted upon you. Seizing your lifeless body, the lurker uses its tentacle-like appendages to draw you to its mouth, and then, starting with your head and shoulders, begins to voraciously devour you...

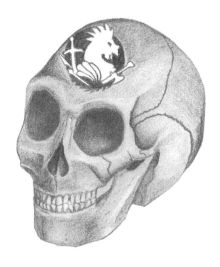

276

You have barely gone ten paces when you abruptly come upon a well-used door on the left-hand side of the corridor...

If you decide to investigate, **turn to 459**

If you choose to carry on, **go to 34**

277

A short time later, you find yourself in an enormous chamber that was obviously used at one time to keep prisoners captive. Several large jail cells line the wall adjacent to you, and with the exception of a few skeletal remains in some of them, all appear to be empty. At the far end of the room is an exit, which you begin making your way toward.

You are well on your way out, when much to your surprise, you hear a voice calling out to you from inside the last of the cages.

"Please, I beseech you! Do not leave me here to perish!" pleads the voice.

Turning, you see a young wood elf, his hands desperately clutching the bars of his prison.

"Please..." the wood elf begs once more, "Free me and I will join you in your quest as your comrade-in-arms. To die in glorious battle at your side is far better than the fate that awaits me here..."

If you choose to free the wood elf, **turn to 474**

If you decide instead to leave the room and the wood elf to his eventual end, **go to 170**

278

"You're wastin' your time, mate," declares the voice. "That door ain't going nowhere no time soon, and me shoulder's got the bruises to prove it!"

Seated a short distance from you with his back pressed against the wall is a wild-looking brute of a man with long, tangled hair and a matted beard. He is wearing a dirty sailor's tunic and his trousers are in absolute tatters.

"Who are you?" you ask.

"Name's Mateo," replies the man. "I became a castaway on this island when the ship I was first mate on ran aground."

"And what of the rest of your crew?" you ask.

"Includin' the Captain and meself, twas fifty of us aboard the Serpent's Wake," Mateo recounts. "I can remember that day like it was only yesterday. The sea was a dead calm and there was no wind — not even so much as a whisper in our sails. We'd been driftin' fer days, ya see, and then all of a sudden, the ship began to move like it had a life of its own. It was like somethin' had taken o'er the Serpent's Wake and was now controlling it! Brought us here, it did! Brought us to this infernal island of death! Fifty of us landed on this accursed rock! Fifty men strong we were, but this island demanded sacrifice and sacrifice it took! The first night we lost ten good men when the vampires came. Some nights the vampires didn't come at all and some nights we were able to fight them off. One by one, we were slaughtered like human cattle and those the vampires didn't take, the island did..."

Mateo pauses here, a faraway look of reflective thought in his eyes. "Of the Serpent's Wake crew, only I am left to tell the tale..."

"Any idea what our mysterious captors have planned for us?" you ask.

Mateo shakes his head.

"Well, I for one don't think we should wait around to find out," you say, as you immediately begin examining the walls, floor, and ceiling of your prison much more closely.

Running your hands along every square inch, you discover a loose stone with a hidden lever behind it that uncovers a secret passage when pulled. Stepping through the doorway with Mateo, you hear it closing behind you as the two of you escape down the narrow and dimly lit tunnel beyond...

(You may now utilize Mateo in combat. Simply roll an additional 1d6 for the sailor along with your roll. Mateo has an LF score of 25 and a Combat Skill Score of 3).

Turn to 482

279

Shrieking loudly, the undead dwarf collapses, its body crumbling into a pile of dust and empty garments even before it has hit the floor. You quickly go through the vampire's garments, but come up empty-handed. A search of the mess hall itself also turns up nothing, prompting you to exit via a door at the end of an adjoining hallway...

Turn to 396

280

Moving forward at a steady but somewhat cautious pace, you suddenly hear the unmistakable sounds of a child weeping coming from somewhere up ahead. Rounding a sharp bend in the passage, you suddenly find yourself standing in a wide hallway dimly illuminated by torchlight. An open doorway on the left seems to be the source of the sobbing. Readying your weapon, you creep slowly up to the doorway and peer in.

Lying on a makeshift bed in the fetal position and with his back to you is a boy who is crying uncontrollably.

"Hey there, little one," you say, speaking in a soft and reassuring voice. "You're going to be okay. I'm here now, and everything is going to be alright. Are you hurt?"

The child does not respond. Nor does he even acknowledge your presence by turning to face you, but instead, continues to weep bitterly.

"Are you lost? Maybe you and I can find a way out of here together," you say.

You are about to make your way into the room, when suddenly, the boy sits up, and, still sniffling, turns to face you, his jaws dislocating like a snake to reveal two rows of razor-sharp fangs. In another instant, the hideous creature has launched itself into the air and is now clinging upside down from the ceiling by its dagger-like talons.

(Continued on overleaf)

Two, bat-like wings slowly unfold from its back as it lets out a growl-like hiss and springs from the ceiling at you...

CHILD VAMPIRE Life Force 25 Combat 4

If you defeat the vampire, **turn to 331**

281

Looking up, you are startled to see a half-naked man wearing nothing but a tattered loincloth running towards you. His eyes are as wild as the hair on his head and his face is frantic with desperation and fear.

The man shouts something unintelligible, before stopping and looking apprehensively over his shoulder. No sooner has he turned, when suddenly, something swoops down from above and the man is born away kicking and screaming. In another instant, the man, along with his mysterious assailant, are gone, leaving you momentarily stunned and standing there in terrified disbelief.

Moving quickly, you beat feet to the nearest shipwreck, where a substantial breach in its hull grants you immediate ingress. Inside, you discover many more of the very same talismans as before, all of them strategically placed in abundance around the opening.

Hearing several growl-like hisses coming from just outside, you ready your weapon, but see nothing framed within the opening in the hull from where you are standing.

Moving closer to get a better view, you are startled by a gruff voice behind you...

Turn to 427

282

After doing a quick scan of your surroundings, you notice a sconce with a torch burning brightly on one of the adjacent walls nearby. Grabbing the torch, you enter the web-filled room, swinging the torch before you as you go. The webbing dissolves almost instantly in the flames, clearing a wide path before you.

Aroused by your approach, the spider immediately begins to advance toward you, its deadly fangs glistening and the light of the torch reflected in its many eyes...

GIANT SPIDER   Life Force 28   Combat 3

If you defeat the spider, **turn to 19**

283

Though you fight valiantly, you are eventually overwhelmed and then overcome by the brutal havoc wrought by the massive brute's vicious onslaught. Standing over your mangled and bloody corpse, the tauregg lets out a long and savage roar, and then, pounding on its chest triumphantly, literally tears your lifeless body limb from limb before devouring you...

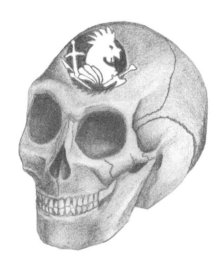

284

For a moment, you are certain you have been made and your ruse uncovered, but then, another chorus of "Arachnae be praised" assures you that your identity is safe for now as the cultists continue on their way and you and Avril-Lyn on yours.

The hallway soon finds its end at an adjoining corridor heading left — this one quickly resolving at a wall with the image of a large spider carved into it in bold relief. Next to the wall and on the right-hand side of the corridor is a door.

Proceeding with caution, you open the door and quietly enter the room beyond...

Turn to 154

285

After a time, you notice that the passage has gradually begun to swing to the right, eventually taking you in a large circle and leading you back to the junction where you originally started...

Please go back to 385

286

The corridor takes you directly to the edge of an enormous cavern. Long before you have even reached the perimeter of the cavern, your ears are immediately met with the unmistakable sound of weeping.

Using the corridor to stay somewhat concealed, you peer into the cavern and are surprised by the scene before you. Sitting on a large rock some distance from you is a gigantic humanoid with its face buried in its palms and crying uncontrollably.

With the giant completely self-focused, you would definitely have the upper hand if you decided to attack it. On the other hand, maybe it would be better to just sneak past the giant instead...

If you decide to attack the giant, **turn to 33**

If you would rather sneak past the giant instead, **go to 485**

287

The queen, it turns out, is a much more formidable opponent than the other wasps, aggressively swooping in and circling you, and all the while trying to bite and sting you.

You fight hard and even valiantly, but are soon overcome by the incredible amount of toxin that has been injected into your body. Immediately, your limp and nearly lifeless body is dragged into the nearby hive, where, preserved by the matriarch's venom, it will eventually become a host as well as food for the wasp queen's parasitic larvae...

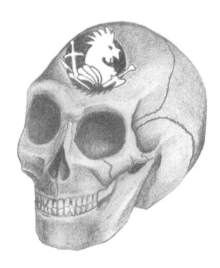

288

Almost immediately, your mouth and throat begin to burn. This is followed swiftly by severe abdominal pain which causes you to double over and then collapse to the floor in agony. Necrosis is instantaneous as the highly corrosive acid you consumed wreaks massive cellular damage to every part of your body it comes in contact with.

Fortunately, your death is swift!

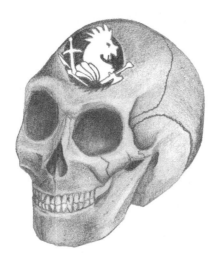

289

Walking over to a series of interconnected cogs, the lizardman begins turning a large crank handle, immediately setting the cogwheels in motion and activating an internal winch within the rough-hewn walls. With a loud rumble, the iron portcullis raises via its attached chains, allowing you to enter the tunnel beyond...

Subtract 10 gold pieces from your PURSE and then **turn to 41**

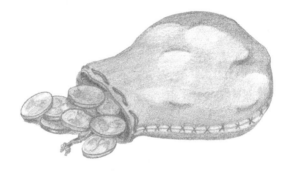

290

Feeding at the base of the carcass is what looks like a giant bird, but without wings. The creature is easily one-and-a-quarter times your height, with a massive head and thick neck. In lieu of wings are two small stumps with feathers, while its two powerful legs culminate in heavy feet equipped with deadly talons. You quietly watch as it uses its enormous beak to tear off chunks of flesh, which it quickly gulps down.

The options before you are clear...

If you decide to wait until it is done feeding and leaves, **turn to 458**

On the other hand, there is a real possibility that the dragon might also return. Maybe it would be better to attack the creature so you can continue on your way. If this is your choice, then **go to 187**

291

You push the boat into the water, hopping in as you are quickly and immediately borne away. Grabbing the paddles, you try to steer the boat, but are helpless and completely at the mercy of the rapidly moving waters. The current carries you swiftly downstream, until finally, the river empties into a huge underground lake sending you drifting out into the open water.

You reach for the paddles and make your way to the shore. Dragging the boat onto the beach, you decide to make camp and get some much-needed rest.

You must have fallen asleep, for you awaken to the sound of an angelic voice singing. The melody is so hauntingly beautiful that you find yourself unable to resist its call. Before you even realize what you are doing, you are waist-deep in the water and are wading farther and farther out...

(You have been bewitched by a siren. At this time, please perform a Resistance check).

If you successfully resist the siren's song, **turn to 301**

If, however, the song's hold on you is too strong, **go to 50**

292

Bleeding profusely from multiple wounds inflicted by the pseudopods, as well as the many mouths of your opponent, it is not long before the extreme loss of blood causes you to expire, and in the ensuing moments, your body is quickly and voraciously devoured...

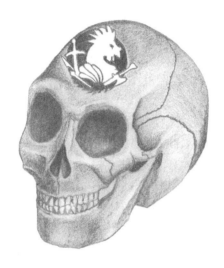

293

After following the shoreline for a time, sandy beach eventually gives way to coastal wetland, transitioning into a tidal, saltwater marsh soon after. Small, mirror-like pools filled with brackish water and surrounded by reeds, tussocks, and low-lying shrubs teem with all manner of aquatic life. Strange and exotic birds are startled into flight by your coming, while miniature boar-like creatures dart in and out of the underbrush.

The ground is wet and spongy underfoot as you make your way through the marsh and proceed further and further inland. Out of nowhere, a low-lying, knee-high mist begins to sweep in, and before long, the marsh has disappeared and you now find yourself trudging through a gloomy and dismal swamp. Ancient cypress trees, overgrown with hanging moss, tower all around you, their twisted and gnarled branches creating a thick canopy overhead that almost completely blocks out the life-giving, light-bringing rays of the sun. Aberrant plants, deprived of sunlight and having a sickly and unhealthy pallor, grow unchecked throughout...

Turn to 391

294

You find yourself standing in a large chamber filled with bookshelves from one end of the room to the other. Each one is crammed from top to bottom with books. In the middle of the room and seated in a plush chair behind a fancy, oak table is an old man in a gray robe — his snow-white beard so long it is literally laying across the table. The man is completely bald, and at first glance, appears to be blind, but then, as you approach the table where he is sitting, you are startled to discover that he does not have any eyes at all!

Immediately aware of your presence, the man says, "Ah, someone who thirsts for the treasure of Exponential Knowledge."

"How does a scholar end up in this maze of madness and monsters?" you ask.

"I have diligently studied every book in this room, but my devotion to the words contained within these many volumes in no way makes me a scholar..." he replies, ignoring your question entirely.

"So you were not always blind then?" you ask.

"I was born without sight and yet see all things," the old man replies almost cryptically. "I am Althaeus, the Oracle of Old, known to some as the Chronicler, the Librarian, the Keeper of Knowledge, and the Cataloger of Secrets."

(Continued on overleaf)

"You seek the Lich Lord's treasure, yes?" he continues. "But what I now offer you is something far greater and more valuable than any treasure this world could bestow."

"I'm listening," you reply, more than just a little intrigued.

"Abandon your foolish and reckless quest," the old man admonishes, "and you will have Exponential Knowledge of the Secret Things as your unfettered mind travels the cosmic, interplanetary paths of True Enlightenment..."

If you decide to accept Althaeus' offer for Exponential Knowledge, **turn to 323**

If you decide instead to leave the library and see what is behind the second door, **go to 114**

You can also check out the third and final door if you have not already done so. If this is your choice, **proceed to 73**

You could also just continue onward down the corridor and forego the remaining doors. If this is your choice, **turn to 199**

295

Free from the changeling's deadly embrace, you quickly and easily dispatch the hideous monstrosity and watch as it falls to the floor in a revolting mass of flesh. In its place, you discover the opening to a narrow corridor...

Turn to 48

296

Suddenly, you are startled by the sight of a wild-looking, brute of a man running full-speed towards you. His face is frantic with fear and desperation as he repeatedly looks over his shoulder at something behind him, but whatever it is, is still not visible.

You are not left to wonder long, for tearing down the path in close pursuit and rapidly gaining on the man is what appears to be a large, wolf-like creature. At times, it seems to be running on two legs and at other times on all fours and you quickly realize that the terrifying beast that is now heading straight for you is no ordinary wolf!

Readying your weapon, you brace yourself for the ensuing battle as the werewolf sets its sights on you, abandoning the chase in lieu of easier prey...

WEREWOLF   Life Force 30   Combat 4

If you defeat the werewolf, **turn to 440**

297

Searching the orc's corpse, you find a smelly, leather pouch on the creature's belt reeking of rot and decay. Inside of it, is a decomposing, human foot and 10 gold pieces.

(Add the gold to your PURSE now. You may also take the severed, decomposing foot if you wish as well and add it to your INVENTORY).

A search of the room reveals nothing else of interest, use, or even value, so you return to the chamber outside...

Please go back to 214

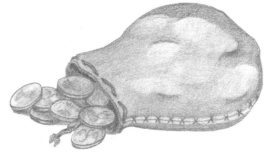

298

You are standing on a massive shelf of rock that juts out from the precipitous face of a cliff. Below you, gigantic waves crash violently and relentlessly against its rocky base — the thundering impact of the pounding surf punctuated only by the stuttering squawks of the seagulls circling overhead.

Doing a quick visual scan of the jagged cliff's exterior, you discover what appears to be hand and footholds carved into the cliffside, starting right where you are standing and going all the way to the very top.

To your right, you can see a pathway that precariously hugs the precipice as it descends, gradually making its way down the side of the cliff until it reaches a sand-covered beach at the very bottom.

On your immediate left and disappearing over the edge of the shelf of rock on which you are standing is a crude ladder constructed out of rope and driftwood. Peering downward, you see another outcropping of rock a short distance below and what looks like the entrance to a small cave...

If you decide to scale the cliff face, **turn to 347**

If you want to head down the path, **go to 466**

Maybe the rope ladder is the safest bet. If this is your choice, **proceed to 87**

299

Up ahead, you see an old, dilapidated shack of a house by the water's edge. Creeping stealthily up to one of the windows, you peer inside and see three bugbears seated at a table playing what appears to be some sort of card game. They are arguing and the gist of the conversation seems to be that one of them may or may not have been cheating. The argument escalates, with one of them angrily turning over the table and then burying its battle-axe in the skull of the one sitting directly across from it. Almost simultaneously, the other remaining brute draws its own weapon and cleaves the first one in two. The creature then kneels down and begins to pick up the gold pieces scattered across the floor.

With its attention completely diverted and you having the element of surprise, this would definitely be the most opportune time, if any, to attack...

If you would rather press on instead, **turn to 49**

(Otherwise, at this time, please perform a Stealth check. If successful, your attack completely takes the bugbear by surprise and it is killed instantly. If, however, your check is unsuccessful, add 1 point to your Stealth score, and prepare to engage this monster in combat).

BUGBEAR   Life Force 25   Combat 3

If you defeat the bugbear, **turn to 397**

300

A wide, but short hallway awaits, with hundreds of votive candles running its entire length along the base of both walls. On the opposite end of the hall is a door which opens into a large, hexagonal chamber, with the only door being the one that brought you here! You also notice a gold square on the floor in the very center of the room that is just large enough for a single person to stand on, and upon closer examination, realize it is a pressure plate.

Puzzled, you step onto the pressure plate and the door you came through closes. There is the distinct sound of hidden machinery engaging, and almost immediately, the chamber begins to make a slow, counter-clockwise revolution...

(At this time, please roll a 1d6).

If you roll a 1, **turn to 32**
If you roll a 2, **go to 100**
If your roll is a 3, **proceed to 263**
If you roll a 4, **turn to 446**
If you roll a 5, **go to 377**
If your roll is a 6, **proceed to 164**

301

As the water level reaches your chin, you suddenly awaken like someone startled from slumber. For only a moment, you are disoriented, confused, and afraid, and then, realizing that you are standing neck-deep in the water, come to your senses and begin to swim back to the beach.

Immediately upon reaching the shore, you head straight for your camp and quickly grab your satchel. Inside of it, is some old candle wax, which you hurriedly stuff into both ears, and not a moment too soon, for the evocative song of the siren begins to fill the air once more. The candle wax works beautifully, making you invulnerable to the siren's enchanting melody.

It is not long before you see something stirring in the water not far from the shore where you are standing. For a moment, you are certain you must still be dreaming, for swimming toward you is one of the most beautiful women you have ever seen. You find yourself strangely captivated by her beauty and even smitten as you gaze into her eyes, but this quickly passes.

Even as you are coming back to your senses, the woman has already dragged herself onto the beach, but the creature now crawling towards you is anything but a woman. Only from the torso up does the creature look like a woman, but that is where the similarity stops, for in lieu of a pair of legs, its entire lower half is that of a fish. Webbed fingers culminate in deadly, dagger-like talons, and two rows of razor-sharp teeth round out the awful picture before you.

(Continued on overleaf of illustration)

The siren opens and closes its mouth, its jaws dislocating like a python, and then, like a snake, begins to slither towards you...

SIREN   Life Force 25   Combat 3

If you kill the siren, **turn to 417**

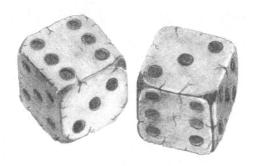

302

With the mantle of nightfall nearly upon you, you quickly seek refuge within the hollowed-out trunk of a massive, fallen tree. Here, too, and strategically placed in abundance around the opening are the very same talismans that were garnishing the entrance of the cave you stayed in the night before. Exhausted, you make your way inside and to the very far back, sitting with your back braced against the wall with your weapon in hand...

Turn to 75

303

As quietly as you are able, you open the door. The room is empty except for a pile of filthy rags in one corner. You are about to leave the room, when suddenly, out of the corner of your eye, you see the rags move. The movement was only ever so slight and barely noticeable, but nonetheless, you know there is no way you imagined it.

Readying your weapon, you cautiously approach the crumpled heap. Suddenly, the pile of rags stands erect to reveal an extremely thin and frail, old man. The man is nothing more than just skin and bones and is so skinny he is practically swimming in the clothes that he wears. His grayish, white beard is so long that it literally touches the ground where he stands. The old man is unarmed.

"You fool!" he begins to shout. "That which you seek can never be obtained by any mere mortal! Death is whispering your name as we speak, calling you home to the destruction of your very soul!"

And then, with a loud cry and a crazed, maniacal look in his eyes, the deranged, old man rushes you...

OLD MAN   Life Force 13   Combat 1

If you defeat the old man, **turn to 54**

304

You have maybe advanced but fifty paces when the passageway abruptly splits into two more corridors...

If you decide to head down the left passage, **turn to 193**

If you choose the passage on the right, **go to 79**

305

You continue down the passage, and several paces later, the large corridor you have been following abruptly terminates. A large fissure, barely wide enough for someone to squeeze through, divides the rocky face of the cavern wall. You take a deep breath and then step into the crevasse, slowly shuffling sideways until you emerge on the other side.

You find yourself in an enormous chamber, and as your eyes scan your new surroundings and its contents, you realize you are standing in a large tomb. The floor is littered with broken pottery and there are burial urns randomly placed throughout the room. There is a dais in the center of the room with what appears to be a large, stone sarcophagus. Circling the dais are several smaller, stone sarcophagi — each one in symmetrical order around the larger one. From where you are standing, it appears that all of them are still sealed and undisturbed.

On the other side of the chamber is a tunnel...

If you would like to search the sarcophagi, **turn to 147**

If you would rather exit through the tunnel on the far side of the chamber, **go to 105**

306

Swimming down to the opening in the cavern floor, you discover a downward-leading passage that carries on for a short distance, but then runs horizontally for a span before bending again. This time it makes its way upwards, and soon thereafter, you and Avril-Lyn unexpectedly find yourselves breaking the surface of the water.

You are floating in what appears to be a large, man-made pool in the center of a spacious and well-lit, rectangular chamber. Votive candles burn brightly throughout, and as you are treading water and trying to get some sense of your surroundings visually, you are stunned by what you see, for beautifully carved in bold relief and set in a breathtaking mosaic of tiles are various depictions of spiders on the walls and ceiling.

"The Temple of Arachnae..." says the sorceress, confirming what was already going through your mind. "We will have to proceed with much greater caution from here on out!"

A short flight of stairs on the far side of the ceremonial pool grants you egress from the crystal clear waters, with the discovery of a corridor you did not notice initially affording you an exit...

Turn to 276

307

Clearly outmatched from the very beginning, you are completely overwhelmed by the brutal and vicious savagery of the manticore's onslaught, eventually conceding through your death.

Standing over your mangled and bloody corpse, the manticore lets out a long and triumphant roar, carrying you in its mouth back to its lair, where it immediately begins to gorge itself upon your flesh...

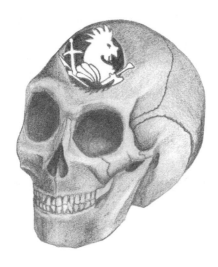

308

Rounding a sharp bend in the passage, you stumble head-on into the ghastly and horrific scene of a man literally being devoured alive by several large, rodent-like creatures with wings. Startled into flight by your unexpected arrival, the filthy, hairless beasts scatter, but then regroup, each one baring their needle-like fangs as their powerful echolocation quickly locks onto your position...

VAMPIRE BAT	Life Force 8	Combat 2
VAMPIRE BAT	Life Force 7	Combat 2
VAMPIRE BAT	Life Force 7	Combat 2

If you defeat the vampire bats, **turn to 212**

309

Staying low and moving quietly between the various rock formations and stalagmites, you slowly make your way around the giant wasps. You have almost reached the exit on the far side of the cavern when suddenly, one of the flying insects discovers you, quickly alerting the rest of them to your presence.

Within seconds, the giant wasps surround you and begin to attack...

GIANT WASP	Life Force 5	Combat 2
GIANT WASP	Life Force 5	Combat 2
GIANT WASP	Life Force 4	Combat 2
GIANT WASP	Life Force 4	Combat 2

If you defeat the wasps, **turn to 61**

If, however, it is you who are killed, **go to 165**

310

You soon find yourselves in the majestic cathedral of a giant cavern, and for more than a moment, you and the sorceress are held captive by its grandeur — the breathtaking splendor of every formation truly a divine masterpiece of water and time.

Picking your way through and around them, you eventually discover a fissure that quickly transitions into a wide corridor...

Turn to 128

311

Grabbing onto your head with its powerful jaws, the giant serpent wraps itself around you, its heavy, muscular coils rapidly tightening. Unable to breathe and your blood circulation cut off, you expire quickly, but not before feeling every bone in your body literally breaking from the force and power of the snake's constriction!

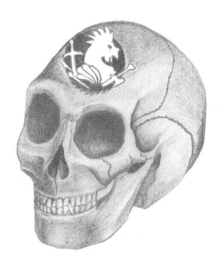

312

Rushing into the cave, you easily sidestep the first of the giant clams as it swings towards you, but are almost immediately swept off your feet by another clam when it suddenly changes directions unexpectedly. You try desperately to scramble to your feet, but each time an enormous shellfish slams into you, knocking you back down into the knee-deep water.

Brutally buffeted by the moving clams and tossed helplessly about by the ever-shifting water, you gradually succumb to exhaustion and eventually drown...

313

With an ear-shattering shriek, the vampire falls to her knees, and then, throwing her hands up into the air, begins to crumble, disintegrating until all that remains of her is a pile of dust and the garments she was wearing. A search of the vampire's garments proves fruitless.

The rest of the night passes without incident, but you are unable to get any kind of restful sleep...

Turn to 14

314

You have not traveled far down the corridor when up ahead, you make out the outline of a wide doorway opening up on the left. Muffled voices are coming from the space beyond, but you are not near enough to make out what they are saying. Ever so cautiously, you make your way over to the doorway and peer into the room.

Seated at a huge, wooden table are three large, goblin-like creatures eating, drinking, and making merry. You immediately recognize them as being goblinoids. Goblinoids are of the same race as goblins, but are considerably larger than their smaller and less aggressive cousins.

You could fight them, but perhaps the best strategy here is for you to sneak past them and avoid any kind of confrontation altogether...

(At this time, please perform a Stealth check).

If you successfully sneak past them, **turn to 250**

If the goblinoids see you, add 1 point to your Stealth score and then **go to 39**

315

It is only moments later that you and the sorceress come to a door on the left-hand side of the passage. The door is slightly ajar, and when you give it a gentle push, opens to reveal a room that is empty, except for a small stool that has been toppled over.

Continue down the corridor **by turning to 434**

316

The passage curves sharply to the left, immediately doubling back to the right. Up ahead and on the left-hand side, you can see a large, wooden door, which you cautiously and quietly open so as to see into the room beyond.

Lying in the center of the empty room is what looks like your typical, everyday, ordinary, black house cat. For a brief moment, the cat watches you intently and then seems to forget you are there at all, grooming itself and purring softly as it does so.

You also note that there appear to be no other means of exit, other than the doorway where you are standing...

If you decide to enter the room, **turn to 42**

If you choose to continue moving forward down the corridor instead, **go to 199**

317

As you are rounding the corner, you run headlong into two more of the Spider Queen's Faithful — a man and a woman, approaching rapidly from the opposite end of the corridor.

"Arachnae be praised!" they declare almost in unison, pressing the palms of their hands and fingers together and bowing their heads as they draw near.

You and Avril-Lyn respond in kind without breaking stride, but then, the woman suddenly stops, and addressing you, says, "Your face is unfamiliar to me. How is it that I have never met you until now?"

"Come to think of it," adds her companion, now eyeing you suspiciously, "I don't believe I've ever seen you before either..."

If you decide to bluff your way past them, **turn to 113**

If you decide to attack them instead, **go to 480**

318

The corridor eventually culminates at a large door. The wood on it has begun to deteriorate in places and the metal bands and handle are completely encrusted with rust, testifying to the door's great age.

You are reaching for the handle of the door, when suddenly, an enormous mouth filled with jagged, dagger-like teeth appears in the center of the door. Too late, you realize that what you had thought to be a door is none other than a creature known as a changeling! Because they are quite slow and unable to move with any kind of speed whatsoever, changelings will often mimic inanimate objects in order to lure and capture unwary and unsuspecting prey.

Before you can even react, the changeling's tongue has already lashed out at you, wrapping itself tightly around your body...

(At this time, please perform a Strength check).

If you are able to free yourself, **turn to 295**

If, however, you are unable to break free from the changeling's grasp, **go to 492**

319

Shrieking in agony, TitusMirror's skin begins to blister and bubble, the flesh literally sliding off of his skull as it becomes a slime-like paste and drips down his armor. With an outstretched, taloned hand, the ancient vampire staggers towards you, and then, falling to his knees, is suddenly engulfed by green, supernatural flames. Within minutes, the strange fire has consumed every part of him, until nothing, not even the armor he was wearing, remains.

In his place, and suspended in midair, is the artifact that you seek — an amulet of unimaginable and indescribable beauty, and resplendent with power and energy! Momentarily transfixed by its dazzling radiance, you are not immediately aware of Glorandol, Eloshann and Maegyddo's coming.

"You have done well, champion!" says Glorandol. Eloshann and Maegyddo say nothing, instead acknowledging you with a nod.

The elven kings gather around the artifact and in another instant, they and the amulet are gone.

Turning, you are startled to discover the elven sorceress who accosted you in the wilderness standing behind you.

"The amulet... What have you done with it?" the woman demands, as she frantically begins searching for it.

"It's gone," you answer.

"Then... I am too late," says the sorceress, her voice trembling with a mixture of anguish and despair. "If you only knew what it is that your actions have set into motion, for the very fate of Ataraxia now hangs in the balance."

"I... I don't understand," you reply.

The woman spends a moment or two in quiet reflection, and then, using her staff to strike the air, causes a shimmering portal to suddenly appear close by.

"Come, and quickly!" declares the woman, as she makes for the magical gateway. "All things will be explained, but for now, we must not tarry, for time is of the absolute essence!"

Without thinking, you quickly follow suit, and in the proverbial blink of an eye, you and the mysterious woman are gone...

Turn to 236

320

Knowing that an extra blade can have its advantages, you elect to accept Laurick's offer of service, and with your new ally close on your heels, resume your march through the labyrinthian network of tunnels.

Laurick tells you that he, too, had come in search of the Lich Lord's legendary treasure, only to fall captive to an orc ambush. The orcs then locked the elf within the prison cell in which you found him, with plans to cook and eat him when they returned.

(You may now utilize Laurick in combat. Simply roll an additional 1d6 for the wood elf along with your roll. Laurick has an LF score of 25 and a Combat Skill Score of 3).

Turn to 69

321

Clearly outmatched by your skill and ferocity as a warrior, you quickly make short work of the undead before they even have a chance to get close to you. A search of their tattered garments yields 5 gold pieces and a giant, nearly flawless ruby.

(Add these items to your PURSE and INVENTORY now).

After resting, you exit the hallway, continuing down the adjoining corridor...

Turn to 235

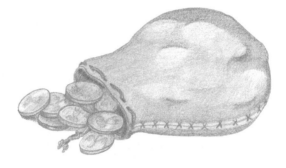

322

Arachnae's brood of evil no more, Avril-Lyn uses her magic to dispel the webbing so you can access the passage beyond. Almost immediately, the two of you are ushered into an immense, cyclopean chamber. A wide and seemingly bottomless rift divides the chamber in two, with the opposite side being completely enveloped by a gigantic, tangled mass of webs. Spanning the chasm's empty void is a massive, gossamer-wrapped bridge, but as you and Avril-Lyn start towards it, you quickly make the gruesome discovery that it has been constructed entirely out of the skeletal remains and desiccated corpses of the Spider Queen's many victims!

"The inner sanctum..." says Avril-Lyn in a voice only slightly louder than a whisper.

"What now?" you ask.

"Now, we lure her out," replies the sorceress, directing your attention to a gong that you had not previously noticed before.

Making your way over to the gong, you strike it with the pommel of your longsword, your pulse quickening as the gong reverberates loudly throughout the entire chamber. And then, you see her — Arachnae, in all of her beautiful and terrifying glory, emerging from a funnel-like orifice near the top. Much to your horror, she is carrying what was clearly her last meal — the desiccated remains of a human form wrapped in silk which she discards as she descends from her web onto the opposite side of the bridge. Upon seeing your elven companion, her countenance quite suddenly and noticeably changes to one of surprise.

"Avril-Lyn!" hisses the Spider Queen. "How very unexpected! An eternity has passed since our paths last crossed... but perhaps it is best we forgo any and all pleasantries, especially in the light of the obvious reason for your coming! And now, you will find out what happens to those who dare to profane my holy temple!"

ARACHNAE   Life Force 45   Combat 6

If you defeat the Spider Queen, **turn to 461**

323

"You have chosen wisely," declares the old man, and motioning for you to sit, hands you a small decanter containing some sort of purple, pudding-like substance. "You must drink this in order for your journey to begin."

Taking a deep breath, you down the entire decanter, and within moments are shocked to discover that you are completely paralyzed!

"Exponential Knowledge of the Secret Things does not come without sacrifice, my child," the Oracle of Old says in a calm, but hardly reassuring voice. "I can say with the utmost confidence your sacrifice will not be in vain."

Completely helpless and unable to move, you watch in absolute horror as Althaeus pulls out his dagger, and making his way over to you, gouges both of your eyes out. Unfortunately for you, it is the last thing that your earthly, mortal eyes see on your way to the place of True Enlightenment...

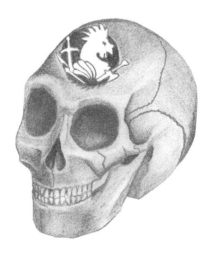

324

It is not long before you find yourself standing at the edge of a wide, but gentle stream — its soothing murmur a welcome respite from the uncanny silence of the forest around you. On the opposite side of the stream, the path you have been following has all but disappeared, giving way to a large, grassy clearing.

Kneeling down beside its tranquil waters, you cup your hands together and slake your thirst. The cool water is unbelievably refreshing and immediately gives you renewed vigor.

Briefly lost in a moment of reverie, what you see next immediately snaps you back to reality as you quickly scramble for cover...

Turn to 163

325

An uneventful half-hour finds you and Avril-Lyn at a junction, with the passage you have been following maintaining its forward course, while to your immediate right, rough-hewn stairs descend into the darkness...

If you decide to see where the stairs lead, **turn to 7**

If would rather keep moving forward instead, **go to 169**

326

You follow the corridor for a short span before coming abruptly to a dead end. With no other option but to head back, you turn around and make your way back to the junction that brought you here, this time proceeding down the other tunnel...

Turn to 15

327

With the sunlight rapidly retreating like a defeated king and twilight nearly upon you, you quickly realize that it is imperative you find shelter to wait out the night, and soon! Your search becomes even more frantic as nightfall overtakes you.

Suddenly, out of nowhere, you distinctly see a small, bluish-green light flickering on and off in the semi-darkness up ahead. In that same instant, you also notice a large tree nearby with a small, cave-like opening between its roots that could possibly afford you some shelter for the night...

If you decide to investigate the light, **turn to 108**

If you choose to take shelter inside of the tree instead, **go to 31**

328

Trembling violently and screeching like a banshee, the last remaining mushroom slumps to the cavern floor in a puddle of its own slime.

You immediately press on, eager to find a means of exit, but the remainder of your trek through the forest of fungi is uneventful and passes without incident.

Eventually, a way out presents itself...

Turn to 24

329

Carefully making your way up the wide staircase to the keep, you guardedly approach the now gaping opening that is its entrance. Just beyond, you can see a foyer that almost immediately transitions into the main hall, and except for the crackling flicker of torch flames, the hall is quite still and ominously quiet as you make your way in. The broad hallway quickly finds its end at a set of hand-hewn, double wooden doors...

Turn to 269

330

You have not ventured far when suddenly, four undead monstrosities with cutlasses stumble awkwardly out of the nearby wreckage of a ship half-buried in the sand. Hollow and empty eye sockets stare blankly at you, and so advanced is their decomposition, that, if not for their distinctly male sailor outfits, it would be impossible to tell whether they had once been men or even women.

Blind but somehow able to sense your presence, the zombified cadavers come at you and Mateo with cutlasses swinging, the sickening smell of putrefying flesh so strong that you nearly vomit as you prepare to engage them in combat...

(Don't forget that you can now utilize Mateo in battle as well. Simply roll an additional 1d6 for the sailor along with your roll. Mateo has an LF score of 25 and a Combat Skill Score of 3).

(At this time, you can also exercise the option of trying to flee by performing an Agility check).

If you are able to successfully flee, **turn to 66**

If not, add 1 point to your Agility score now and...

UNDEAD PIRATE	Life Force 12	Combat 2
UNDEAD PIRATE	Life Force 11	Combat 2
UNDEAD PIRATE	Life Force 10	Combat 2
UNDEAD PIRATE	Life Force 10	Combat 2

If you defeat the undead pirates, **go to 182**

331

With a shrill and haunting screech, the vampire throws its hands up into the air, and then, as if frozen in time, begins to crumble, disintegrating until nothing remains but a pile of dust and the clothing it was wearing.

The encounter leaves you visibly shaken. Nevertheless, you do a quick sweep of the room and discover a small lockbox hidden underneath the bed. Inside of the lockbox is an emerald ring, a HEALTH potion, and 25 gold pieces, which you immediately add to your satchel.

(Add these to your PURSE and INVENTORY now) and then **proceed to 78**

332

"There is definitely something in there," says the sorceress, matter-of-factly. "What it is exactly, I'm not quite sure..."

If you have not already done so and would like her to cast a *detect traps* spell, **turn to 118**

If you decide to enter the chamber anyway, **go to 428**

Or, perhaps Avril-Lyn was right when she suggested you head back to the three-way junction. If this is what you would like to do now, **proceed to 264**

333

The passageway continues for some time before once again splitting into three smaller halls. At the end of the middle corridor, you can just make out what appears to be a door. You can also hear the distant, but loud hum of machinery coming from the right-most corridor...

If the corridor on the left is your choice, **turn to 421**

If you decide to take the corridor on the right where you can hear some sort of machinery, **go to 27**

Or, perhaps it would be to your advantage to see what lies beyond the door at the end of the middle corridor. If this is your choice, **proceed to 126**

334

Suddenly, and before you are even aware of what is happening, you feel yourself being lifted into the air by many cold and invisible hands, and though you fight desperately, you are unable to break free from your unseen assailants. You are taken down a long flight of stairs and at the bottom are dropped roughly onto the hard, stone floor of a holding cell. The door is slammed shut and you hear the unmistakable sound of a key turning in the lock.

Quickly taking stock, you are very much surprised to find that all of your personal effects, including your weapon, are still intact.

Rising to your feet, you prepare to use your shoulder as a battering ram, but are startled from doing so by a gruff voice behind you...

Turn to 278

335

Making your way over to the first portcullis, you note the timing as it comes crashing down and just as quickly rises and falls again...

(Because there are three portcullises, you will have to perform an Agility check for each one).

If you are successful in making it past all three portcullises, **turn to 249**

If, however, you failed any of your three Agility checks, **go to 62**

336

The corridor eventually splits in two, with one tunnel branching sharply to the left and the other continuing on nearly the same course like the one you have been following. You decide to head down the tunnel on the left, but this one dead ends, forcing you to head back and take the other one...

Turn to 199

337

You have been following the monotonous stretch of shoreline for what seems like the better part of the afternoon, when you spot the wreckage of a large ship partially grounded on the beach just ahead. More than half of the ship is still in the water, and as you get closer, you notice the hull has a sizable breach into which the water rushes with each breaking wave. With the blisteringly hot day just hours from being swallowed up by nightfall's coming, you decide that perhaps it might be best to remain here overnight.

You are about to make your way into the ship via the jagged opening in its side when suddenly, you distinctly see movement from within. Instinctively, and with the swiftness that only comes from being a seasoned warrior, you quickly leap clear of the opening, simultaneously bringing your weapon to combat readiness.

Emerging from the ship's hull is an enormous crocodile that is easily two-and-a-half times as long as you are tall. Unbelievably agile for its size, the scaly, reptilian beast immediately comes for you...

SALTWATER CROC   Life Force 35   Combat 4

(When you have brought the crocodile's LIFE FORCE down to 20, DO NOT continue fighting it, but instead, **proceed to 205**)

338

You and Avril-Lyn are just mere paces from the door when suddenly, you realize that you no longer hear the humming of Arachnae's Faithful. Turning around, you are alarmed to find the cultists standing directly behind you, and within the span of just a few moments, they have completely overwhelmed, disarmed, and bound the two of you...

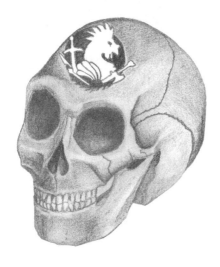

339

With the inevitable invasion of nightfall rapidly approaching, you diligently begin seeking out shelter.

Suddenly, you hear a man crying out in pain, followed by cruel and merciless laughter. Leaving the path to investigate, you ready your weapon and cautiously enter the thicket. As you make your way further into the dense underbrush, you hear what is definitely the sound of voices just ahead. Using the heavy vegetation around you for concealment, you creep as quietly and as far forward as you are able to. What you see fills you with indignation.

Bound securely to a tree is a wild-looking brute of a man with long, tangled hair and a matted beard. He is wearing a dirty sailor's tunic and his trousers are in absolute tatters. Standing in front of him are two short, squatty, imp-like creatures, who appear to be torturing him. You watch as one of them uses its needle-like teeth to tear one of the man's fingernails from his finger, causing him to scream in agony, at which point, both of the little monsters erupt into vicious laughter.

Stepping out from hiding, you call out to them to get their attention. Startled by your sudden appearance, the two creatures immediately make a run for it, stumbling over each other as they quickly disappear into the forest...

Turn to 213

340

The door reveals an extremely well-lit corridor which you follow for quite some time until it eventually finds its end at a good-sized chamber. In the very center of the room is a small table hewn from stone. Perched on top of it is a small handbell and a sign that reads: RING ME!

There is also a wooden door on the far side of the chamber...

If you decide to ring the bell, **turn to 177**

If you would rather head for the door instead, **go to 426**

341

Several minutes elapse, but nothing happens. Replacing the stopper, you quickly stash the empty flask in your satchel and press on...

(Add this item to your INVENTORY now) and then **turn to 253**

342

Using hand signals, you motion for Mateo to remain in the corridor as you silently make your way into the room. By this time, the man is snoring quite loudly, and it is at that moment that your attention is drawn to something that you did not notice before. Dangling from the man's belt is a golden key and it is a safe bet that it probably fits the lock on that chest!

(At this time, please perform a Pickpocketing check).

If you successfully retrieve the key, **turn to 223**

If you are caught in the act, add 1 point to your Pickpocketing score and then **go to 453**

343

After dispatching the last of the giant ants, you decide to make haste and get as far from the vicinity as possible, knowing full well there are certain to be more of the aggressive insects nearby.

Eventually, the corridor you are following splits into a T-junction…

If you decide to take the tunnel going left, **turn to 143**

If your choice is the tunnel heading right, **go to 84**

344

Slipping through the dense, underwater vegetation that nearly covers the opening to the large passage, you are astounded by the awesome scene that meets your eyes.

Drifting lazily before you are literally dozens of the very same jellyfish-like creatures you saw in the grotto earlier — their combined, bioluminescent glow brightly illuminating the entire passageway.

Momentarily transfixed by their ethereal beauty, you are unaware they have been moving towards you, until it is too late! Within moments, you are completely surrounded by them on all sides and are now cut off from Avril-Lyn and the tunnel exit.

Suddenly, you feel tiny stabs of excruciating pain coming from different parts of your body, especially from your hands, face, neck, and ears! Almost immediately, you find yourself struggling to breathe as anaphylaxis sets in and your gills begin to fail. In the ensuing panic, you begin to thrash about the tunnel wildly, incurring many more painful stings from the tentacles of the mysterious creatures all around you. The lethal venom aggressively attacks your nervous system and within the short span of only a couple of minutes, you die an agonizing and extremely painful death!

Grieving your unexpected loss, Avril-Lyn, who remained close to the entrance, turns and swims back into the grotto...

345

Slowly coming to, you open your eyes, and as they adjust to the semi-darkness, discover you are resting on what appears to be a wide outcropping of rock. A stygian void of blackness and oblivion beckons to you from the abysmal depths below. Training your gaze upwards, you see the chasm's opening framed out of reach and high above you, and after examining the sheer face of the chasm wall, you quickly determine it to be unscalable.

Dismay soon turns into abject hopelessness as the full realization of your situation begins to weigh upon you. You are trapped, with no hope of escape or even rescue! There is also little doubt in your mind that the Legorian Kings now have the last of the artifacts in their possession.

And what has become of Avril-Lyn? Surely, if she was still alive, she would have come for you.

It is at that moment that you suddenly remember the amulet that was given to you by the sorceress.

'Should you and I ever become separated, simply hold this amulet in your hand while saying my name and you will immediately be transported to wherever it is that I am...'

"Avril-Lyn," you say while holding the amulet.

There is a blinding flash of light, and —

Turn to 273

346

Surprisingly, the mouse proves to be much more formidable than you had anticipated, but ultimately, you and Avril-Lyn make short work of it.

You and the sorceress continue following the fissure, eventually emerging from its opposite end. It is here that Avril-Lyn restores you both back to your normal size.

Turn to 26

347

Reaching for the nearest handhold and getting a firm grip, you pull yourself up until one of your feet is planted firmly on the first foothold and begin making your way up the sheer face of the precipice. Your progress is extremely slow and every movement physically demanding, but eventually, you reach the summit.

Utterly exhausted as you drag yourself up and over the brink, you collapse onto a grassy knoll, your body completely spent. A light and gentle breeze caresses the hilltop as you lay there with your eyes closed...

Turn to 44

348

Slowly and cautiously opening the door, you peer into the room and quickly realize that you have stumbled upon the sleeping quarters of the Faithful. Several bunk beds, each one built three high, are butted perpendicular against the opposite wall. Right away, you notice that three of the beds have somebody sleeping in them. There is also a large chest sitting at the foot of the bunk bed farthest from you...

If you decide to sneak into the room and find out what is inside the chest, **turn to 433**

If you would like to see what lies beyond the other door across the hall, **go to 141**

Otherwise, **turn to 45,** to continue down the hall.

349

Brutal and unforgiving, the Legorian Sentinel decimates you with the power of its attacks, leaving you bloody and barely able to move as you lay defeated on the polished, marble floor. The last thing you remember is seeing the goliath gatekeeper raising one of its gigantic feet directly above you, before literally stomping you into oblivion!

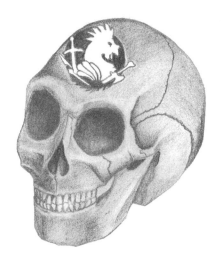

350

Unable to withstand the surprising strength of your attack against her, the sorceress backpedals, and then, with a wave of her hand, disappears...

Turn to 180

351

Vultures, startled into flight by your sudden appearance, continue circling above as you and Mateo cautiously approach — the sickening smell of carrion and charnel rot now so unbearable as to make you want to vomit. By far the largest corpse of any creature you have ever seen, it suddenly becomes abundantly and frighteningly clear as you look more closely that you have stumbled upon the remains of Ataraxia's most fearsome and formidable apex predator — a dragon!

Without warning, Mateo, who is following behind you, lets out a blood-curdling scream. Quickly turning around while simultaneously drawing your weapon, you are horrified to discover the decomposing dragon clutching Mateo's limp and bloodied body in its powerful jaws. Utterly helpless and unable to come to the aid of your companion, you watch wide-eyed and aghast as Mateo is bitten in two.

Suddenly, the ghostly forms of what appear to be three elven kings materialize close by. It is at almost the same instant that a strange fire spews forth from the three spectral beings, immediately turning the undead monstrosity into a pile of ash...

Turn to 254

352

With a banshee-like scream, the sea hag slumps to the hard stone floor of the cave.

Making your way over to the chest, you discover that it is securely locked, and although you carefully examine the chest, you can find no obvious or hidden means of unlocking it.

Perhaps the lock can be picked...

(At this time, please perform a Lock Picking check).

If you successfully pick the lock on the chest, **turn to 135**

If you are unable to open the chest, add 1 point to your Lock Picking score and exit the cave **by going to 40**

353

Up ahead, and just out of sight beyond a bend in the corridor, you can hear what sounds like a creaking noise with a hissing *whoosh*. Cautiously making your way forward, you round a corner and discover the origin of the mysterious sounds. Swinging back and forth in front of you and across the corridor itself, are three pendulums with blades. Each one of the pendulums is moving at a different speed than the others and not one of them is in sync. Even as you are watching, a large subterranean rat wanders too close to the sweep of the first blade and is instantly cut in two.

It is definitely going to take more than just calculated timing to make it past all three unscathed!

(Because there are three portcullises, you will have to have a TOTAL OF THREE successful Agility checks. For each failed check, you must roll a 1d6 to determine how much DAMAGE you have sustained. You may roll as many times as necessary, until you have either made it past all three pendulums or are dead. Any damage you receive will be retained until you use a HEALTH potion. You may also add 1 point to your Agility score for all of your combined failed checks, but only ONE).

If you succeed, **turn to 10**

354

The heavy stench of putrefaction now permeates the air as you near a sharp bend in the corridor. Slowly making your way forward, you stop just shy, and with your weapon in hand, cautiously peer around the corner.

It is here that the passage you have been following abruptly terminates at the edge of a spacious, cavern-like room. At its center is what appears to be a mound literally composed out of the decomposing carcasses of men and beasts alike. With your weapon combat-ready, you make your way in, gagging on the smell of charnel house rot — the stench now so intolerable that you are almost at the point of vomiting.

Suddenly, several long, tendril-like appendages burst forth from the mound, rapidly snaking their way through the air towards you...

(How quick are you on your feet? Find out now by performing an Agility check. If your check is successful, then you either dodged the tendrils or they missed. If, however, your check failed, you have been struck by them. Add 1 point to your Agility score for failing, and then roll a 1d6 to determine how much DAMAGE you have sustained. Subtract this amount from your LIFE FORCE now. Any damage you receive will be retained until you use a Health potion).

Turn to 202

355

With a loud, snake-like hiss, the lizardman immediately launches an offensive, aggressively lunging at you with its broad-headed spear...

LIZARDMAN SENTRY   Life Force 29   Combat 3

Did you kill the lizardman? If so, **turn to 404**

356

It is during the hottest part of the day that you unexpectedly happen upon the most bizarre collection of statues that you have ever laid eyes on. Carved from solid stone and no two alike, each one of them is amazingly life-like and vividly detailed, but what you find most alarming is the expressions of absolute terror that the artist chose to put on their faces. Equally as disturbing is the fact that many of them have their hands up and their heads turned to the side as if trying to shield themselves and avert their eyes from gazing at some ghastly and horrific scene. Some even appear to be cowering in fear. Even their very placement seems to be completely random and oddly irregular, with some of the statues even standing partially in the water.

Not far from where you are standing, a wide flight of stairs weaves its way around the boulders and up the hillside, culminating at the entrance of what appears to be the remnants of an ancient temple...

If you decide to investigate the temple ruin, **turn to 224**

If you decide to continue following the shoreline instead, **go to 483**

357

Suddenly, excruciating pain, unlike anything you have ever experienced before, racks your entire body as literally every one of your bones begin to break and shift inside of you. Falling to your hands and knees in agony, your eyes change to an insane, yellow glow as your rapidly changing frame and expanding muscles burst from your clothing and armor. Coarse, dark fur sprouts all over your body and your now contorted face dramatically elongates into a slavering, canine-like snout.

Your transformation at its end, you let out one last, final scream, which abruptly becomes a long howl as an insatiable hunger quickly overtakes you...

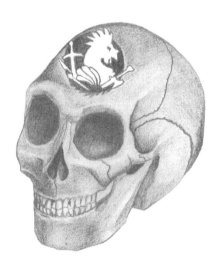

358

Beyond the doorway is a wide and extremely well-lit corridor that twists and turns, eventually opening up into a large cavern. It is what you see next that makes you glad you did not just rush in.

Squatting at the far end of the cavern and gorging itself upon the flesh of what is obviously a human body, is the largest baboon you have ever seen. You watch in horror as the brute beast uses its sizable canine teeth to effortlessly tear gigantic chunks of meat from the corpse it is holding.

It is then that the unthinkable happens. Without any warning whatsoever, you sneeze!

Suddenly aware of your presence, the baboon immediately stops feeding, tossing the half-eaten cadaver aside and erupting into a series of bone-chilling screams and howls. You barely have time to ready your weapon before the savage creature has sprinted on all fours across the cavern and is upon you...

GIANT BABOON   Life Force 35   Combat 4

If you defeat the giant baboon, **turn to 16**

359

As the mummy's grip tightens around your wrist, you watch in absolute horror as your skin begins to shrivel up and your arm starts to wither. You try desperately to reach for your weapon with your other hand, but the rest of your body has already started to deteriorate as well. You feel yourself growing weaker and weaker by the moment as your life force ebbs away, until finally, you succumb to the power of Umra, the Resplendent...

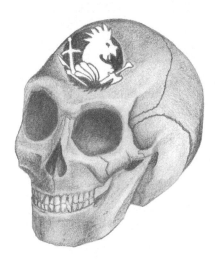

360

You have not ventured far down the hole when suddenly, the rung supporting all of your body weight gives, coming out of the wall and causing you to lose your footing. For a brief moment, you are holding on with both hands, your feet dangling in the air. Then, without warning, the rung your hands are wrapped around also comes loose, sending you plummeting downward. On the way down, you hit your head and lose consciousness before hitting the hard floor of the chamber below...

(At this time, please roll 2d6 to determine how much DAMAGE you sustained from the fall and subtract this amount from your LIFE FORCE now. Any damage you receive will be retained until you use a HEALTH potion).

A wide chamber greets you at the bottom when you come to, and in the semi-darkness, you can just make out a door on one of the walls. Moving towards it, you press your ear to the wood, but are unable to discern any sounds whatsoever through the solid, oaken panel. As you slowly and cautiously open the door, brilliant, unfiltered light floods into the chamber, momentarily blinding you in the process.

An extremely well-lit corridor awaits you on the other side...

Turn to 286

361

Mortally wounded, the mantis backs away from you slowly and then retreats into the dense understory of the forest. After a brief rest, you search the partially-eaten body of the mantis' victim and are rewarded with 15 gold pieces.

(Add these to your PURSE now).

Turn to 242

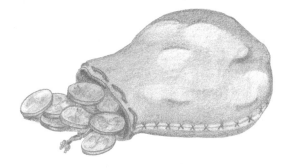

362

The skeletons prove to be no match for you and you quickly dispatch them. A search of the garments they were wearing yields a couple of small coin purses containing a total of 15 gold pieces as well as a HEALTH potion...

(HEALTH potions can be used at any time to restore lost LF points, except when you are in combat. Each HEALTH potion can be used ONE TIME to restore 5 points. You are also free to use as many of them as you wish at any time, but your LIFE FORCE can never ever exceed its original default of **25**).

(Add these items to your PURSE and INVENTORY now).

Did you already search the chest? If not, **go to 162**

Otherwise...

Finding nothing else of interest in the room, you make your way through the door and back into the passage you were following...

Turn to 484

363

Several minutes elapse, but nothing happens. Replacing the stopper, you quickly stash the empty flask in your satchel and press on...

(Add this item to your INVENTORY now) and then **turn to 253**

364

Without warning, the tunnel swings abruptly to the right and you find yourself in a large, rectangular chamber. The tunnel seems to pick up again on the other side, and other than the above-ground well in the center of the room, there appears to be nothing else of any significance.

You are about to make your way over to the well to investigate when quite unexpectedly, one of the vilest creatures you have ever laid eyes on emerges from the tunnel on the far side of the room. Filthy and ravenous in appearance, its emaciated body resembles that of a woman, with its torso, arms, and revolting face being almost human in semblance. From the waist down, its features become more and more bird-like, with its lower half like that of a vulture and cruel and deadly talons on its ugly feet. Dirty wings, with tons of missing feathers, sprout from its bony shoulders, making it truly something hideous and repulsive to behold.

The harpy leaps up from the ground and alights on the edge of the well. Before it is even aware of your presence, you have already rushed into the room and dispatched it. The creature slumps backward, bouncing off the walls of the well as it plummets downward. You hear a sickening *thrumpf* as its body meets the ground below.

You are about to exit the room via the tunnel on the other side when suddenly, two more of the horrid

(Continued on overleaf)

creatures emerge from the well, flapping their grimy wings as they advance through the air towards you...

| HARPY | Life Force 15 | Combat 2 |
| HARPY | Life Force 13 | Combat 2 |

If you kill the harpies, **turn to 227**

365

You successfully traverse the room and are about to open the trunk when suddenly, the cultist in the bed closest to you wakes up. Upon seeing you, she cries out, and in an instant, both of them are on their feet with their shortswords drawn...

CULTIST   Life Force 25   Combat 3
CULTIST   Life Force 25   Combat 3

If you defeat the acolytes, **turn to 160**

366

It is not long before you stumble upon the entrance to a small cave. Readying your weapon, you cautiously approach the opening of the grotto and peering inside, see a skeleton chained securely to a large boulder. Its matted beard, dirty sailor's tunic, and tattered trousers immediately tell you this was once a man and most likely a sailor as well. Lying in the dirt not far from him is a HEALTH potion, which you immediately collect and add to the contents of your satchel.

(Add this item to your INVENTORY now).

You are about to head out when suddenly and much to your complete surprise and amazement, the skeleton addresses you.

"Hey, mate! How 'bout helpin' a feller out and gettin' me outta these 'ere chains?" says the skeleton.

"Who are you?" you ask, not exactly sure how to respond, "and how is it that you are still... you know... alive?

"Aye, now that be the magical question I wish me knew the answer to meself, mate!" replies the skeleton. "Name's Mateo. I became a castaway here when the ship I was first mate on ran aground."

"And what of the rest of your crew?" you ask, still very much in disbelief that you are having a conversation with a skeleton.

"Includin' the Captain and meself, twas fifty of us

aboard the Serpent's Wake," Mateo recounts. "I can remember that day like it was only yesterday. The sea was a dead calm and there was no wind — not even so much as a whisper in our sails. We'd been driftin' fer days, ya see, and then all of a sudden, the ship began to move like it had a life of its own. It was like somethin' had taken o'er the Serpent's Wake and was now controlling it! Brought us here, it did! Brought us to this infernal island of death! Fifty of us landed on this accursed rock! Fifty men strong we were, but this island demanded sacrifice and sacrifice it took! The first night we lost ten good men when the vampires came. Some nights the vampires didn't come at all and some nights we were able to fight them off. One by one, we were slaughtered like human cattle and those the vampires didn't take, the island did..."

It is here that the skeleton momentarily pauses, as if in reflective thought. "Of the Serpent's Wake crew, only I am left to tell the tale, and as ya can see, mate, there isn't much left of me at that," he says with a laugh.

"I will free you," you say, as you begin working on the chains that bind him, "but be forewarned, skeleton, I will not tolerate any trickery on your part."

Within moments, Mateo is free and has pledged his life and blade to you in service and gratitude.

You decide to give the grotto one more sweep and discover a small, earthen pot that you did not notice before. Inside of it, is a large coin purse containing an unbelievable haul — two gold rings, a gold coin, and

30 gold pieces to be exact!

(Add these to your PURSE and INVENTORY now).

With your undead companion, Mateo, at your side, you immediately resume your trek up the rocky ravine...

(You may now utilize Mateo in combat. Simply roll an additional 1d6 for the sailor along with your roll. Skeleton Mateo has an LF score of 15 and a Combat Skill Score of 2).

Turn to 112

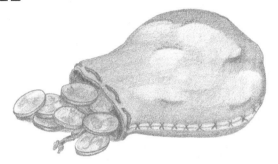

367

The corridor you are now following begins to grow noticeably wider and higher, eventually transitioning into an enormous cavern. Jagged rocks and stalagmites rise up from the cavern floor, while high above, stalactites taper down from the ceiling like gigantic icicles, mirrored in the crystal clear pool of water below.

Kneeling down beside the water, you cup your hands together and slake your thirst. The water is unbelievably refreshing and gives you renewed vigor.

Suddenly, you see movement within the water, but quickly realize what you are seeing is actually the reflection of something stirring directly above you. Looking up, you see a gigantic, blob-like mass slowly descending from the roof of the cave. In an instant, you are on your feet and have retreated to a safe distance away.

It drops down into the water and then begins to slide across the cavern floor towards you...

If you decide to fight the black ooze, **turn to 203**

Perhaps this is a fight best avoided. If this is your choice, **go to 451**

368

Suddenly, you are startled by the voice of a woman behind you.

"I really wish that it did not have to come to this, but I am afraid I have no other choice," says the woman.

Looking up, you see a beautiful, elven maiden standing some distance from you. In her hands, she holds a mage's staff, which is pointed directly at you.

"I'm not quite sure I understand," you say.

"I am sorry... truly I am, but there is no other way! I cannot allow you to continue any further!" replies the woman, as she brings her staff back and launches a ball of fire at you...

(At this time, please perform an Agility check. If your check fails, you have been struck by the fireball and must roll a 1d6 to determine how much DAMAGE you have sustained. Also, make sure to add 1 point to your Agility score for failing).

ELVEN SORCERESS   Life Force 25   Combat 5

(When you have brought the sorceress' LIFE FORCE down to 15, DO NOT continue fighting her, but instead, **proceed to 22**).

369

Like a cruel and unyielding mistress, the sun ruthlessly beats down upon you as you hike across the broken land, and with not even a wisp of a cloud to diffuse the devastating heat, you find yourself forced to rehydrate frequently.

You are progressing up a short, but somewhat steep and rocky incline, when much to your surprise, you suddenly hear the sound of a woman singing. Making your way to the crest of the hill, it is what you see when you reach the top that makes you begin to question the very testimony of your ears and eyes.

Dancing on a low, table-like rock just ahead is a beautiful, young maiden — her eyes tightly closed as she sings an ancient song in an unknown tongue. Her every movement is sensual and almost hypnotic, and you quickly find yourself strangely bewitched by her beauty and instantly captivated by her mysterious allure.

Snapping back to your senses, you call out to her, but the woman has already crumbled into a pile of sand...

Turn to 490

370

A palpable and extremely unsettling quiet accompanies you as you begin your ascent up the stairwell — the flickering of your torch's flame and the soft footfalls of your feet upon the stone uncomfortably loud in the oppressive, tomb-like silence. Like an animal fleeing for its life, the stygian blackness retreats before the invasive light of your torch — the resulting shadows openly taunting and mocking you as your mind starts to play tricks on your eyes.

Eventually, you reach a wide upper landing, where a short tunnel brings you abruptly to a heavy, wooden door that has been reinforced with bands of iron. The door is ajar, and for several moments, you stand there, head tilted and ears inclined, listening. Hearing nothing, you extinguish your torch and then inch the door open, but only just wide enough for a peek at what lies beyond...

Turn to 144

371

Emerging from the thicket is an abomination straight out of your worst nightmares — a multi-legged monstrosity; a hideous amalgamation and what can only be the perversion of a spell gone horribly and terribly wrong. With no apparent rhyme or reason, spindly, insect-like legs of varying sizes and lengths randomly sprout from its severely disfigured mass of a body, while the placement of its head, eyes, and mandibles seem to be nothing more than just an afterthought.

Completely oblivious to your presence, the terrifying creature moves about the clearing for a bit before eventually scuttling back into the underbrush from whence it came...

Turn to 490

372

Slipping on the mysterious ring, you cry out as it immediately tightens around your finger. Try as you might, you cannot get it to come off, and as the flesh and tissue of your hand begin to die and decay rapidly, you realize that what you thought was just an ordinary ring is actually a cursed object known as a Ring of Rot. The decomposition of your body is swift and the pain is excruciating. In a matter of moments, you become one of the undead — a ghoul — suffering a fate far worse than any death...

373

A hidden doorway appears in the wall almost immediately after pulling the lever on the right. You step through the doorway and watch as it closes behind you. You have no other option now but to continue moving forward and down the hall...

Turn to 76

374

Even without a weapon, the centaur still proves quite formidable, but eventually succumbs to your prowess. Bleeding profusely from its many wounds, the centaur's breathing becomes more labored with each breath and its movements slow, until finally, exhaling one last time, it stumbles forward and slumps to the ground...

Turn to 58

375

Silently but swiftly crossing the room, you kneel down before the chest and as you are slowly raising its lid, the chest lets out a loud squeal, awakening the cultist in the bed closest to you. She immediately cries out to alert her sleeping companions, all of them scrambling out of their beds and onto their feet with their shortswords drawn...

CULTIST	Life Force 25	Combat 3
CULTIST	Life Force 25	Combat 3
CULTIST	Life Force 25	Combat 3
CULTIST	Life Force 25	Combat 3

If you defeat the cultists, **turn to 233**

376

Instinctively, you reach out to catch hold of the chasm's edge, your grasp falling short by mere centimetres! Unable to recover, you fall to your death, your body making a sickening noise as it literally explodes upon impact when you hit the rocky bottom of the chasm far below...

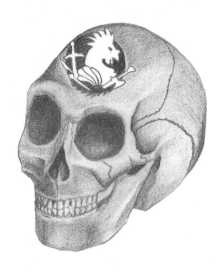

377

You step off of the pressure plate, and right away, the chamber comes to a grinding halt as the door swings open and four cultists armed with shortswords step out...

CULTIST	Life Force 25	Combat 3
CULTIST	Life Force 25	Combat 3
CULTIST	Life Force 25	Combat 3
CULTIST	Life Force 25	Combat 3

If you defeat them, **return to 300 and roll again**

378

"Finally, I am free," the spirit says, smiling.

There is a look of peace on his face as he closes his eyes and falls to his knees, and then, in another instant, the apparition has vanished...

Turn to 247

379

In a fit of sadistic rage, the troll-gre grabs you by the legs, and with barbaric savagery, swings your body into the trunk of a nearby tree. The sheer force of the impact alone causes every bone in your body to break as well as your organs to rupture inside of you. The troll-gre then takes your limp and lifeless body, and, throwing it over its shoulder, trudges back to its lair, where you will be devoured at its leisure...

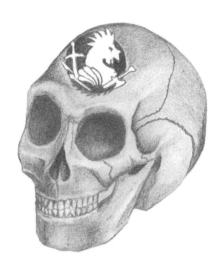

380

The corridor terminates at the edge of a giant pool of stagnant, green slime. With little choice but to stay the course, you step down into the knee-deep, foul-smelling ooze. You are about to take a step forward when suddenly, the muck up ahead is clearly disturbed by something moving just beneath the surface.

Moments later, a muscular, worm-like body with a sucker-like orifice breaches just ahead of you. Another pops up just to the left of the first and another just behind. Somehow aware of your presence, the gigantic leeches quickly disappear beneath the green sludge, the movement of the slime telling you they are headed directly for you...

GIANT LEECH	Life Force 7	Combat 1
GIANT LEECH	Life Force 6	Combat 1
GIANT LEECH	Life Force 5	Combat 1

If you defeat the giant leeches, wade through the pond of green slime and **turn to 277**

381

Much to your surprise, the giant stops weeping, and, suddenly aware of your presence, quickly leaps to its feet. Too late you realize that the creature now towering above you is no ordinary giant at all, but is composed entirely out of solid rock. It is a stone golem, and unfortunately, your weapon is completely ineffective against it!

Also unfortunate for you is that the stone golem immediately seizes you, and with brute force savagely throws you against the cavern wall. The impact is the equivalent of you falling from a great height, literally causing your body to burst open, spilling your intestines and your vital organs all over the ground.

Why this stone golem was crying will forever remain a mystery...

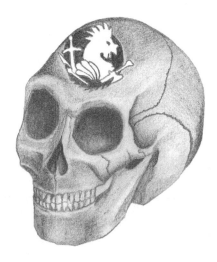

382

Your head is still spinning when you finally regain consciousness, and as the objects around you gradually come into focus, you make the shocking discovery that you have been tied to a large spit and are suspended helplessly over a pile of wood. Even more horrifying still is the fact that the inbred you killed earlier is already cooking on another spit close by — the foul stench of its burning flesh overwhelming your nostrils.

Craning your head as far as you can in all directions, you quickly appraise your surroundings. You are in a village and flanked on all sides by crude dwellings constructed out of tree branches and daubed with mud. Alive and bustling with activity, you watch as women just as repulsive as their male counterparts busy themselves with everyday chores, while all around you, freakishly ugly children run to and fro as they play. One of the children — what may or may not be a little girl — rushes up to you and smacks you several times with a thick stick before scampering off.

It is at that very moment that you hear the steady, rhythmic pounding of tribal drums, and turning your head slightly, see a large procession of swamp folk making their way towards you. At their head is their chieftain — a hulking, inhumanoid brute with the skull of some ferocious beast adorning his head like a crown. Hobbling beside him is a squatty, hunch-backed creature carrying a torch.

(Continued on overleaf)

The chieftain begins speaking to his people in an unintelligible language, and then, with a wave of his seven-fingered hand, motions for the torch-bearer to step forward and set the wood beneath you ablaze.

Suddenly, the ghostly forms of what appear to be three elven kings materialize close by. It is at almost the same instant that a strange fire spews forth from the three spectral beings, immediately turning the inbred torch-bearer and the chieftain into ash. The fire also completely consumes your restraints, causing you to drop from the spit and sending you tumbling down the woodpile before coming to rest at the feet of the apparitions.

Leaping quickly to your feet, you discover that all of the swamp folk have fled, and with the exception of the spirits standing before you, there is not a soul to be seen anywhere in the village...

Turn to 178

383

You have barely even dispatched the two cultists, when perhaps two dozen or more of the Spider Queen's Faithful suddenly pour into the hall from both sides, attracted by the noisy clamor of your recent battle. Within moments, they have completely overwhelmed, disarmed, and bound the two of you...

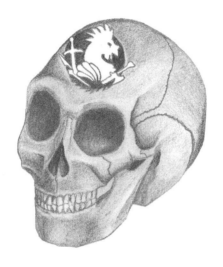

384

After a time, the passage begins to swing in almost a full circle to the right, eventually doubling back on itself before turning sharply to the left. It is here you suddenly find yourself standing before a wide hallway constructed entirely from top to bottom from tight-fitting blocks of white stone. A series of consecutive, evenly-spaced torches running its full length burn brightly on one side and there is a door at the far end of the hall.

"What do you make of this?" you ask, stopping at the very threshold of the hallway without entering.

"Maybe it's just me," replies the sorceress, the apprehension quite apparent in her voice, "but my intuition is telling me something isn't quite right here..."

If you decide to continue down the hallway anyway, **turn to 121**

On the other hand, if Avril-Lyn is right, maybe it would be better to turn back and take the other passage instead. If this is your choice, **go to 175**

385

The corridor breaks off into three passageways, with one going sharply to the left, one continuing straight ahead, and the other doing a gradual twist to the right...

If you decide to head down the left passage, **turn to 285**

If your choice is the middle corridor, **go to 52**

Or if you choose instead to go down the right-most tunnel, then **proceed to 104**

386

Convulsing violently and spasmodically, the loathsome creature shudders and is suddenly still.

Making your way around its revolting carcass, you quickly move on, and after trudging along for the better part of nearly two hours, you and Avril-Lyn agree to stop for a brief, but much-needed rest.

"Do you have any idea what we should expect when we find the temple?" you broach.

Avril-Lyn shakes her head. "There is no telling what awaits us, but I can assure you we are not going to be able to just march right in through the front gate. The very temple itself is constructed like a fortress and it's a safe bet the entrance is going to be heavily guarded by Arachnae's disciples and their acolytes. We are definitely going to have to find an alternative means of entry..."

The Faithful, otherwise known as the Children of Arachnae or the Spider Cult, had been around for hundreds of years, and yet very little was known about this sect and their highly secretive, religious practices.

After rehydrating and eating some food, you and Avril-Lyn set out once more...

Turn to 410

387

Moving forward, you and your elven companion, Laurick, eventually come to an entire stretch where the structure of the passage appears to be unstable and in serious disrepair. Makeshift braces and temporary beams have been erected and randomly placed throughout, precariously holding the deteriorating walls and the crumbling canopy above in place. Filled with apprehension and not just a little uneasiness, you and Laurick begin to carefully and cautiously make your way through, many times having to step over and around the supporting timbers and fallen rock.

You are almost in the clear when suddenly, without any warning whatsoever, the entire ceiling starts to give. Before you even have time to react, Laurick has already shoved you out of harm's way before being lost from your field of vision in an avalanche of falling stone and debris.

You call out to the wood elf several times, but there is no reply. When the cloud of airborne dust and dirt has settled, you begin a quick sweep of the rubble, only to make the gruesome discovery that Laurick's lifeless body lies crushed beneath a gigantic boulder.

Grieving the sudden and unexpected loss of your newfound friend and comrade-in-arms, it is with a heavy heart that you press onward...

Turn to 41

388

Lumbering down the hallway is a monstrous creature literally straight out of your childhood nightmares. Nearly one-and-a-half times your size and having four powerful arms and two heads, the hulking brute is the living epitome of absolute terror. Its colossal frame is wrapped with several lengths of rusty chain, making it truly an intimidating and terrifying foe!

It is only but an instant before the savage creature is upon you, and taking the loose and dangling chains hanging from its body, it begins to swing them ferociously through the air as it advances towards you...

TWO-HEADED CAVE TROLL   Life Force 35   Combat 4

If you defeat the cave troll, **turn to 136**

If, however, the cave troll kills you, **go to 472**

389

Almost immediately after rotating the last turn-stone, a barrage of darts spews forth from multiple hidden apertures, with some of them hitting you.

(To determine how much DAMAGE you sustained, roll a 1d6 and subtract this amount from your LIFE FORCE now).

You have obviously chosen the wrong combination of symbols!

Please return to 87

390

Unable to withstand the surprising strength of your attack against her, the sorceress backpedals, and then, with a wave of her hand, disappears...

Turn to 232

391

You are skirting the edge of a large bog when suddenly, your eyes are drawn towards something moving across the mire and headed directly for you. It is still quite some distance away and seems to be traveling via a succession of quick hops.

Readying your weapon, you soon discover the nature of the creature that is now stalking you. Hopping across the boggy ground towards you is something that resembles a giant toad, but as it draws nearer, you quickly realize that this is no ordinary amphibian. Its large mouth is filled from top to bottom with razor-sharp teeth and each one of its webbed feet culminates in a set of deadly talons.

Launching itself into the air, the giant toad clears the remaining distance between you and itself...

(At this time, you can exercise the option of trying to flee by performing an Agility check. If you fail, add 1 point to your Agility score).

If you successfully flee, **turn to 89**

If you decide to fight the giant toad or were unable to successfully flee, **go to 198**

392

Looking ahead, you see a half-naked man running down the shoreline towards you. His eyes are as wild as the hair on his head and he seems to be shouting something, but is still too far away for you to even make out what he is saying. Perhaps this is nothing but the ramblings of a deranged lunatic, but it is also possible he might be trying to cast a spell on you...

If you decide to attack the man before he can attack you, **turn to 94**

You could also wait and see what this man's intentions are. If this is your choice, **go to 188**

393

Searching the borc's body, you discover a coin purse with 25 gold pieces inside of it.

(Add the gold to your PURSE now) and then **proceed to 9**

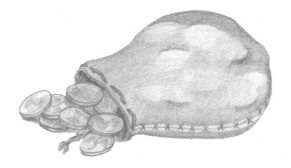

394

The orc is snoring quite soundly as you quietly enter the room, make your way around the table, and then kneel down beside it...

(At this time, please perform a Pickpocketing check).

If you successfully pickpocket the orc, **turn to 101**

If you are discovered, add 1 to your Pickpocketing score and then **go to 491**

395

After a time, the terrain begins to change quite dramatically, with the way ahead becoming more and more difficult to navigate with each passing moment. The path itself has all but disappeared and you quickly find yourself having to circumvent geothermal pools and small but scalding hot, geysers as you make your way across a now volatile and unpredictable landscape. Clearly a dangerous hotbed of volcanic activity, you begin to wonder if it would be wise to even continue moving forward. It is what you see next that immediately makes you regret that you did not turn back when you had the chance.

Not even ten paces in front of you is a shallow, bowl-like depression in the earth with three large, oval-shaped objects inside of it. With a shudder, you realize that you have unwittingly stumbled upon a nest, and judging by the size of the eggs, it must belong to a creature of considerable size!

You are about to turn and head back the way you came when suddenly, the eggs begin to rock violently back and forth. Even as you are watching in horrified fascination, several winged, reptilian-like somethings burst from their shells, each one advancing towards you hungrily on all fours...

DRAGON HATCHLING   Life Force 15   Combat 2
DRAGON HATCHLING   Life Force 14   Combat 2
DRAGON HATCHLING   Life Force 13   Combat 2

If you defeat the dragon hatchlings, **turn to 95**

396

You find yourself outdoors. A surreal, almost phantasmagorical mist completely envelops the ground with a thick, low-lying veil of white, while above, a rough, woolen blanket of mottled gray now hides any traces of the Ataraxian sun.

You are standing in what is clearly the inner courtyard. To your immediate left, is a stable with several empty stalls running consecutively along almost the entire length of the inner, curtain wall. It is there, where the stable ends, that you notice another door going directly into the castle keep itself. From where you are standing, you can also see a short flight of stairs leading up to the double doors of the keep's main entrance.

If you decide to enter the keep via the main entrance doors, **turn to 185**

On the other hand, perhaps it would be much wiser entering by way of the door at the far end of the stables. If this is your choice, **go to 64**

397

The bugbear quickly succumbs to the ferocity of your attacks and collapses to the floor like a tree that was just felled.

A search of all three bodies, as well as the shack itself, yields 5 gold pieces. You also find a hollow place under one of the floorboards containing a small chest. Inside of the chest, are a HEALTH potion, 5 more gold pieces, a large bear claw, and a mysterious key. Upon closer examination of the key, you quickly realize that this is no ordinary key, but is actually a skeleton key! Skeleton keys are able to unlock virtually any lock.

(Add these items to your PURSE and INVENTORY now).

Turn to 49

398

You try to kick the door down but to no avail. Unfortunately for you, the loud noise you made while doing so has attracted the attention of a wandering monster...

(Roll a 1d6 to determine which monster from the table below you will have to face).

1	RABID DOG	Life Force 5	Combat 1
2	REANIMATED CORPSE	Life Force 8	Combat 2
3	UNDEAD DWARF	Life Force 8	Combat 2
4	GIANT CENTIPEDE	Life Force 13	Combat 2
5	GIANT MOLE RAT	Life Force 18	Combat 2
6	HOBGOBLIN	Life Force 25	Combat 3

(You can also exercise the option of trying to flee by performing an Agility check).

If you are able to successfully flee, **turn to 59**

If not, add 1 point to your Agility score and prepare to face the monster in battle...

WANDERING MONSTER   Life Force ?   Combat ?

If you defeat the random, wandering monster, **turn to 59**

399

Following the course of the river seems as good a path as any, and so, walking along the river's edge, you begin making your way downstream. After a time, you find a small boat that appears to have washed up on the beach...

You could try to navigate the river in the boat. If this is your choice, **turn to 291**

If you decide it would be best to just continue downstream on foot, **go to 140**

400

By far the most formidable opponent you have faced thus far, the Legorian Sentinel nearly decimates you with its size and by the sheer dominance of its attacks! But it is your speed that ultimately hands you the victory, for the gatekeeper, a powerful foe in many ways, is no match for your light-footed quickness and your calculated attacks eventually take it down. It staggers forward, each step more labored than the last, until finally, it can no longer stand. The sound of its body hitting the floor reverberates throughout the chamber, and within moments, the gentle purring of its internal motors cease, followed by a very perceptible silence.

You are about to move on when you notice that a small compartment has opened on the back of the colossus. Inside, is a strange object, which after closely examining, leads you to believe it was probably the device that powered this fallen wonder of ancient, Legorian technology.

You also find a small, inconspicuous chest near the dais, inside of which, is a HEALTH potion.

(Add these items to your INVENTORY now).

Quietly making your way up the stairs, you step through the massive doors and into the hallway from whence the mighty guardian came...

Turn to 63

401

With the rapidity of thought itself, you instantly find yourself standing on top of a huge outcropping of rock jutting outward from a cliff. A tempestuous and angry sea ravages the rocky base of the precipice far below, while above you, the vertical face of the cliff extends upward until it is eventually lost in the fog-like mist high above.

Before you is the dark and ominous opening of a tunnel, and almost immediately, your nostrils are met by the heavy stink of carrion and rotting flesh coming from within. Lighting your torch and readying your weapon, you enter the tunnel, the slime-covered floor causing you to slip and slide as you carefully pick your way through the putrefying remains of humans and beasts alike. That this is a passage frequented by vampires is more than obvious and you quickly realize that this is probably one of the exits used by them when hunting at night.

Gagging and nearly vomiting every step of the way, you are greatly relieved when the passage finds its end at a large, wooden door...

Turn to 251

402

The dark lord throws his head back and lets out a blood-curdling shriek as his convulsing body begins to levitate upwards, dragging the phantasmagorical mist with him into the air. You watch in horrified fascination as the Lich Lord's eye sockets and mouth erupt into beams of explosive light and energy, until eventually, the undead necromancer is consumed and disintegrates right before your eyes!

Knowing a lich can never truly die unless the phylactery containing its soul essence is also destroyed, you begin a thorough sweep of the throne room. Your diligence is soon rewarded, for you discover a hidden partition in the wall just behind the Lich Lord's throne, and behind it, a secret chamber overflowing with gold and precious things, but also containing the powerful artifact that you seek.

It is an hourglass of all things, and ironically, the last remnants of sand trickle to the bottom just before you smash it using the very staff of the Lich Lord, himself. The sand within pours out onto the floor, scattering, and then dissipates as if swept away by the wind...

Turn to 475

403

Placing the scroll back onto the podium, you decide against reading the incantation, opting instead to exit the chamber...

Turn to 336

404

The reptilianoid is truly a savage and deadly opponent, unmatched in its use of the spear, but in the end, it is you who prevails. A search of the lizardman's body rewards you with 15 gold pieces.

(Add the gold to your PURSE now).

You find the control mechanism that operates the heavy gate nearby, and with several steady turns of the large crank handle, activate the interconnecting cogs controlling the internal winch within the rough-hewn walls. With a loud rumble, the iron portcullis raises via its attached chains, allowing you to pass through to the tunnel beyond...

Turn to 41

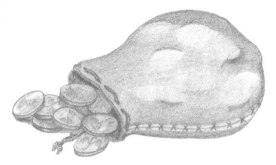

405
(At this time, please perform a Stealth check).

If your check is successful, **turn to 274**

If, however, your check failed, add 1 point to your Stealth score and then **go to 309**

406

Finding nothing of value or of any use on the bodies of the mummies, you make your way to the dais and find that the larger sarcophagus is still completely intact. A thick layer of dust has settled on top of its lid, the accumulation of perhaps centuries of dirt and debris. You brush it off, only to discover that the lid of the sarcophagus is not stone at all, but made out of solid gold and encrusted with all manner of precious stones and jewels.

Using the blade of an old sword you find lying nearby, you begin prying on the edge of it until the seal finally breaks and the lid pops free. It takes nearly all of your strength to slide the heavy gold lid off of the sarcophagus.

Inside, are the mummified and withered remains of a man dressed in a fine purple robe and wrapped in tattered, linen strips. His arms are folded across his chest and there is a gold necklace around his neck. A golden, bejeweled crown adorns his head, affirming this man was once royalty.

You are reaching for the necklace when suddenly, the mummy's hand grabs onto your wrist...

(At this time, please perform a Strength check).

If you are able to break free, **turn to 216**

If, however, you are unsuccessful, **go to 359**

407

Soft and diffused light fills the grotto as daybreak silently announces its return. Emerging from the cave, you step out into the crisp, early morning air. Just ahead, a dark and forbidding forest looms in stark contrast against the azure blue, Ataraxian sky. Ominous and foreboding, its ancient trees rise up from the primeval landscape — their gnarled roots extending in all directions and their tops quickly lost in the vaulted canopy of the leaves and branches high above. A wide and twisting path, choked on both sides by brambles, weaves its way through the thick and matted understory of the forest floor.

With the only other recourse being to head back down the face of the cliff, you enter the forest. It is immediately obvious to you that something is amiss. A palpable, almost tomb-like silence surrounds you as you travel deeper and deeper into the ominous woods. Disturbingly absent is the noisy drone of busy insects filling the air. Noticeably missing, too, are the occasional melodic choruses of birds at play. In fact, the forest seems to be an uncanny void when it comes to the usual sounds of nature.

Rounding a sharp bend, you are alarmed to see a gigantic humanoid-like creature lumbering out of the thicket and onto the path before you. The monstrous brute is easily one-and-a-half times your size and is carrying what appears to be the bone of some large animal for a club.

(Continued on overleaf)

Upon discovering you, the half-troll, half-ogre lets out a loud cry, abruptly breaking into a full-speed charge...

TROLL-GRE   Life Force 35   Combat 4

If you defeat the troll-gre, **turn to 159**

If the troll-gre defeats you, **go to 379**

408

Shuddering violently with its tentacles flailing uncontrollably about, the lurker lets out one last shriek before crumpling to the ground in front of you. Weary from the encounter, you collapse beside its smelly carcass and decide to rest for a spell so that you can dress your wounds. You also take some of the lurker's meat and then cook it and eat it. Finding renewed vigor, you resume your trek, shadowing the river's edge, this time, at a much safer distance...

Turn to 327

409

The changeling is surprisingly strong, nearly pulling your arm into its gaping, tooth-filled mouth. Miraculously, you are somehow able to pull your arm free, and quickly retreat to a safe distance away, your weapon now in hand. The changeling, however, does not attack, instead reverting back to its clever disguise right where it is sitting.

Giving the monstrosity a wide berth, you hastily exit via the tunnel on the other side of the room...

Turn to 388

410

A short time later, you and the sorceress once again find yourselves at another junction — this one presenting you with three avenues.

Stopping just shy of the entrance to the larger tunnel on the left, you distinctly hear the steady percussion of what can only be droplets of water hitting the surface of a pool. There is also the heavy smell of putrefaction coming from this passage as well. The other two tunnels are as silent as a tomb...

If you decide to investigate the passage with the heavy sound of dripping water, **turn to 81**

If you decide to maintain the same general course by continuing down the middle passage, **go to 110**

If your choice is the tunnel on the far right, **proceed to 304**

411

A short while later, you arrive at a locked, iron door, which effectively blocks you from traveling any further...

(At this time, please perform a Lock Picking check).

If you successfully pick the lock, **turn to 358**

If, however, you are unsuccessful, add 1 point to your Lock Picking score and when you finally succeed, **go to 358**

412

With a loud rumble, the iron portcullis raises via its attached chains, allowing you to enter the tunnel just beyond.

You have not ventured far, when quite suddenly and without any warning whatsoever, you come face-to-face with a wandering monster...

(Roll a 1d6 to determine which monster from the table below you will have to face).

1	VENOMOUS INSECT	Life Force 3	Combat 1
2	GIANT LAND LEECH	Life Force 8	Combat 1
3	GIANT CAVIE	Life Force 8	Combat 2
4	CAVE CRAWLER	Life Force 16	Combat 2
5	CARRION CREEPER	Life Force 28	Combat 3
6	REPTILIAN BEAST	Life Force 30	Combat 3

(You can also exercise the option of trying to flee by performing an Agility check).

If you are able to successfully flee, **turn to 194**

If not, add 1 point to your Agility score and prepare to face the monster in battle...

WANDERING MONSTER   Life Force ?   Combat ?

If you defeat the random, wandering monster, **turn to 194**

413

Making your way into the forest, you are at once completely captivated by its surreal and dream-like beauty. Suddenly, you catch a brief glimpse of a feminine form flitting through the trees, followed by flirtatious laughter. You try calling out to her, but the only reply you receive is the ambient noise of the birds and insects around you. Again and again, she appears, and in an instant is gone. Each time you give chase, calling out to her, and before you know it, have been led deep into the forest. You soon realize that you are now quite possibly and even hopelessly lost.

As you are reflecting on your situation, it is at that very moment you wander into a clearing, and there before you is a large table literally overflowing with food and drink. A beautiful, young maiden stands beside the table and as you approach, motions for you to sit. Without saying a word, she quietly sits down beside you, and smiling, indicates for you to eat.

As you begin to dine, you are immediately taken aback by the bountiful meal set before you. It is a king's feast to be sure! The woman says nothing, but instead watches you intently, while batting her big, blue eyes. After you have eaten your fill, you politely thank the woman for her kindness, but find you are unable to stand because you are completely paralyzed from the waist down...

(You have been bewitched by a dryad and must now perform a Resistance check in order to free yourself).

(Continued on overleaf of illustration)

413 Continued

If you are able to break free from the dryad's spell, **turn to 258**

If, however, you are unable to resist, **go to 71**

414

Almost immediately, you can feel your body being rejuvenated and your vigor renewed.

(Add 5 points to your LF score now. If your LIFE FORCE is already at its default score of 25, then you may add 1 to all of your dice rolls during your next combat encounter instead, but only for the duration of that encounter).

Replacing the stopper, you quickly stash the empty flask in your satchel and press on...

(Add this item to your INVENTORY now) and then **turn to 253**

415

Even before the life has completely left your body, the cyclotaur grabs you and with a loud shriek literally tears you in half, spilling your internal organs and intestines everywhere. It cries out again and then lets the two halves of your corpse fall where they land before heading back into the waterfall...

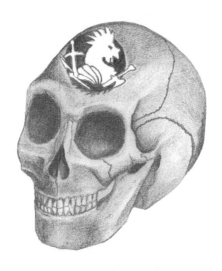

416

As you are rounding the corner, you see another of the Spider Queen's disciples approaching from the opposite end of the corridor.

"Arachnae be praised!" declares the cultist, pressing the palms of his hands and fingers together and bowing his head as he is passing by.

You and Avril-Lyn respond in kind and without breaking stride continue down the hallway, which soon finds its end at an adjoining corridor heading right — this one quickly resolving at a wall with the image of a large spider carved into it in bold relief. Next to the wall and on the left-hand side of the corridor is a door.

Proceeding with caution, you open the door and quietly enter the room beyond...

Turn to 154

417

The creature lets out one last, unearthly shriek, writhing and convulsing in the gravelly sand before breathing its last and collapsing in a puddle of its own blood.

The siren is wearing a gold necklace, which you quickly remove and add to the contents of your satchel.

(Add this item to your INVENTORY now).

After breaking down your camp, you decide against going back onto the water, instead, continuing on foot and following the shoreline around the lake...

Turn to 204

418

You have stopped to rest beside a large boulder when suddenly, you are startled by the voice of a woman.

"I really wish that it did not have to come to this, but I am afraid I have no other choice," says the woman.

Looking up, you see a beautiful, elven maiden standing some distance from you. In her hands, she holds a mage's staff, which is pointed directly at you.

"I'm not quite sure I understand," you say, as you slowly rise to your feet.

"I am sorry... truly I am, but there is no other way! I cannot allow you to continue any further!" replies the woman, as she brings her staff back and launches a ball of fire at you...

(At this time, please perform an Agility check. If your check fails, you have been struck by the fireball and must roll a 1d6 to determine how much DAMAGE you have sustained. Also, make sure to add 1 point to your Agility score for failing).

ELVEN SORCERESS   Life Force 25   Combat 5

(When you have brought the sorceress' LIFE FORCE down to 15, DO NOT continue fighting her, but instead, **proceed to 17**).

419

You have just spread out the bedroll on the floor and are getting ready to settle down for the evening when suddenly, you are startled by the voice of a woman crying out for help. Cautiously peering out the window, you are alarmed to see a young maiden covered in blood and stumbling across the clearing towards the cottage. The woman appears to be in a lot of pain and is sobbing uncontrollably. Moments later, you watch as she collapses, struggling to drag herself forward and across the ground.

Whatever it is that attacked this young maiden could very well still be out there, and venturing from the cottage to come to her aid could put you at significant risk...

If you decide to help the woman, **turn to 206**

If you think it would be best to let the woman fend for herself, **go to 151**

420

The passage carries on for only a short distance and then abruptly terminates before a set of double doors with the matching halves of a spider web masterfully carved in bold relief onto both of them. The sound of humming suddenly prevails over all others as you push the doors open and make your way into the space beyond.

You are standing in an enormous, rectangular chamber. At its far end, is a huge pedestal base with a large, stone representation of Arachnae prominently displayed upon it. Lying prostrate on the floor in front of the base are two dozen of the Spider Queen's devotees, each one of them in a trance-like state and humming in unison as they worship the carved image of their demonic deity. A door to the right of the base appears to be the only other exit from the chamber, other than the double doors you came through.

Knowing full well that you and Avril-Lyn could never hope to best so many of the Faithful at once, you realize that the only viable option here is to sneak past them...

(At this time, please perform a Stealth check).

If your check was successful, **turn to 158**

If, however, it was not, add 1 point to your Stealth score and then **go to 338**

421

Proceeding down the corridor, you notice a large wooden door just ahead and to the left. Weapon readied, you cautiously open the door and peer into the chamber on the other side.

The large room beyond is well-lit and is literally strewn from one end to the other with human bones, tattered garments, and pieces of armor. On the far side is a wooden chest. There is also a large pile of bones in one of the far corners of the room.

There could be something useful or even valuable in both...

If you decide to investigate the chest, **turn to 162**

If you would like to search the bone pile, **go to 221**

If you choose to leave the room instead, **proceed to 484**

422

Her insatiable bloodlust now at a furious level, the vampire grabs your nearly lifeless body with one of her hands and uses her other one to savagely tear your head from your body. A crimson mist spews forth, covering the entire area. There is a brief moment when the vampire revels over her blood feast, and then, ripping your heart from your chest, ravenously devours it...

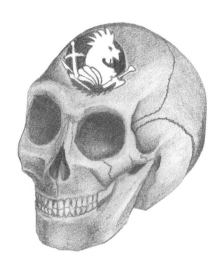

423

To your right, an unscalable wall of rock rises high above you as you follow the narrow strip of shoreline that hugs its base. It is not long before you stumble upon the entrance of a cave. Cautiously peering into the dimly-lit grotto, what you see inside literally causes every hair on your body to stand on end.

Sitting at a large wooden table is what appears to be, at first glance, a very old woman, but as you look more closely, you quickly realize that the creature before you is anything but. Its bluish-gray skin is covered with seaweed and dirty, matted white hair hangs down in a disheveled mess across its grotesque face, covering everything except for its hideous mouth. Gnarled, skeletal fingers culminate in long and deadly, black talons.

Moments later, you watch in horror as the sea hag sinks its disgusting snaggleteeth into what is clearly a severed, human arm!

Still shaken by what you have just witnessed, it is then that you notice a small, wooden chest sitting just behind the sea hag. The chest could very well contain something of use or even value, but is it worth the risk?

If you decide to attack the sea hag, **turn to 241**

If you decide that this is a conflict not worth initiating, **go to 40**

424

The minotaur stumbles towards you a few more steps, exhaling weakly before finally keeling over. Knowing full well that minotaur horns can fetch quite a high price on the market, you remove them from the creature's head and put them in your satchel. You also find a small coin purse on a nearby skeleton containing 25 gold pieces.

(Add these items to your PURSE and INVENTORY now).

You search the cavern thoroughly, but are unable to locate anything else of worth.

Turn to 219

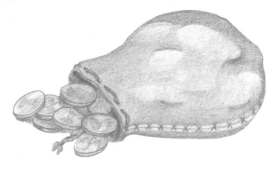

425

The passage continues for a time before curving sharply to the right and then heading in a different direction. At the bend is a large, wooden door. Placing your ear to the wood, you listen closely, but are unable to discern any sound whatsoever through the heavy, oaken panel. Slowly and cautiously opening the door just wide enough to have a look at what awaits you on the other side, what you see immediately gives you pause in wonder.

From the floor to the ceiling, the chamber beyond has literally been invaded by what appears to be some sort of strange, reddish-colored fungus. In the farmost corner of the room, sits a large chest...

If you decide to investigate the chest, **turn to 138**

If you would rather press on instead, **go to 280**

426

Up ahead you can see three doors on the left-hand wall of the corridor. Approaching the first of the three, you press your ear against the hard, wooden exterior, but hear nothing...

If you decide to open the door, **turn to 294**

If you decide to investigate the second door, **go to 114**

If you choose to open the very last door instead, **proceed to 73**

If you decide to forego the doors entirely and continue following the corridor, then **turn to 199**

427

"I wouldn't do that if I were you, mate!" declares the voice.

Trying not to make any sudden moves, you turn around slowly and in the semi-darkness of the ship's interior can just make out the outline of a figure not even five paces away.

"Fortunately for us, those talismans keep the vampires at bay," the stranger continues, as he lights a torch to dispel the darkness. "In here, you're safe... at least, for the time bein'."

Seated on a crate a short distance from you is a wild-looking brute of a man, with long, tangled hair and a matted beard. He is wearing a dirty sailor's tunic and his trousers are in absolute tatters.

"Who are you?" you ask.

"Name's Mateo," replies the man, as he reaches for a bottle of ale at his feet. "I became a castaway here when the ship I was first mate on ran aground."

"And what of the rest of your crew?" you ask.

"Includin' the Captain and meself, twas fifty of us aboard the Serpent's Wake," Mateo recounts. "I can remember that day like it was only yesterday. The sea was a dead calm and there was no wind — not even so much as a whisper in our sails. We'd been driftin' fer days, ya see, and then all of a sudden, the ship began to move like it had a life of its own. It was like somethin' had taken o'er the Serpent's Wake and was now controlling it! Brought us here, it did! Brought us to this infernal island of death! Fifty of us landed on this accursed rock! Fifty men strong we were, but this island demanded sacrifice and sacrifice it took! The first night we lost ten good men when the vampires came. Some nights the vampires didn't come at all and some nights we were able to fight them off. One by one, we were slaughtered like human cattle and those the vampires didn't take, the island did. Of the Serpent's Wake crew, only I am left to tell the tale..."

Finishing off the bottle, Mateo is silent for many moments as if in reflective thought and then tosses you some dried fish. "It would do you well to eat somethin' and then try to get some rest, mate," he says as he reaches for another bottle of ale.

After yet another night of restless sleep, you immediately set out at first light, this time with your newfound companion and comrade-in-arms, Mateo, at your side...

(You may now utilize Mateo in combat. Simply roll an additional 1d6 for the sailor along with your roll. Mateo has an LF score of 25 and a Combat Skill Score of 3).

Turn to 330

428

Proceeding cautiously and carefully stepping over a chest plate lying just on the other side of the opening, you make your way into the chamber while Avril-Lyn watches from the passage. A casual scan of the room and the items on the floor turns up nothing.

"I'm not seeing anything," you say, unconsciously breathing a sigh of relief.

Suddenly, something drops onto the top of your boot with a soft *plop* from above. Glancing down, you are shocked to discover a small, greenish-gray glob that has already eaten its way through the leather of your boot. Within seconds, it has completely dissolved all of the tissue and bone of your foot, and as you collapse to the floor and begin screaming in agony, the last thing you see is a large, gelatinous mass directly above dropping down from the ceiling on top of you...

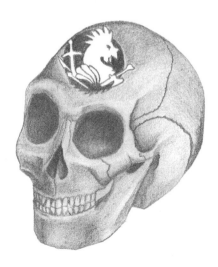

429

Suddenly, your eyes are drawn towards the figure of something extremely large moving rapidly across the desert floor in your direction. It is still too far away to make it out in any great detail, but whatever it is, it is definitely closing in on you and fast! With nowhere to run and hide, you and Mateo brace yourselves for the inevitable face-to-face confrontation.

Bounding straight for you is an enormous, humanoid-like creature. Clothed in tattered and filthy rags and hunched over like an ape, it stands nearly twice your height. Jagged teeth protrude unevenly from its horrible, skull-like jaws, but perhaps its most distinctive and terrifying feature is its three eyes!

Without slowing, the triclops lunges for you with outstretched hands, but you successfully evade it. Mateo, on the other hand, is not so lucky, and even as you are watching in complete and utter helplessness, the triclops tears the struggling sailor in two, sending his organs and intestines flying everywhere. Savagely tossing the two halves of Mateo's body aside, the monstrous fiend throws its hands up into the air and then lets out a savage, blood-curdling roar as it begins advancing towards you.

Suddenly, the ghostly forms of what appear to be three elven kings materialize close by. It is at almost the same instant that a strange fire spews forth from the three spectral beings, immediately turning the brute behemoth into a pile of ash...

Turn to 152

430

Within minutes, the zombified cadaver has been decimated by your attack. By this point, the smell of decomposing flesh is literally so unbearable that you decide against searching its body, instead, moving on and continuing down the corridor...

Turn to 210

431

More than a little troubled by your encounter with the mysterious woman, you set out once more. Directly ahead and extending as far as the eye can see is a broad chaparral consisting of mostly scrub oak, bushes, and a few small trees. In the far-off distance, you spot what might possibly be a range of small mountains, and it is towards these, the only visible landmark, that you head.

A meandering maze confronts you at every turn, and you quickly realize that without the mountains as your reference and guide, one could easily become disoriented and even lost in this labyrinth of brush and shrubbery.

You unexpectedly find yourself standing in a small glade and what you see next literally sends shivers down your spine...

Turn to 234

432

Suddenly, you are startled by the voice of a woman.

"I really wish that it did not have to come to this, but I am afraid that I have no other choice," says the woman. "Stand up... slowly, and do not make any sudden moves!"

Rising to your feet, you see a beautiful elven maiden standing some distance from you. In her hands, she holds a mage's staff, which is pointed directly at you.

"I'm not quite sure I understand," you say.

"I am sorry... truly I am, but there is no other way! I cannot allow you to continue any further!" replies the woman, as she brings her staff back and launches a ball of fire at you...

(At this time, please perform an Agility check. If your check fails, you have been struck by the fireball and must roll a 1d6 to determine how much DAMAGE you have sustained. Also, make sure to add 1 point to your Agility score for failing).

ELVEN SORCERESS   Life Force 25   Combat 5

(When you have brought the sorceress' LIFE FORCE down to 15, DO NOT continue fighting her, but instead, **proceed to 65**).

433

Sheathing your weapon, you quietly and cautiously make your way into the room...

(At this time, please perform a Stealth check).

If your check is successful, **turn to 190**

If, however, it is not, add 1 point to your Stealth score and then **go to 375**

434

After a time, the faint but harsh and discordant clang of metal striking stone begins to resound throughout, its volume increasing as every step brings you closer to its source. Rounding a sharp bend in the passage, you are very much disconcerted by what you see directly ahead of you.

Blocking your movement forward are three iron portcullises, one after the other in succession and each one moving up and down rapidly as if automated.

Owning the realization that turning back is just not feasible, you thoughtfully weigh your options...

If you decide to utilize your speed in conjunction with timing to maneuver your way past them, **turn to 335**

"I could cast a spell to shrink us," suggests Avril-Lyn. "We might have a much better chance of getting past them if we are smaller." If this is your choice, **go to 134**

435

"You are the same three spirits who appeared after I defeated the Lich Lord," you say, addressing the ghostly entities standing before you. "You took his staff and now have rescued me from certain death. Why?"

"I am Glorandol and this is Eloshann and Maegyddo," replies the spectre in the middle, speaking in an ancient and unknown tongue that you should not be able to understand and yet somehow do. "Many, many millennia ago, we three kings ruled as One. Ours was a kingdom of love, peace, and prosperity, and one abounding in the wisdom and knowledge of the Ancient Ones. A mecca of peace and academic pursuits, the glorious Kingdom of Legoria existed as such for many, many thousands of years, untouched by the sins of war and undefiled by the greed and lust that so characterizes humankind."

"But that would all change when four, extremely powerful sorcerers would unite to overthrow us and all that Legoria represented, seeking for themselves that which we had created for good, that they might use it for their dark intents and evil purposes. Our collective, intellectual minds, the greatest the world of Ataraxia has ever seen, gave us unparalleled advances in the sciences, birthing many untold technological wonders. It was this technology that they sought to make their own and in a twist of ironic fate, that very same technology would also bring about the total annihilation of our people, as well as the end of Legorian civilization itself."

"The sorcerers forced us to watch as they mercilessly

slaughtered every last one of our people. Then, using their combined dark magic and three, incredibly powerful artifacts, they banished us to the Realms Beyond, sending us to a perpetual prison without walls, where we are neither alive nor truly dead."

"When you defeated the Lich Lord, we knew that in you we had found our champion and the one that could free us from the chains of eternal exile..."

"I'm not sure I understand," you say.

This time, it is the one called Eloshann who speaks. "In the very same way that the sorcerers were able to use those three artifacts to banish and bind us, so, too, when they are again reunited, those same artifacts also have the power to release us..."

"These artifacts... how could one even possibly know where to begin looking for them?" you ask, somewhat intrigued.

"Of the two remaining artifacts, we know that one of them is here on this island and the other somewhere deep within the endless Warrens of Wvanderfell," answers Maegyddo. "Both are guarded by a fearsome and formidable monster."

"Didn't you say there were three artifacts?" you interject. "Why now are there only two?"

"Because one of the three has already been recovered," Glorandol says in a matter-of-fact voice.

"The Lich Lord's staff..." you reply.

The three spectral kings nod their heads in affirmation.

"So then, this... place... this island and my being here... none of this is by any means a coincidence, is it?" you say.

"It would seem that fate has bound you to this island, but to what end and for what purpose, of that we cannot say for certain," says Maegyddo.

"So why not simply recover the artifacts yourselves?" you ask.

"Our powers are limited beyond the veil of our torment," replies Eloshann. "There is also a powerful magic that not only binds the artifacts to the monsters that guard them, but also restrains us from even coming anywhere near them. Unfortunately, that same enchantment also prevents any and all from leaving this island..."

"Of course..." you mumble under your breath.

"Find the castle," Glorandol adds. "It is there that the master of this island dwells — an ancient and powerful evil unlike anything you have ever faced and whose origin predates perhaps even history itself — the Vampire Sovereign and blood sire of the vampire race, TitusMirror! But finding the castle will be far from easy, for each day at sundown, the castle disappears, only to reappear again in a different place on the island. Unspeakable horrors await you, but it is there that you will find the artifact, and quite possibly, your freedom. May the gods give you strength and grant

you success."

And then, just as suddenly and mysteriously as the apparitions appeared, they are gone.

Sifting through the scattered and grisly remains of the creature's victims, your search nets you a small booty of 5 gold pieces, which you quickly secure in your satchel before moving on...

(Add these to your PURSE now) and then **proceed to 171**

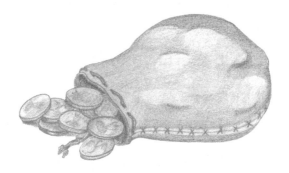

436

"Thank you, friend," says the old man as you help him to his feet. "Those miserable creatures would surely have gotten the best of me if you hadn't shown up."

After dressing his wounds, the old man thanks you again, and before you even know what is happening, hands you a small vial and then vanishes right before your eyes. The vial turns out to be a HEALTH potion, which you immediately place inside your satchel.

(HEALTH potions can be used at any time to restore lost LF points, except when you are in combat. Each HEALTH potion can be used ONE TIME to restore 5 points. You are also free to use as many of them as you wish at any time, but your LIFE FORCE can never ever exceed its original default of **25**).

(Add this to your INVENTORY now).

Pressing on, you arrive at yet another four-way junction...

If you decide to head down the left-most corridor, **turn to 88**

If you would like to take the one in the middle, **go to 267**

Or, if the corridor on the right is your choice, **proceed to 314**

437

Cautiously approaching the severed head, you begin to gag as the smell of rot intensifies the nearer you get to it. It becomes so overpowering that you literally vomit as you reach the edge of the table.

Even as close as you are, you still cannot tell what is in the severed head's mouth. You reach for the mysterious object, but then suddenly, the eyes of the decomposing head snap wide open and the head lunges forward, its teeth latching onto your hand. You scream out in pain (deduct 1 point from your LF score), and then with one strong motion, shake the head free, sending it flying across the room. The head erupts into sinister laughter as it watches you from the floor, but though it rocks back and forth and shakes furiously, is unable to move from the spot where it landed.

Glancing back at the table, you notice a large gold coin now laying there. This must have been what was in the jaws of the severed head!

(Add the coin to your PURSE now).

Finding nothing else of interest in the room, you exit through the door that you noticed when you first came in. You can still hear the head hissing and growling as you quietly close the door behind you...

Turn to 244

438

With the hobgoblins' attention completely invested in their game, you easily sneak past them without being seen...

Turn to 334

439

With your weapon readied, you cautiously approach the mysterious object. Like the thing hovering overhead, it, too, seems to be composed out of the same strange, liquid metal-like substance. A soft, almost ethereal hum emanates from it and you find yourself unable to resist its hypnotic call. Without even a second thought, you step onto the disc and in an instant, you and the disc are gone!

Turn to 168

440

With a loud cry, you deliver the final, death-dealing blow and watch as the werewolf collapses at your feet and returns to its human state.

(During your battle with the lycanthrope, were you at any time wounded? If so, do not read any further, but instead, **turn to 357**).

"Bloody beast would've been the end of me if ya hadn't come along, mate," says a gruff voice behind you.

Turning, you see a man with long, tangled hair and a matted beard standing nearby. He is wearing a dirty sailor's tunic and his trousers are in absolute tatters.

"Who are you?" you ask.

"Name's Mateo," replies the man. "I became a castaway on this island when the ship I was first mate on ran aground."

"And what of the rest of your crew?" you ask.

"Includin' the Captain and meself, twas fifty of us aboard the Serpent's Wake," Mateo recounts. "I can remember that day like it was only yesterday. The sea was a dead calm and there was no wind — not even so much as a whisper in our sails. We'd been driftin' fer days, ya see, and then all of a sudden, the ship began to move like it had a life of its own. It was like somethin' had taken o'er the Serpent's Wake and was now controlling it! Brought us here, it did! Brought us to this infernal island of death! Fifty of us landed on this accursed rock! Fifty men strong we were, but this island demanded sacrifice and sacrifice it took! The first night we lost ten good men when the vampires came. Some nights the vampires didn't come at all and some nights we were able to fight them off. One by one, we were slaughtered like human cattle and those the vampires didn't take, the island did. Of the Serpent's Wake crew, only I am left to tell the tale..."

Mateo pauses here, a faraway look of reflective thought in his eyes. "Ya saved me life. For that, I am indebted to ya and if ya'll have me, mate, then me blade is yours."

After dressing your wounds and having a bite to eat, you immediately set out, this time with your newfound companion and comrade-in-arms, Mateo, at your side...

(You may now utilize Mateo in combat. Simply roll an additional 1d6 for the sailor along with your roll. Mateo has an LF score of 25 and a Combat Skill Score of 3).

Turn to 131

441

Suddenly, you are startled abruptly from slumber, only to discover that you are being dragged roughly across the ground and out from beneath the tree. Standing over you is a humanoid-like creature who is clearly the result of years and years of inbreeding. Its face is hideously deformed and its filthy body, although muscular, is grotesquely disfigured. It is wearing nothing but the remnants of a tattered animal hide and brandishes a crude club.

Quickly scrambling to your feet, you bring your weapon to combat readiness...

SWAMP FOLK INBRED   Life Force 27   Combat 3

If you defeat the inbred, **turn to 226**

442

Slipping the shield onto your arm and readying your weapon, you carefully make your way around a fallen pillar and into the temple ruin. Right away, you experience the uncomfortable sensation that you are being watched. Steeped in a veil of shadows with only a few randomly-placed torches for light, you discover that much of the temple sanctum is in ruins. Fallen rubble and debris are everywhere, as well as many more of the medusa's hapless victims. The temple is also partially flooded, no doubt due to heavy rainfall coming in.

Suddenly, you hear a hiss coming from directly above you. Before you even have time to react, heavy, snake-like coils have already wrapped themselves around your body, simultaneously lifting you into the air and spinning you around to face your unseen nemesis hiding in the stonework above. Forced to gaze upon her loathsome visage, the petrification of your flesh is almost instantaneous.

The medusa lets out a cruel laugh, and then loosening her muscular coils, lets your cold and lifeless body of stone fall to the floor below, where it shatters into dozens of pieces...

443

"As much as it grieves me to tell you this, I am sorry to say that your answer is incorrect," replies the halfling. "That being said, unfortunately, we do have an agreement and I am afraid that it is time to settle."

(Your INVENTORY up to this point should look like the following, this, of course, being contingent on whether or not you have used up all of your HEALTH potions:

1   Smoked fish and dried fruit
2   Large, uncut diamond
3   Half of your gold pieces
4   Health Potion
5   Blade of Alakara
6   All of your gold pieces

Roll a 1d6, and the number that it lands on will determine what item(s) from above you MUST give to the halfling. If you do not have any HEALTH potions left or have already used the Blade of Alakara, then simply leave those items off of the list and roll until one of the other remaining items is forfeited. If your roll is a 4, even though you might have more than one HEALTH potion, you only have to give Tomlin ONE. If your roll is a 3 or a 6, unfortunately, you MUST give the entire amount of gold pieces specified to the halfling. Subtract the item/items given to the halfling from your INVENTORY now).

"Well met, traveler!" declares the halfling, as he places the item(s) inside his leather satchel. "And just so there are no hard feelings between us, I have decided that I am going to help you anyway!"

443 Continued

The halfling snaps his fingers and you suddenly find yourself standing on the other side of the gorge. Looking across to the other side, you discover that Tomlin Underhill, along with his table and chairs, has vanished...

Turn to 339

444

With a loud cry, you deliver the killing blow. The kraken convulses violently, until finally, its body is completely limp and still. Pieces of its tentacles are literally strewn all over the beach, testifying to the ferocity of your attacks. You collapse next to its slimy carcass, and, utterly exhausted, decide this is as good a place as any to make camp and get some rest.

You wake up feeling refreshed, and having renewed vigor, set out once more. While making your way along the river's edge, you discover a small chest half-buried in the sand with a HEALTH potion inside of it.

(Add this item to your INVENTORY now) and then **turn to 299**

445

Stealthily making your way across the room, you are able to open the trunk and get in and out without alerting the room's occupants to your presence. Unfortunately, the trunk is empty...

Turn to 45

446

You step off of the pressure plate, and right away, the chamber comes to a grinding halt as the door swings open to reveal a passage with hundreds of votive candles sitting on the floor next to the walls on both sides. You immediately recognize this as the passage that brought you here...

Please return to 300 and roll again

447

Up ahead, you can just make out the outline of an open doorway on the left. Creeping silently forward, you stop just shy of it and peer into the chamber beyond.

Floating in midair with his legs crossed and his open palms extended upward is an old man in a gray robe — his snow-white beard so long it is literally dangling below him as he levitates. The man is completely bald and at first glance, appears to be blind, but then you quickly make the startling discovery he does not have any eyes at all!

Somehow aware of your presence, the man says, "Ah, as foretold, you have come, but then, there was no doubt in my mind that you would."

There is something deeply unsettling, and, at the same time, altogether intriguing about his words, so much so that you find yourself wondering if the old man, himself, might hold the answers to the many pressing questions in your mind...

If you decide to speak with the old man, **turn to 70**

If you think that it would be better to continue on your way, **go to 354**

448

Searching the body of the ogre, you find 70 gold pieces, the large claw of a bear, and a HEALTH potion.

(Add these items to your PURSE and INVENTORY now).

You also search the body of the half-naked man that it was pursuing, but find nothing of value or use on his person.

Continuing your trek along the river's edge, you eventually discover a tunnel leading upwards and out of the cavern...

Turn to 353

449

No sooner have you unlocked the door and swung it open than your throat is torn wide open, killing you almost instantly! Even before your body has hit the hard, stone floor, Avril-Lyn has already fled via a portal, just as a large vampire steps out from the inky black confines of the holding cell...

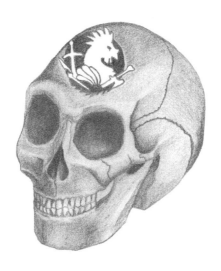

450

"You are the same three spirits who appeared after I defeated the Lich Lord," you say, addressing the ghostly entities standing before you. "You took his staff and now have rescued me from certain death. Why?"

"I am Glorandol and this is Eloshann and Maegyddo," replies the spectre in the middle, speaking in an ancient and unknown tongue that you should not be able to understand and yet somehow do. "Many, many millennia ago, we three kings ruled as One. Ours was a kingdom of love, peace, and prosperity, and one abounding in the wisdom and knowledge of the Ancient Ones. A mecca of peace and academic pursuits, the glorious Kingdom of Legoria existed as such for many, many thousands of years, untouched by the sins of war and undefiled by the greed and lust that so characterizes humankind."

"But that would all change when four, extremely powerful sorcerers would unite to overthrow us and all that Legoria represented, seeking for themselves that which we had created for good, that they might use it for their dark intents and evil purposes. Our collective, intellectual minds, the greatest the world of Ataraxia has ever seen, gave us unparalleled advances in the sciences, birthing many untold technological wonders. It was this technology that they sought to make their own and in a twist of ironic fate, that very same technology would also bring about the total annihilation of our people, as well as the end of Legorian civilization itself."

"The sorcerers forced us to watch as they mercilessly

slaughtered every last one of our people. Then, using their combined dark magic and three, incredibly powerful artifacts, they banished us to the Realms Beyond, sending us to a perpetual prison without walls, where we are neither alive nor truly dead."

"When you defeated the Lich Lord, we knew that in you we had found our champion and the one that could free us from the chains of eternal exile..."

"I'm not sure I understand," you say.

This time, it is the one called Eloshann who speaks. "In the very same way that the sorcerers were able to use those three artifacts to banish and bind us, so, too, when they are again reunited, those same artifacts also have the power to release us..."

"These artifacts... how could one even possibly know where to begin looking for them?" you ask, somewhat intrigued.

"Of the two remaining artifacts, we know that one of them is here on this island and the other somewhere deep within the endless Warrens of Wvanderfell," answers Maegyddo. "Both are guarded by a fearsome and formidable monster."

"Didn't you say there were three artifacts?" you interject. "Why now are there only two?"

"Because one of the three has already been recovered," Glorandol says in a matter-of-fact voice.

"The Lich Lord's staff..." you reply.

The three spectral kings nod their heads in affirmation.

"So then, this... place... this island and my being here... none of this is by any means a coincidence, is it?" you say.

"It would seem that fate has bound you to this island, but to what end and for what purpose, of that we cannot say for certain," says Maegyddo.

"So why not simply recover the artifacts yourselves?" you ask.

"Our powers are limited beyond the veil of our torment," replies Eloshann. "There is also a powerful magic that not only binds the artifacts to the monsters that guard them, but also restrains us from even coming anywhere near them. Unfortunately, that same enchantment also prevents any and all from leaving this island..."

"Of course..." you mumble under your breath.

"Find the castle," Glorandol adds. "It is there that the master of this island dwells — an ancient and powerful evil unlike anything you have ever faced and whose origin predates perhaps even history itself — the Vampire Sovereign and blood sire of the vampire race, TitusMirror! But finding the castle will be far from easy, for each day at sundown, the castle disappears, only to reappear again in a different place on the island. Unspeakable horrors await you, but it is there that you will find the artifact, and quite possibly, your freedom. May the gods give you strength and grant

you success."

And then, just as suddenly and mysteriously as the apparitions appeared, they are gone.

After recovering your weapon and all of your belongings from a nearby chest, you quickly secure the use of a lifeboat and make your way back to shore...

Turn to 146

451

Using the stalagmites and the rocks for cover, you successfully maneuver your way around the sluggish, black slime and are able to safely reach the corridor leading out of and away from the cavern...

Turn to 6

452

Almost immediately, you can feel your body being rejuvenated and your vigor renewed.

(Add 5 points to your LF score now. If your LIFE FORCE is already at its default score of 25, then you may add 1 to all of your dice rolls during your next combat encounter instead, but only for the duration of that encounter).

Replacing the stopper, you quickly stash the empty flask in your satchel and press on...

(Add this item to your INVENTORY now), and then **turn to 253**

453

Sliding the key off of the man's belt, you are silently congratulating yourself, when the unthinkable happens! The key accidentally slips from your grasp, landing loudly on an empty bottle sitting on the floor. Startled from his drunken slumber, the man immediately sits up, and seeing you, leaps to his feet.

Suddenly, the man begins to transform right before your very eyes, his stature increasing and his frame becoming noticeably larger. Coarse black hair starts to sprout all over his entire body, and even as you are watching in fearful fascination, the man's jaws elongate into a muzzle-like snout filled with razor-sharp teeth. Exaggerated fingers are soon armed with cruel and deadly claws and human ears quickly become more wolf-like in appearance.

Its metamorphosis complete, you barely have time to ready your weapon as the werewolf attacks...

WEREWOLF   Life Force 30   Combat 4

(Don't forget that you can now utilize Mateo in battle as well. Simply roll an additional 1d6 for the sailor along with your roll. Mateo has an LF score of 25 and a Combat Skill Score of 3).

If you defeat the werewolf, **turn to 72**

454

Moving at a steady pace, you come to a bend in the corridor and can distinctly hear the noisy clamor of celebration and the festive sounds of many making merry just ahead. Creeping stealthily forward, you cautiously peer around the corner and are instantly wonderstruck by the scene now visiting your eyes.

The corridor you have been following terminates, opening up into an enormous banquet chamber with a gigantic wooden table surrounded by chairs and set with the most glorious and bountiful feast you have ever laid eyes on. The sight and smell of the food is almost overwhelming and intoxicating, but as captivated as all of your senses are, you are immediately drawn back to the fact that you can hear a room active and alive with people, but there is not a soul to be seen anywhere within the banquet chamber.

Suddenly, a loud voice proclaims a toast, and even as you are looking on in fascinated disbelief, every goblet on the table rises into the air as if raised by unseen hands. A quick succession of cheers erupts from the room's invisible occupants, followed by tumultuous laughter and conversation as goblets are lowered and tipped back like they are being drunk from. You watch in utter amazement as the unseen dinner guests begin to eat, all manner of tabletop delicacies and eating utensils floating through the air as the ghostly festivity carries on.

Seeing a corridor just before the banquet chamber you had not noticed before, you quietly slip into it...

Turn to 364

455

Trapped in a veritable hall of horrors, you must now fight the undead to gain passage to the other side...

CRAWLING SKELETON   Life Force 7   Combat 1
CRAWLING SKELETON   Life Force 6   Combat 1
CRAWLING SKELETON   Life Force 5   Combat 1
CRAWLING SKELETON   Life Force 5   Combat 1

If you defeat them, **turn to 321**

If, however, the skeletons defeat you, **go to 231**

456

The corridor makes a sharp left and then a sharp right, before finally culminating at a large cavern. Water is dripping heavily from the ceiling and has collected in several large, but shallow pools on the cavern floor. Small fish dart back and forth within them, startled by your sudden appearance.

You are about to make your way in, but then notice just the hint of movement in the farmost corner of the cavern as something begins to stir, its gigantic coils slowly unraveling as it begins to slither across the floor. Quietly you watch as the biggest snake you have ever seen emerges from the shadows. Its triangular head is the size of a good-sized shield and its body is fully as thick as the trunk of a large tree.

The enormous serpent raises its head, its forked tongue flicking in and out and its movements cautious and calculated as it slides its head beneath the water of one of the pools...

Perhaps you could sneak past it. If this is your choice, **turn to 12**

If you decide to fight the snake instead, **go to 195**

457

Opening the double doors and stepping through them, you find yourself immediately awestruck by the breathtaking and truly captivating sight before you. A perfect garden utopia awaits you, with beautiful and exotic flowers, topiaries that are shaped like animals, and gentle cascading waterfalls. Masterfully carved statues and majestic, hanging gardens only add to its already stunning magnificence, while at its very center is its crown jewel — a gigantic, but lavish water fountain! A flagstone walkway casually winds its way throughout.

Suddenly, one of the larger statues moves — its batlike wings unfolding from its back as it steps down from its marble pedestal. Throwing its head back, the gargoyle lets out a hair-raising shriek and then quickly advances towards you...

(At this time, you can exercise the option of trying to flee by performing an Agility check).

If you are able to successfully flee, **turn to 116**

If not, add 1 point to your Agility score, and prepare to face this monster in battle...

GARGOYLE   Life Force 28   Combat 3

If you defeat the gargoyle, **go to 208**

458

After eating its fill, the giant, flightless bird scampers off, quickly disappearing into the forest.

Sliding down the side of the bloody carcass, you land firmly on your feet and straight away resume your trek...

Turn to 228

459

The door opens to reveal a good-sized room that is obviously for storage. A single shelf filled with an array of miscellaneous items runs along the wall closest to where you are standing, while stacked in the middle of the room are several wooden crates along with a number of empty barrels. There is also what appears to be a straw bed on the far side of the chamber...

If you decide to search the room, **turn to 120**

If you would rather press on, **go to 34**

460

You are about to kneel down and grab the hand so that you can remove the ring when suddenly, it leaps up from the floor, going straight for your neck! Before you even have time to react, the hand has already wrapped its slime-covered fingers around your neck and is choking you — the reek of rot and decaying flesh filling your nostrils as you struggle to breathe.

Despite showing signs of advanced decomposition, the hand is surprisingly strong, but so is your will to live. Grabbing onto it with both of your hands, you are able to successfully prise it loose and toss it across the room.

As soon as it hits the floor, the hand immediately begins crawling back towards you...

SEVERED HAND   Life Force 1   Combat 1

If you defeat the hand, **turn to 211**

461

Stumbling backward, Arachnae shudders and then lurches to one side before collapsing lifeless onto the floor just beside the bridge. In that same instant, her body takes on the hard appearance of stone, and then, begins to crumble into pieces, until all that remains of the Spider Queen is a myriad of small fragments, dust, and the crown she was wearing.

What ensues in the moments that follow, happens so quickly that you literally have no time to even react.

As you are reaching for the artifact, the Legorian Kings suddenly appear, simultaneously hurling a ball of explosive energy at you. The force of the blast knocks you unconscious and sends you tumbling over the chasm's edge...

Turn to 345

462

After a time, the white sand gives way to more rocky terrain, until eventually, you find yourself standing at the base of a vertical rock face that effectively blocks any progress forward. Undaunted, you decide to make your way back to the ravine you saw hours before, with the hope it might take you further inland and maybe even closer to your destination.

Turning to head back, you are startled to see a table and chairs where there were none before, and much to your amazement, a halfling seated at the table as well! He is wearing an appallingly bright, multi-colored tunic with matching trousers and there is a leather satchel sitting on the ground beside his chair.

"Greetings, adventurer!" declares the halfling. "It certainly is a lovely day for an outing at the beach, wouldn't you say? Ah, but where are my manners? Tomlin Underhill at your service! It would seem that this cliff has put you at somewhat of an impasse. Perhaps I can be of some assistance with that!"

"Alright then," you reply. "You have my ears, halfling. What exactly are you proposing?"

Motioning for you to have a seat in one of the empty chairs, the halfling removes a good-sized scroll from his leather satchel, and then, carefully unrolling it, spreads it out on the table before you.

"What you are seeing here is a puzzle," Tomlin explains. "In fact, this very puzzle just so happens to be one of my own creations! The terms are simple. Solve this puzzle, and I will get you to the top of that cliff. If, however, you are unable to solve the puzzle, then I get to take an item from your satchel."

With the only other alternative being to retrace your steps and make your way back to the ravine, you reluctantly accept the halfling's offer.

Taking a much closer look, you see a grid consisting of 25 squares total beautifully inked onto the scroll. Five of the squares have bold outlines around them and you also notice that more than half of the grid's squares have the silhouettes of one or more animals inside of them. Just above the grid is a horizontal table with ten different animal silhouettes, along with what is obviously their assigned numeric values.

(To solve this puzzle, START WITH THE SQUARE designated by the ARROW and fill in all of the EMPTY SQUARES with their CORRECT NUMERIC VALUES. Use the TABLE above the grid as your KEY. Once you have filled in all of the squares, ADD UP all of the NUMBERS in the FIVE SQUARES WITH BOLD OUTLINES around them. Their SUM TOTAL, if the numbers inside of them are correct, is the puzzle's SOLUTION! It is also the MAGIC NUMBER and the section that you must turn to in this book in order to continue! There is only ONE CORRECT ANSWER to this puzzle! The puzzle's solution can be found on the last two pages of this book).

Did you solve this puzzle? If so, then **turn to that section number now**

If, however, you are unable to figure out the puzzle, then **go to 268**

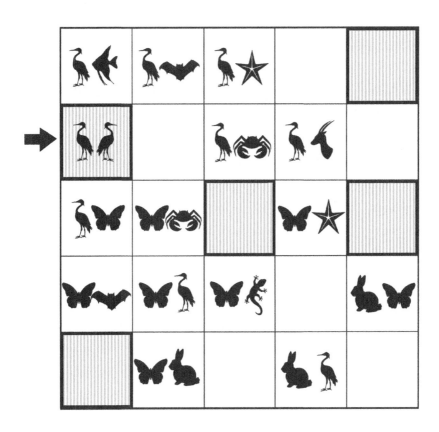

463

The corridor continues for some distance before abruptly merging into a large, circular chamber. Still standing in the tunnel, you peer cautiously into the room and are shocked to discover what appears to be a dead body lying facedown on the floor.

There is also another corridor on the other side of the chamber directly opposite you...

If you decide to investigate the body, **turn to 222**

If you decide to make your way to the corridor on the far side of the room instead, **go to 316**

464

Up ahead, you can see what appears to be a wide chasm. A flimsy, wooden bridge spans the gap, stretched out over a dark and bottomless abyss. Carefully and cautiously, you start making your way across, every step one of uncertainty as the bridge strains under your weight and begins to rock back and forth uncontrollably.

You have almost reached the other side when suddenly, one of the support ropes snaps unexpectedly, causing the bridge to flip violently to one side as well as catapulting you in the process...

(At this time, please perform a Luck check).

If luck is on your side, **turn to 252**

If, however, your check failed, **go to 376**

465

Doing a quick search of the grisly and decomposing remains of the tendril beast's many victims, you discover 15 gold pieces and a HEALTH potion, which you quickly add to your satchel before moving on...

(Add these to your PURSE and INVENTORY now) and then **turn to 21**

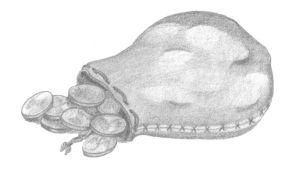

466

Your descent is guardedly slow and quite difficult, the slope of the pathway with the scree and crumbling rock making for a treacherous combination. Each and every step is a struggle to maintain your footing and your balance, but eventually, you make it to the bottom unscathed.

Here, the surf is much more forgiving, gently lapping at the golden sands of the seashore and filling rock pools with its briny water as it comes and goes. The smell of salt and seaweed saturates the air as you begin to follow the shoreline.

Suddenly, a large, triangular dorsal fin breaches the sand some distance ahead of you, slicing through the sandy beach as easily as a newly-sharpened knife cutting flesh as its owner moves swiftly beneath the granular surface. Two more dorsal fins emerge to the right and left of the first and soon all three are making their way full speed towards you.

With the sand sharks nearly upon you and there being little hope of outrunning them on foot, you have no choice but to engage them in combat...

SAND SHARK	Life Force 27	Combat 2
SAND SHARK	Life Force 26	Combat 2
SAND SHARK	Life Force 24	Combat 2

If you defeat the sand sharks, **turn to 38**

467

Suddenly, Mateo lets out a blood-curdling scream. With your weapon combat-ready, you turn just in time to see the sailor hoisted into the air by a tentacle-like appendage plunged deep into his chest. Still kicking and screaming, you watch helplessly as Mateo is dragged into the leafy canopy high above and is lost from view. You call out his name several times, but to no avail.

Grieving the tragic and unexpected loss of your new friend, it is with a heavy heart that you press on...

Turn to 262

468

Weary from your encounter with the centipedes, you decide to rest for a spell. Finding a gigantic toadstool with a bed of moss-like vegetation around it, you plop down underneath it with your back braced against its thick trunk.

You must have fallen asleep, for you awaken to find yourself being dragged slowly across the ground feet first. Wrapped tightly around your ankles is what appears to be a tubular vine of some sort. Instinctively and without even thinking, you immediately take your weapon and strike the vine, freeing yourself. Instantly, you are on your feet, ready to face your unknown opponent, but what you see fills you with surprise and terrified wonder.

Shambling toward you is perhaps the weirdest creature you have ever laid eyes on. By all appearances, it looks just like a large mushroom, only slimy and with a gaping mouth full of jagged teeth. There are no eyes that you can see and what you had originally thought to be a vine around your ankles are none other than one of its incredibly long, tentacle-like roots.

Moments later, the creature is joined by more of its kind, hungry spittle running down each of their trunks as they shuffle menacingly toward you...

(Continued on overleaf)

Resolve this encounter:

CARNIVOROUS MUSHROOM Life Force 7 Combat 2
CARNIVOROUS MUSHROOM Life Force 6 Combat 2
CARNIVOROUS MUSHROOM Life Force 6 Combat 2
CARNIVOROUS MUSHROOM Life Force 5 Combat 2

If you defeat the carnivorous mushrooms, **turn to 328**

469

You are nearly in the clear when suddenly, the unthinkable happens! The toe of your boot catches on a portion of the floor that is uneven, causing you to stumble uncontrollably, instantly drawing attention to your presence.

Within mere moments, the zombified cadaver has shambled over to your position and its master is not far behind...

LADY NECROMANCER   Life Force 25   Combat 3
REANIMATED CORPSE   Life Force 10   Combat 2

If you defeat both of them, **turn to 29**

470

Her insatiable bloodlust now at a furious level, the vampire grabs your nearly lifeless body with one of her hands and uses her other one to savagely tear your head from your body. A crimson mist spews forth, covering the entire area. There is a brief moment when the vampire revels over her blood feast, and then, ripping your heart from your chest, ravenously devours it...

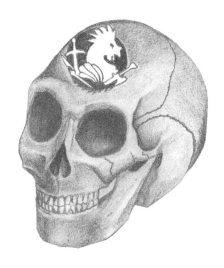

471

The queen, it turns out, is a much more formidable foe than her minions, aggressively swooping in and at times even circling you, and all the while trying to bite and sting you. The battle is an intense one, but eventually, you are victorious, delivering the final killing blow to the wasp queen.

After a well-deserved rest, you make your way into the hive itself and discover the corpses of several fallen adventurers. A quick search of their decomposing bodies adds 75 more gold pieces and a HEALTH potion to your satchel. You also do a quick sweep of the cavern before leaving, but find nothing else worth keeping.

(Add these items to your PURSE and INVENTORY now) and then **proceed to 199**

472

The cave troll raises your lifeless body in triumph, and then, with all four of its arms, tears your rib cage and stomach open, spilling your intestines to the ground and exposing all of the organs within. It has been quite some time since this cave troll tasted human flesh and it is not about to waste even one morsel of you...

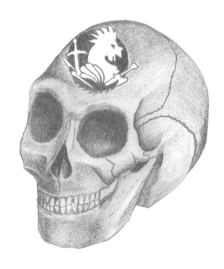

473

Emerging from the portal, you find yourself standing in the midst of a primeval forest — its massive and towering trees testifying to its great antiquity. A low-lying mist completely obscures the forest floor from view and there is an uncanny and almost oppressive silence hanging heavily over the entire area.

"Where are we?" you ask.

"We are in a place that has been warded by powerful magic. The spell protects a secret entrance leading to the Warrens," replies the sorceress, nodding towards something behind you.

Turning, you see the stump of what was once a gigantic tree, now completely overrun with vines and all manner of creeping vegetation.

"Once inside," Avril-Lyn continues, "we must find our way to the Temple of Arachnae, the dreaded and terrible Spider Queen. It is deep within her sanctum that the final artifact is hidden. To the best of my knowledge, this hidden entrance is the closest access point to getting us there."

Arachnae... the very name itself is enough to send chills down your spine as you suddenly recall the terrifying tales told to you as a child by the firelight of a demonic, taurian monstrosity with the head and torso of a woman and the body of a gigantic spider.

"Before we enter the Warrens, there is something that

I want you to have," says the sorceress.

From inside of her robe, Avril-Lyn produces a small, bejeweled amulet on a leather cord and places it around your neck.

"Should you and I ever become separated, simply hold this amulet in your hand while saying my name and you will immediately be transported to wherever it is that I am. It will also protect you from certain kinds of magical attacks."

(Add the amulet to your INVENTORY now).

Using the tangled mass of vines to scale it, you discover when you reach its top that the stump has been hollowed out, eventually becoming one with the inky, black void directly below. A crude, wooden ladder mounted to the stump's interior leads down into the stygian depths.

Straddling the rim of the giant tree stump, you carefully position yourself onto the makeshift ladder and slowly begin your descent one precarious rung at a time. Avril-Lyn is not far behind, immediately conjuring a glowing orb to dispel the darkness as the two of you continue making your way downward...

Turn to 130

474

After a cursory search of the chamber, you soon have the keys in hand and have freed the wood elf from his imprisonment.

"I am Laurick," the elf says, stepping out of the cell and kneeling before you. "If it be your pleasure, my blade is yours..."

If you decide to have Laurick accompany you, **turn to 320**

If you choose instead to press onward on your own, **go to 170**

475

Suddenly and quite unexpectedly, the ghostly forms of three elven kings materialize before you. The apparitions do not speak, but instead, simply acknowledge you with a nod. In another instant, the mysterious spirits are gone, and with them, the Lich Lord's staff.

The rippling effects of the Lich Lord's defeat are immediately seen and felt throughout the Kingdom of Olomar. The heavy and unseen hand of Sineus' oppression has now been removed, broken, and shattered, along with the dreaded curse that once consumed and blighted the land. Vegetation is now fuller, greener, and healthier in appearance, and animals long gone, and at one time a staple food source for the land's inhabitants, are now returning in droves. All of the Lich Lord's undead constructs crumble where they stand and are no more — each one finally laid to rest in peace!

The fabled treasure is also yours — wealth beyond anything you could ever have imagined, but the true reward is knowing that the Kingdom of Olomar is now free! Bards will write and sing songs of your valor and your heroic deeds will become the stuff of legend, inspiring a new generation of adventurers, both men and women alike!

Life is great and better than you could ever have imagined, but that would soon change...

Turn to 5

476

Directly adjacent to the living quarters is another chamber that was undoubtedly used as a mess hall for the castle guards. Imperfectly centered in the room are two massive, wooden tables — each one having benches on both sides. One of the benches is toppled over and there are eating bowls, goblets, and various utensils strewn haphazardly all over the table and the floor.

Suddenly, you hear a low, growl-like hiss on the far side of the chamber and look up just in time to catch a brief glimpse of something disappearing under the farmost table.

Bringing your weapon to combat readiness, you back away slowly so as to put some distance between yourself and the table. You are not left to wonder long about the identity of your mysterious stalker, for even before you have repositioned yourself, your assailant is already emerging from beneath the table in front of you.

It is a dwarf — or at least, it WAS a dwarf before joining the ranks of the undead! Bat-like wings unfurl themselves from behind it as the vampiric creature springs at you...

VAMPIRE DWARF   Life Force 28   Combat 4

If you defeat the vampire, **turn to 279**

477

You rush into the room, intending to make short work of the spider, but in your haste forget that the purpose of a web is to capture prey. In only a moment's time, you quickly find yourself completely entangled in the sticky, white strands and unable to free yourself. Though you fight to break loose, your struggle only causes you to become more hopelessly ensnared.

You watch in utter horror as the giant arachnid approaches and sinks its fangs deep into your flesh. The effects of the spider's neurotoxin are almost instantaneous as paralysis sets in. Enzymes within the venom begin to liquefy your body from the inside out, and although you cannot feel a thing, you are still fully conscious as the spider begins to feed on you...

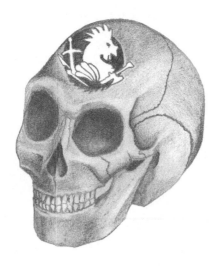

478

You have stopped to rest beside a large boulder when suddenly, you are startled by the voice of a woman.

"I really wish that it did not have to come to this, but I am afraid I have no other choice," says the woman.

Looking up, you see a beautiful, elven maiden standing some distance from you. In her hands, she holds a mage's staff, which is pointed directly at you.

"I'm not quite sure I understand," you say, as you slowly rise to your feet.

"I am sorry... truly I am, but there is no other way! I cannot allow you to continue any further!" replies the woman, as she brings her staff back and launches a ball of fire at you...

(At this time, please perform an Agility check. If your check fails, you have been struck by the fireball and must roll a 1d6 to determine how much DAMAGE you have sustained. Also, make sure to add 1 point to your Agility score for failing).

ELVEN SORCERESS   Life Force 25   Combat 5

(When you have brought the sorceress' LIFE FORCE down to 15, DO NOT continue fighting her, but instead, **proceed to 350**).

479

A dimly lit chamber greets you on the other side, and other than a large, wooden chest in one of the corners, the room is completely empty. There is another door directly opposite of you on the far-facing wall.

Making your way over to the chest, you discover that it is unlocked and carefully raise the lid, knowing full well that it might potentially be booby-trapped. You are astonished by what you find, for inside of it is an incredible assortment of items, mostly weapons, but every one of them forged out of silver!

(From the list below, please select your weapon(s) now:

SILVER TWO-HANDED BROADSWORD
SILVER TWO-HANDED BATTLE AXE
SILVER TWO-HANDED MACE
SILVER ONE-HANDED SWORD
SILVER ONE-HANDED BATTLE AXE
SILVER ONE-HANDED MACE
SILVER ONE-HANDED BALL AND CHAIN
SILVER DAGGER (x 2 IF YOU ARE DUAL-WIELDING)
and a SHIELD*

*The shield may be used in conjunction with any of the one-handed weapons.

The chest also contains a torch, two HEALTH potions, a PURSE, and a SATCHEL (a.k.a. your INVENTORY). Presently, the only item that you should have in your INVENTORY is the chainmail armor that you are currently wearing. Add the weapon(s) you chose, as well as the torch and HEALTH potions, to your INVENTORY now).

After arming yourself and listening briefly at the other door, you cautiously open it and exit the chamber...

Turn to 124

480

Even before you have drawn your weapon, the cultists already have theirs in hand and are rushing madly towards you and the sorceress...

CULTIST	Life Force 25	Combat 3
CULTIST	Life Force 25	Combat 3

If you defeat them, **turn to 383**

481

The corridor abruptly dead-ends at a stone block wall. The wall is solid, but seems strangely out of place — almost as if it was added after the fact! A careful search reveals two small levers cleverly hidden in plain sight next to the wall...

(At this time, please roll a 1d6).

If your roll is an EVEN number, **turn to 265**

If your roll is an ODD number, **go to 373**

482

The passage eventually splits into two, with one tunnel branching sharply to the left and the other continuing on nearly the same course as the one you have been following. Deciding to head down the tunnel on the left, you quickly discover that this one dead ends, forcing you and Mateo to double back and take the other one...

Turn to 56

483

You have not traveled far when suddenly, you see something making its way out of the water and onto the shore not far from where you are standing. Unfortunately, your presence on the beach has attracted the attention of a roaming sea monster...

(Roll a 1d6 to determine which monster from the table below you will have to face).

1	WATER LIZARD	Life Force 6	Combat 1
2	SPITTER	Life Force 18	Combat 1
3	GIANT WATER SPIDER	Life Force 20	Combat 2
4	GIANT MUD CRAB	Life Force 32	Combat 3
5	SLUDGE BEAST	Life Force 35	Combat 3
6	SEA SERPENT	Life Force 40	Combat 4

(You can also exercise the option of trying to flee by performing an Agility check).

If you are able to successfully flee, **turn to 337**

If not, add 1 point to your Agility score and prepare to face the monster in battle...

SEA MONSTER   Life Force ?   Combat ?

If you defeat the sea monster, **turn to 337**

484

Charging down the corridor towards you is a large, humanoid-looking creature dressed in tattered, filthy rags and animal hides. It is nearly twice as tall as you and carries a large wooden club made out of an uprooted tree. Around its neck is a necklace made out of human skulls.

With its club reared back to strike, the hill giant comes at you full speed...

HILL GIANT   Life Force 40   Combat 4

If you defeat the hill giant, **turn to 186**

If the hill giant defeats you, **go to 90**

485
(At this time, please perform a Stealth check).

If your check is successful, **turn to 111**

If, however, your check failed, **go to 381**

486

Holding your semiconscious form aloft in triumph, the vampire hisses in delight as she uses her free hand to savagely tear your still-beating heart from your chest...

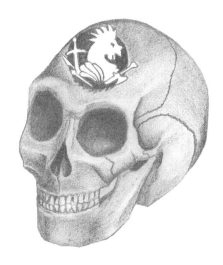

487

Its breathing labored and clearly irregular, you watch as the remaining hollow man staggers awkwardly towards you and then collapses sideways against one of the chamber walls.

A passage on the far side of the chamber affords you and the sorceress an exit...

Turn to 310

488

Up ahead, the tunnel appears to just end, seemingly dropping off into nothing, but as you get closer, you realize it terminates at a spiral staircase leading down into the stygian blackness.

Lighting your torch, you begin making your way downward — the shadows playing and dancing upon the walls of the stairwell as you descend. An eerie and uncomfortable silence accompanies you.

After what seems like an eternity, you finally reach the bottom of the pit and follow a corridor leading out of the stairwell and ending at a large metal door. Using your shoulder and nearly all of your strength, you push it open — the door shrieking loudly as it swings upon rusty hinges to reveal a well-lit corridor just beyond.

Unfortunately for you, the loud noise you made while opening the door has attracted the attention of a wandering monster...

(Roll a 1d6 to determine which monster from the table below you will have to face).

1	GREMLIN	Life Force 3	Combat 1
2	UNDEAD GOBLIN	Life Force 5	Combat 2
3	CAVE CRAWLER	Life Force 10	Combat 2
4	GIANT SCORPION	Life Force 15	Combat 3
5	UNKNOWN CREATURE	Life Force 26	Combat 3
6	REPTILIAN BEAST	Life Force 30	Combat 3

(Continued on overleaf)

(You can also exercise the option of trying to flee by performing an Agility check).

If you are able to successfully flee, **turn to 225**

If not, add 1 point to your Agility score and prepare to face the monster in battle...

WANDERING MONSTER   Life Force ?   Combat ?

If you defeat the random, wandering monster, **go to 225**

489

Kicking your feet and using your hands and arms to maneuver, you are astonished by how clean and clear the water is. The very same bluish-green crystals that illuminated the passages before now light the way forward with a ghostly underwater glow, at the same time, allowing you to see quite some distance ahead.

The watery passage continues its downward slope, simultaneously meandering back and forth in a true aimless fashion. After a span, it begins to rapidly expand, and before long, you find yourselves in a massive, underwater grotto teeming with an abundance of life, both plant and animal. You quickly realize what you initially thought was just a flooded passageway is actually part of a much larger and vibrant, underwater ecosystem fed by an underground spring. Schools of fish swimming in synchronization zigzag as one through the water, while still other, more solitary individuals dart in and out of the aquatic flora growing copiously all over the floor of the cave. You also see several strange, bioluminescent, tentacled creatures closely resembling jellyfish hovering in place as if suspended from above by an invisible line. Fascinated, you stretch out your hand to touch one, but it quickly glides away.

Carefully assessing your underwater surroundings, you notice at least three passages diverging from the cavern you and Avril-Lyn are currently in. A mysterious light source emanates from the passageway to your immediate right. In addition, there is also a passageway almost directly above you and the opening of another just ahead on the cavern floor...

489 Continued

If you decide to investigate the one with the light coming from it, **turn to 344**

If you decide to swim for the opening that is above you, **go to 266**

There is also the passage going downwards. If this is your choice, **proceed to 133**

490

Forced to make a sharp detour around a massive rock formation, you suddenly find yourself sliding uncontrollably down a small embankment as the sand and loose, crumbling rock give way beneath your feet.

"Salutations, bold and fearless adventurer!" declares a disturbingly familiar voice.

Looking up, you are surprised to discover an extremely short and repulsive-looking creature sitting on a rock. The creature is dressed in fine, tailored clothing and is holding a leather travel bag on its lap.

"Grazu?" you say.

"Purveyor of the rare and the exotic, at your service!" declares the goblin, giving you his trademark, awkward and toothy smile.

"Well, well, well!" you reply, your tone clearly marked with an abundance of sarcasm. "If it isn't the lowly and unassuming merchant, himself, and his World-Famous Emporium! Your voice... it's still the same, but how is it that your appearance has changed so much since last we met?"

"Well, if you must know," replies the goblin, "I know this guy who knows a guy who knows a gal who knows another guy whose brother's neighbor's third cousin is a cosmetic surgeon. Long story short, I was starting to notice some crow's feet and smoker's lines, plus I've never been too happy with my nose, so I decided to get a rhytidectomy and some rhinoplasty. What do you think?"

Grazu leaps to his feet, and taking his well-worn travel bag by the handle with both hands, gives it a hard shake. Instantly, it transforms into the same, large vendor's booth from your first meeting with the same, huge, wooden sign that reads: GRAZU'S WORLD-FAMOUS EMPORIUM.

"Welcome, welcome! What a happy coincidence that fortune should bring us together once more!" declares the goblin, beaming proudly. "This time, my travels have taken me to the very edges of the cosmos, itself, to bring you the absolute finest that the universe has to offer, with each and every item personally hand-selected by myself!"

Making your way to the counter, you carefully begin to peruse the menu of items available for sale...

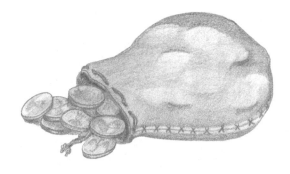

GRAZU'S WORLD-FAMOUS EMPORIUM

ITEM:	PRICE:
HEN'S TEETH	5 GP
HAND SANITIZER	5 GP
THROW PILLOW	10 GP
POTENT POISON AGAINST THE UNDEAD*	10 GP
AIR GUITAR	15 GP
UMRA THE RESPLENDENT, ACTION FIGURE	15 GP
SIAMESE CHICKEN BONES	20 GP
SPEEDO	20 GP
YOGA PANTS	25 GP
HEALTH POTION**	25 GP
RESURRECTION ELIXIR (Limit One)***	50 GP
STEEL-TOED BOOTS	55 GP
MICROWAVE OVEN	60 GP
MRE's (MEALS READY TO EAT)	60 GP
FAIRY DUNG	75 GP
DWARVEN CHASTITY BELT	100 GP
TUSK OF A WOOLLY MAMMOTH	300 GP
IRON MAIDEN	500 GP
WASHER AND DRYER	800 GP
HELL IN A HANDBASKET	1000 GP
FULLY AUTOMATIC ASSAULT RIFLE	SOLD OUT
MALIVOR: CATACLYSM'S EDGE	PRE-ORDER ONLY
HOUSE OF TORMENT	PRE-ORDER ONLY

*   Causes 5 points of instantaneous damage to the undead

**   Restores 5 points to your LIFE FORCE

*** Enables you to rejoin the battle after being killed, without having to start over at the beginning of the book

(This is also your opportunity to sell any items you may have acquired during your quest thus far, and use the gold pieces obtained to purchase any of the items listed in Grazu's inventory. What follows is a list of those particular items and what Grazu, the Goblin Merchant, will purchase them for, should you decide to sell them. Be sure, after selling them, to revisit the menu of items for sale!).

DICE	5 GP
GOLD TOOTH	5 GP
SHARK TOOTH	5 GP
PIECE OF AN OLD MAP	5 GP
GAMEBOOK	10 GP
GOLD RING	10 GP
GOLD COIN	10 GP
HEALTH POTION	10 GP
EMERALD RING	15 GP
SKULL COMPASS	20 GP
RESURRECTION ELIXIR	20 GP
MYSTERIOUS RING	25 GP
LARGE, UNCUT DIAMOND	30 GP

(Be sure to adjust your PURSE and INVENTORY accordingly after you have finished buying and selling).

Turn to 197

491

Awakening from its drunken slumber and seeing you, the orc leaps out of the chair and to its feet, tossing the table aside and staggering toward you...

ORC   Life Force 20   Combat 3

If you kill the orc, **turn to 297**

492

Although you fight desperately, the changeling's grasp upon you is just too strong, and with your arms pinned tightly beneath the creature's tongue, you eventually succumb to physical exhaustion. No longer having the strength to resist, the changeling easily pulls you into its mouth and voraciously devours you and all of your personal effects. It even uses its extremely long tongue to lap up every last drop of your blood from the floor before reverting back to its clever disguise...

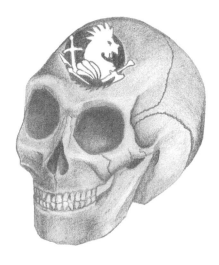

493

After traveling for a span, you reach a section where the corridor suddenly dips down, and due to flooding, is partially submerged underwater. Deciding the best course of action is to keep moving forward, you slowly and cautiously ease into the dirty, waist-deep water, moving at as steady a pace as you are able.

Suddenly, you distinctly feel something swim past you, brushing your leg as it goes by. In another instant, you find yourself being dragged beneath the water. There is a brief struggle as you fight desperately to free yourself from your unseen, underwater captor. You eventually prevail, and whatever it was that was holding onto your leg releases its grip, allowing you to stand to your feet and quickly make your way out of the water.

Retreating to a safe distance away from the water's edge, you watch as something breaches the surface. Moments later, you see three, large, grotesque creatures with snake-like bodies sliding out of the water, and although they do not have any eyes, it is quite apparent that they can either smell you or sense your presence, as all three slither awkwardly across the floor towards you...

GIANT CAVE EEL	Life Force 6	Combat 2
GIANT CAVE EEL	Life Force 5	Combat 2
GIANT CAVE EEL	Life Force 4	Combat 2

If you defeat the cave eels, **turn to 385**

494

Dismounting from your horse, you decide to continue on foot. Your exploration of the plateau base, however, is short-lived, for you soon discover a partially hidden tunnel that appears to have been recently uncovered by a landslide. A strange, almost artificial light emanates from the tunnel walls, illuminating the path before you.

Eventually, you find yourself at a four-way junction...

If you decide to head left, **turn to 156**

If your choice is the middle passage, **go to 229**

If you want to take the right tunnel, **proceed to 333**

495

The corridor meanders to the left and to the right before finding its resolution at a large, wooden door. Placing your ear to the wood, you listen closely, but are unable to hear anything through the heavy, oaken panel. As quietly as you are able to, you slowly and cautiously inch the door open, but only just wide enough for you to see what lies beyond.

In the very center of the room and spinning in place like a giant top is what looks like a swirling vortex of rapidly moving water. Even more amazing to you is the fact that the revolving column of water is suspended in midair and does not seem to originate from any source you can see. Fascinated, you decide to take a closer look.

As you draw near, the liquid vortex begins to spin at a much more decelerated rate. It is almost as if time itself is slowing down. Suddenly, images from your life begin to flicker within the whirling eddy — veritable portraits of your past and your present, along with figments of a future yet to come. Powerful emotions begin to well up from deep within you, as memories both good and bad flash before your eyes, flooding your heart and mind as you are forced to revisit them. For many moments, you are completely overwhelmed, and then, just like that, the mysterious vortex is gone, leaving you standing alone in an empty room...

Turn to 261

496

The reptilianoid is truly a savage and deadly opponent, unmatched in its use of the spear, but in the end, it is you who prevails, thanks in greater part to Laurick's skill as a warrior. A search of the lizardman's corpse rewards you with 15 gold pieces.

(Add the gold to your PURSE now).

Laurick, in the meantime, has discovered the control mechanism that operates the heavy gate. With the steady turn of a handle, a series of interconnecting cogwheels are immediately set into motion, activating an internal winch within the walls.

With a loud rumble, the iron portcullis raises via its attached chains, allowing you and your elven companion to pass through to the tunnel beyond...

Turn to 387

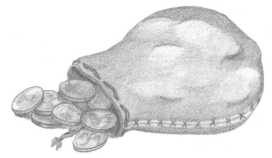

497

With your weapon in hand, you cautiously make your way through the thick underbrush in the direction you believe you last heard the woman's voice coming from. Stumbling as you step out from the treeline, you suddenly find yourself in a small clearing and are immediately filled with horror at the terrible sight that instantly greets your eyes.

Covering the clearing like a blanket from a weavers loom is an enormous spider web — the desiccated and grisly remains of countless victims scattered throughout like fruit on a fruit tree. Right away, you notice the small wood nymph hopelessly ensnared in the webbing — her giant, dragonfly mount also entangled in the sticky, white strands not far from her.

It is then that a sudden and very perceptible movement at the top of the web catches your eye, drawing your focus away from them to a large, funnel-like orifice woven into the canopy of the foliage above. Crouching just beyond its opening but still within view is a gigantic spider!

Suddenly, the dragonfly, who up until this point has remained completely motionless, begins to struggle. Its futile throes immediately arouse the spider above, which emerges from its burrow and rapidly descends upon the helpless insect.

With little time to react, you instinctively reach for a large rock and throw it as hard as you can at the multi-legged monstrosity. The rock strikes one of its legs, causing it to tumble roughly from the web and onto the ground in front of you.

For a brief moment, the giant arachnid appears to be slightly stunned and even disoriented, but then, turns to face you, hungrily advancing towards your position...

GIANT SPIDER   Life Force 28   Combat 3

If you defeat the giant spider, **turn to 106**

498

You have been following the monotonous stretch of shoreline for what seems like the better part of the afternoon when quite unexpectedly, the beach begins transitioning into a steep, rocky knoll. What you see when you reach its summit leaves you speechless with awestruck wonder.

Before you and stretching as far as the eye can see is a veritable graveyard of ships. Dozens upon dozens of seafaring vessels of all shapes and sizes are literally scattered across the white sand landscape, while the wreckage of nearly twice as many lie overturned on their sides in the water.

With dusk so close on the heels of the rapidly dwindling daylight, you realize it is imperative that you secure shelter for the night, and quickly!

Turn to 281

499

Moving on from the living quarters of the servants, it is not long before you stumble upon the kitchen. There being little of interest here, as well as nothing of any real use or value to you, you exit the kitchen and continue your exploration of the keep...

Turn to 269

500

His fellow kings defeated and himself mortally wounded, Glorandol staggers weakly towards you, raising his sword in one last feeble attempt to engage you, but you easily parry his pathetic strike and then lop off his head.

"It is finished!" you declare, and utterly spent, collapse onto the ground next to the sorceress, who is now free from her magical restraints.

"If only that were true," she says. "There is still the matter of making certain the artifacts are destroyed. Should they ever again fall into the wrong hands, the forces of evil would have an unstoppable army at their beck and call!"

"Didn't you tell me yourself they could not be destroyed?" you ask.

"Actually, there is ONE way to destroy the artifacts..." answers the sorceress, "one and only one way, but unfortunately, it means that I, too, must be destroyed."

"But I thought the phoenix were immortal and could not die," you say.

"It is true that we cannot be killed," replies Avril-Lyn. "We can, however, lay down our lives willingly of our own accord, but in doing so, there is no return from death. No ashes will remain that I might be reborn. The blood pact ritual that was performed so many millennia ago did not just bind Sineus, TitusMirror, and Arachnae to the artifacts until death. It also bound me to them as well, and by offering my life now in sacrifice, the artifacts will also be destroyed along with me. It is what I should have done back then, but did not have the courage to do so... Anyway, it's been an honor to know you and to have fought at your side. I am truly grateful for the time that we shared. Farewell, my friend..."

Giving you one last smile, Avril-Lyn places a hand affectionately on your shoulder, and still smiling, gathers up the artifacts and then walks some distance from you. With great sadness, you watch as she bursts into flames, revealing her true form, and in another instant, she and the artifacts are gone...

EndGame Gaming

PRESENTS

SAVAGE REALMS
LABYRINTH:
THE LICH LORD'S LAIR

THE LEGORIAN KINGS SAGA BEGINS....

CREATED BY BRIAN HENSON AND TROYANTHONY SCHERMER

COVER AND INTERIOR ARTWORK BY ILYA SHKIPIN

COVER DESIGN AND CHARACTER PROFILE SHEET BY BRIANNA SCHERMER

**The original, 1st Edition cover of
Labyrinth: The Lich Lord's Lair**

ENDGAME GAMING

Presents

SAVAGE REALMS

Labyrinth:
The Lich Lord's Lair

The Legorian Kings Saga begins...

Created by Brian Henson and TroyAnthony Schermer

EndGame Gaming

Presents

Savage Realms
Escape from Darkmoor Keep

The Legorian Kings Saga unfolds...

Created by Brian Henson and TroyAnthony Schermer

EndGame Gaming

Presents

SAVAGE REALMS

Labyrinth:
The Lich Lord's Lair

The Legorian Kings Saga begins...

Created By Brian Henson and TroyAnthony Schermer
Cover and Interior Artwork By Ilya Shkipin
Cover Design By NiKayla Schermer
Character Profile Sheet By NiKayla Schermer

EndGame Gaming

Presents

Savage Realms
Escape from Darkmoor Keep

The Legorian Kings Saga unfolds...

Created By Brian Henson and TroyAnthony Schermer
Cover and Interior Artwork By Ilya Shkipin
Cover Design By NiKayla Schermer
Character Profile Sheet By NiKayla Schermer

ENDGAME GAMING

THE

SAVAGE REALMS

AWAIT....

The Kickstarter Rewards

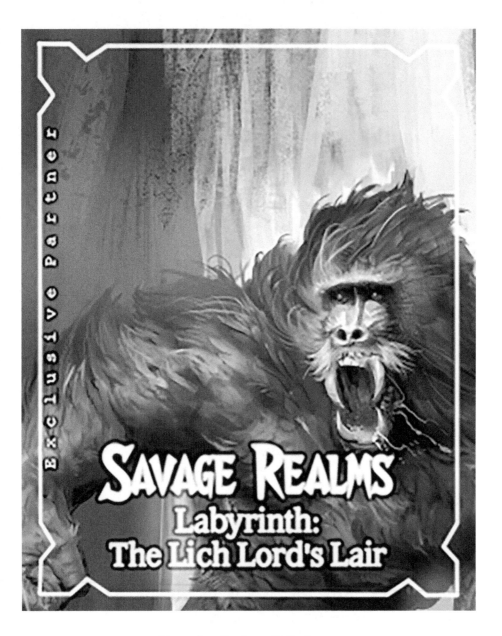

Bookplate Sticker

Bookplate Sticker

Digital Wallpaper

Bookmarks

**The Simplified Company
Logo with the Custom Dice**

**Special Hardback Edition of
Escape from Darkmoor Keep**

Exclusive Poster

Conceptual Art, Preliminary Sketches and More

SAVAGE REALMS

BALANCE OF FATE
The Legorian Kings Saga

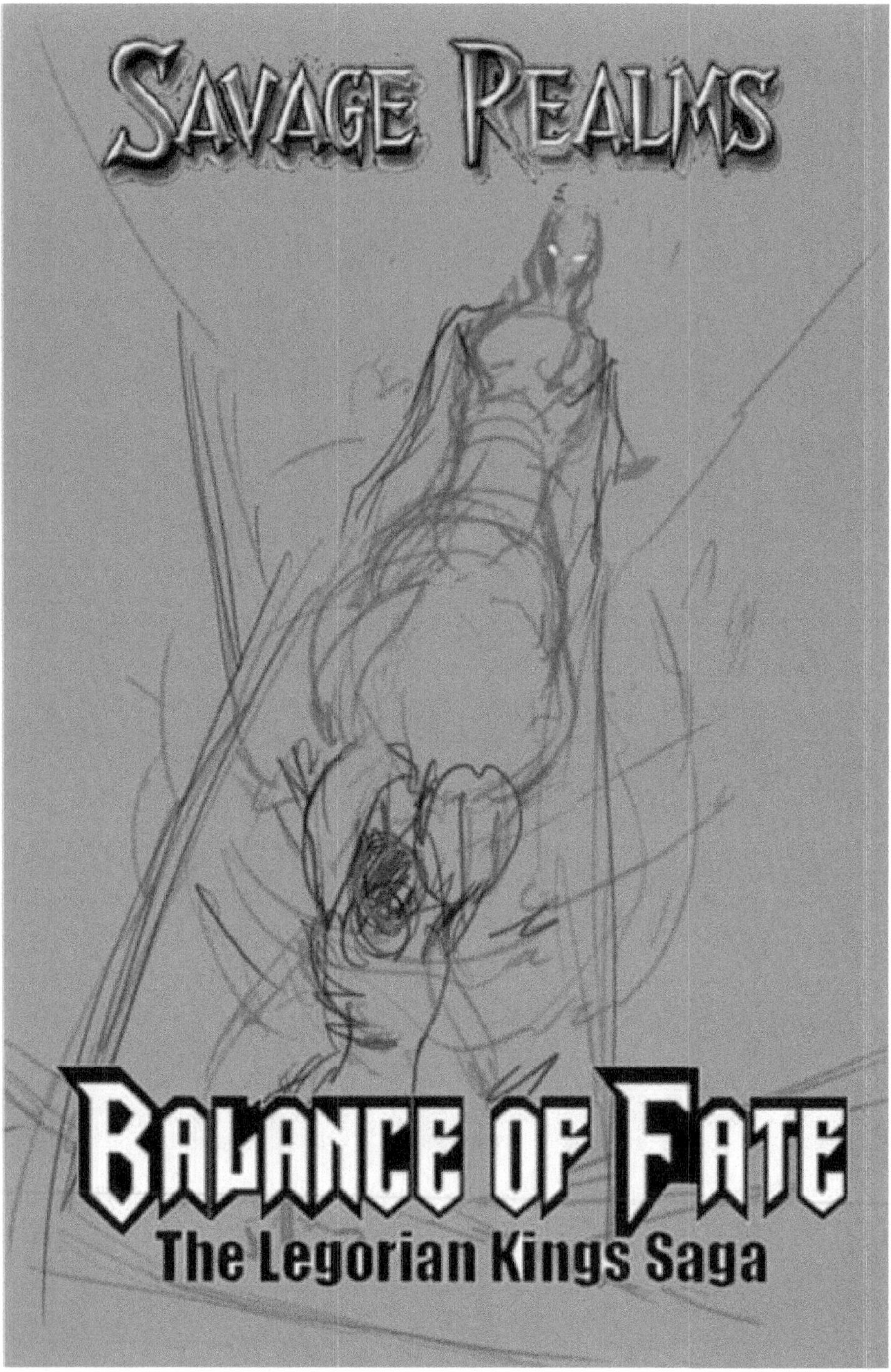
SAVAGE REALMS
BALANCE OF FATE
The Legorian Kings Saga

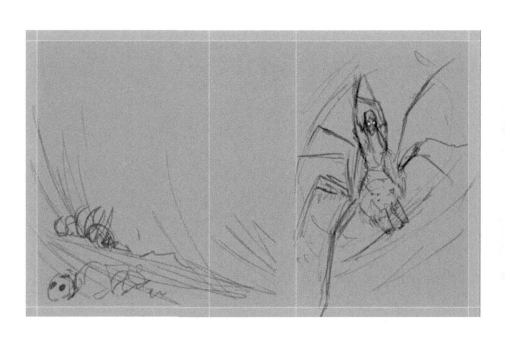

VICTIM

The Kraken with a forest background

**Rejected first draft submission
of the Child Vampire**

Originally commissioned to be a fillustration, this piece by Pat O'Neill is inspired by the book's closing scene...

Puzzle Solutions

The Figure 8 Puzzle in
Section / Reference 126

The hidden number is actually the puzzle's shape, which is the number **8**.

The Turn-Stone Puzzle in
Section / Reference 87

The phrases must be in the following order for the turn-stones to be in their proper sequence:

Earthen born by the darkest night
Forged in fire and bound by light
Washed in rivers of waters pure
Windswept whispers of ancient lore

The correct sequence for the turn-stones is
EARTH, **FIRE**, **WATER**, and **AIR**.

The Grid Puzzle in
Section / Reference 462

After you have used the key to decipher the numeric values of the silhouettes in the grid, it is only a matter then of guessing what the next sequential number is in the adjoining squares. Adjoining squares can be above, below, beside, or even connecting diagonally at the corners. If you filled in the grid correctly, the numbers in the five shaded squares will be **11**, **20**, **24**, **33** and **35**, and when added together, their total will be **123**. This is the section that you must turn to in order to successfully complete the puzzle.

The Stone Door Puzzle in
Section / Reference 473

From the fifth take its seventh
(The seventh letter of the fifth line is **S**)

From the second take its first
(The first letter of the second line is **I**)

From the fourth take its tenth
(The tenth letter of the fourth line is **X**)

From the first take its third
(The third letter of the first line is **T**)

From the third take its fifth
(The fifth letter of the third line is **Y**)

C O **T** N K A E G P S
I Q M X P E R H Z J
U C P S **Y** L A O V K
F W N D O H Q B T **X**
R M G P E Z **S** K Y C

The solution to this puzzle and the section you must turn to in order to continue is **SIXTY** (**60**).

NO TO AI GENERATED IMAGES

At Savage Realms Press, we stand in solidarity with human artists, unequivocally believing in hiring them and supporting their artwork. We have NEVER used AI-Generated images in any of our gamebooks, nor will we ever do so in the future.

#supporthumanartists

Printed in Great Britain
by Amazon

27667310R00401